MW00424892

PASSING THROUGH HAVANA

For Saint Sybil,
Affectionate felis,
Felicie

PASSING
THROUGH
HAVANA

A Novel of a Wartime
Girlhood in the Caribbean

Felicia Rosshandler

St. Martin's/Marek
New York

PASSING THROUGH HAVANA. Copyright © 1984 by Felicia Rosshandler. All rights reserved. Printed in the United States of America. No part of this book may be used or reproduced in any manner whatsoever without written permission except in the case of brief quotations embodied in critical articles or reviews. For information, address St. Martin's/ Marek, 175 Fifth Avenue, New York, N.Y. 10010.

Design by Manuela Paul

Library of Congress Cataloging in Publication Data
Rosshandler, Felicia.
    Passing through Havana.

    I. Title.
PS3568.08469P3   1984   813'.54   83-19284
ISBN 0-312-59779-7

First Edition

10 9 8 7 6 5 4 3 2 1

For Mutti

PASSING THROUGH HAVANA

I

She entertained in the genteel Antwerp apartment that overlooked Avenue de Belgique. Titian-haired, an earring clipped to each lobe, she was Magda Lupescu, mistress of the King of Rumania. She called Lupescu a new Madame Pompadour. Never tired of the Lupescu saga although it had played itself out.

Carol, she would breathe to me. King Carol. It all began at a military ball. His wife on his arm, Carol's eyes searched the room. Fixed on Magda. In a moment they were dancing and drinking champagne.

And then? I would ask.

Threw up his throne and vanished. Gave up everything for love! Paris, London, Biarritz. They caused a sensation wherever they went! And she, that stunning Lupescu woman, the daughter of a Jewish pharmacist, set the style for the whole world!

Standing in the doorway during one of Suze's parties, peeping into the candlelit salon, I would tell myself that no one, not even Magda Lupescu, was more beautiful than my mother. She would flitter about in a room filled with flowers and chocolates, smiling her movie-queen smile while Max, my "industrialist" father, winked at me, his bulging gray eyes a shade brighter than usual as he proffered cigars, cognac, liqueurs, anything you wanted. At parties, my parents were a real team.

But tonight was different. Cordiality had replaced Suze's usual Slavic exuberance. Greetings were as subdued as the pale yellow sunset filtering through the Belgian lace. I knew that some of the guests, refugees from Germany, Czechoslovakia, and Austria, had terrible tales to tell, but just what these might be I couldn't say. Nobody had bothered to explain. It was December 1939—the days were short. Anton, our guest of honor, was fresh out of Poland.

Poland, that's all they ever talk about. Poland, Danzig, and the Corridor. Inside Max's Phillips radio, on its minuscule stage, Neville Chamberlain played master of ceremonies. Quiet, children: Radio London will now balance a rubber ball on the tip of its nose. Twang, twang, crackle. Only Pierre, my fifteen-year-old brother, understood enough English to translate Neville's promises to defend Poland.

Shortwave or long, Max's radio was deemed infallible. For its oracular pronouncements, Franz gave up soccer; Pierre, poets and philosophers; Suze learned how to stay home. And I? Released at last from the tyranny of the pseudo-French governess hired to initiate me in the art of curtsies and unsoiled white gloves.

Merde to you, Mademoiselle!

For a child like me, brought up seen, not heard, the war meant a welcome change. Although I was only nine the night Chamberlain declared his intentions, I'll never forget the outcry he provoked. Chamberlain's a fool . . . a saint. Everyone an expert. As the debate raged, my bedtime was overlooked. I traveled from lap to lap and bustled to and from the kitchen bearing coffee cups and whipped cream, unbelievably helpful, so that I would not be sent to bed. What would I not have done to escape Mademoiselle's ardor for shaping me into *une petite fille modèle.*

Oui, Mademoiselle. Non, Mademoiselle. Merci, Mademoiselle.

2

Were they so enamored of her title, or did she request we ignore her proper name?

Because my brothers were older and freer, I received the brunt of Mademoiselle's meticulous attention. In the morning, while I was at school, she would straighten, launder, starch, iron, plan tasteless nursery meals. Come three o'clock, her sour camomile odor would greet me at the school door where she waved away schoolmates interested in hopscotch, rope-jumping, or any other such "non-useful" amusement. Instead, we would race along cobblestoned Antwerp streets headed for ballet, piano, swimming, orthodontist. What hurts most is the memory of my desire, on bitter winter afternoons, for a cone of street-corner *frites* doused with coarse salt, the very thought of which, Mademoiselle always said, turned her stomach.

Whenever possible, she would squeeze in a visit to Parc Lamorinière, because "A day without fresh air is like a day without food." We would sit on hard benches under high chestnut trees. Sometimes, I would stand by the park's modest lake and rage at the swans. I wondered, even then, if there was more than my well-being involved in those dreary outings, outings made too late in the day to find playmates. Who was that pale man who would occasionally appear? Could it be that Mademoiselle had a suitor? If so, why didn't he visit her at home?

After these encounters, Mademoiselle would appear upset, usually at me. I was pale, I was green, I was dirty. I had not held myself properly when greeting Monsieur. *Comme ça*, like that, she would shout—your eyes cast down in humility, your head high with dignity. *Mon Dieu*, is that so hard?

Once home, she would march me into the tub and examine my orifices for dirt, wax, rashes. Nose, *en ordre;* ears, *en ordre;* now the pipi and we're done.

After dinner, which I ate in the kitchen with my brother Franz, Mademoiselle would present me to Max and Suze like a scrubbed, costumed monkey.

I knew what was expected of me during those parental interludes, and while Max downed his schnapps and Suze puffed on a cigarette that bore the imprint of her rich, red mouth, I would gladly, yes gladly, demonstrate a pirouette or play a very, very simple Clementi sonata. My performance completed, Max usually pinched my cheek and, although it hurt, I chose to receive this as a demonstration of pride, as I did Suze's applause and comments on my tidy, flanneled appearance. I can't recall any dialogue, although we must have spoken. Only a sense of expectation on their part, to which I responded with zest and a genuine desire to please. It was not that I was particularly docile, but rather that I had learned, perhaps as early as the cradle when starched German *Schwester* would hold me up for inspection, that petulance would get me nowhere.

Franz and I had had our eyes on Anton, the "guest of honor," ever since he joined the crowd of regulars at our dinner table a few weeks before. When it came to feeding refugees, Suze had certainly risen to the occasion; there were three, four, even five extra place settings at every meal. Anton's manners had been pointed out to us and we had been told that we would do well to model ourselves after him. Manners and appearance were very important to Max and Suze, and I could not afford a slip if I wanted to eat with the grownups.

But all that was irrelevant tonight. No need to be careful; the house was too full for my manners to show. Antwerp relatives on the blue sofa, Uncle Paul and Tante Caro on the two club chairs, Van Velde, Max's gentile partner, and his wife on a narrow piano bench, all leaning forward, all anxiously awaiting a firsthand account. Anton had Max's old leather wing chair and everyone else sat on the dining room's straight Hepplewhites brought in by my brothers Pierre and Franz. Together, they formed a circle

4

of sorts on the blue and rose oriental. Even the cows in their sepia landscape seemed attentive. I sat on the floor in a far corner and watched Anton's boyish face through knees and elbows.

"His blond hair saved him," I heard Tante Caro whisper to Suze.

"Shh," she replied, silencing her sister with a wave of the hand. "He's about to begin."

Anton, always jumping up to kiss a hand or fetch a chair yet almost too self-effacing to join a conversation, much less lead one, had everyone's attention tonight, three months after the invasion of Poland. He had promised to talk about his experiences under the Nazis, yet at this moment, drawn and perspired, he looked as if he regretted the offer. But no, I watched him sit up, straighten his back, and lean forward almost eagerly. The leather chair creaked as he began:

"I am standing on a street corner chatting with friends," he said in a strong voice. "We are admiring a sleek German motorcycle, the kind with a sidecar. Suddenly, there is a commotion. I look around and see three or four men being shoved by Germans. We wonder whether we should flee or stand still and try to go unnoticed. We decide to run for it but, at the last instant, I turn around. I see the men, very frail against the uniformed figures, being led into a large truck. One of them is my father. . . ."

The sun has set and all reflections have disappeared. Only Anton's hair keeps its golden glow. At twenty, he resembled an old, sad child. During the weeks he ate with us, his vacant eyes made me shudder and I always averted mine.

"One day I am pushed out of the soup line; they know I'm a Jew because of the star, of course. After that, no more star for me. Anything is preferable to being a Jew. I can pass because of my 'Aryan' looks and it's worth

5

the risk not to go hungry." He stopped. Mrs. Van Velde scratched the back of her head. Mr. Van Velde picked his teeth. The room was very quiet until, suddenly, three or four people started to cough.

"Naked men," he resumed in a subdued tone, "naked men and women were assembled in the square, in the frost, and beaten until they bled." He stopped again. He was very still; the only thing moving had been his mouth. Now he was a statue and his eyes were veiled, like cloudy glass. In that instant of absolute silence, I could feel my clean, naked body. I wanted to get up and leave but I couldn't move.

In my short flannel skirt and high socks, I seemed to be all knees as I crouched by the wall. I bent down to examine a gash on my left leg. It had begun to heal and there was a scab. I picked at it and sensed the rawness underneath; I pulled it off anyway and watched it bleed. When I had fallen, the only one who had not laughed had been Maya Buchbinder, a Polish refugee. My other classmates had pulled their aprons over their mouths and giggled. Seeing the blood ooze now as it had then, I felt again the humiliation of that clumsy fall.

Suze was frowning and shaking her head. She reached toward me and pressed a handkerchief into my hand. I think the handkerchief is too fine to soak up my blood, but I do it anyway so as not to displease her further.

"Sold every last thing," I heard Anton say. "A pair of shoes would bring a kilo of bread. . . ." He's mad for sure. I know all about barter societies, but this is 1939! "Feeding pork to pious Jews in Cracow," he said, "all their possessions, even chamberpots, piled onto baby carriages. . . ." This was going too far. I glanced at Pierre and Franz. Pierre had his usual intense stare. Franz was biting his fingernails. What was going on here? Tante Caro crossed and uncrossed her fat legs. The Austrian refugee lit a cigarette and murmured "Schreklich!" I looked at Max,

6

awkwardly perched on a dining chair, eyes half closed. No help there, either. I fixed on the rug's geometric border which, I discovered, was not symmetrical at all. A Jew. A Jew. Twice a year, at Passover and during those dreary Rosh Hashana services, I am a Jew as well. I examined Anton. Good. My hair was even lighter. How many times have Franz and I been complimented on our "darling" Aryan looks!

"Gnaedigste Frau," Anton whispered to Suze, "I'm all talked out."

"My poor boy," she replied. The Austrian woman who had murmured *"Schreklich"* stood up and put her arms around Anton.

"À table," Suze announced, and everyone got up.

The table had been enlarged by three leaves and people moved about awkwardly, seeking a place to sit. I wondered whether they were as relieved as I was that Anton's narrative had ended. I walked over to Uncle Paul and asked him to wiggle his ears.

"Not now," he blew through his mustache.

I cornered Pierre, who was bustling about returning chairs to the dining room. "Where is Cracow?" I asked.

"In Poland. It's the ancient residence of the Polish kings."

"The what? Pierre," I whined, "come back."

Franz, thirteen, walked over. "Just think," he said, "Anton is the only one in his family to escape. Everybody else . . ."

"Escape from what? From what, from what . . ."

"From Hitler, stupid. Hitler wanted to kill him."

What had he done? Why would Hitler, in his open Mercedes . . . surely he knows what he's about? Didn't I see during newsreels every Sunday that the movie screen was blanketed, margin to margin, with cheering, flag-waving crowds?

7

"Austria, the Sudetenland, and now Poland," I had recently overheard Max say. "If I were Hitler, I would be satisfied, too."

If *I* were Hitler, I would line up my army the way Franz lines up his tin soldiers. I would climb a white horse, charge like St. Joan, and, banners flying, conquer the world. Or, dare I dream it? I would be that pigtailed little girl in Bavarian folk dress, smiling and curtseying before the cameras as she hands the Führer a bouquet of wildflowers. But first, I must suggest that he shave off that silly Chaplin mustache. Why does he . . . I started to ask, but no, I'm sick of being called stupid. The thing to do is keep quiet, look at Anton's blond hair, and avoid his eyes. Frankly, I would not mind it one bit if Anton were to disappear for good. That's a terrible . . . I take it back. I'll make it up to him at dinner. Cross my heart.

When the Flemish maid appeared with the sauerbraten, I tried to tell Anton that I had once seen her and the grocery boy kiss on a park bench. But his face stopped me. His cheeks had billowed out as if stuffed with rubber balls, his mouth was so full that gravy oozed at the sides. And Suze was offering him more food with her most seductive smile.

"No, no, dear lady," Anton sputtered. "Not another bite." Still, he picked up his plate and extended it toward Suze. Crazy.

"No," he insisted. "Absolutely nothing." And he retrieved the full plate.

I thought I would explode. Some good manners! His eyes darted about like a thief's as he pulled the meat apart with delicately held knife and fork. Once in, he chewed at breakneck speed to reduce the bulk. That did it. I stared at my fingernails, an old school trick, to still the urge to laugh. It worked briefly but when I looked up, I met Franz's sly eyes at the other end of the table.

"No, no, dear lady," he mimicked, mouthing the words. "Absolutely nothing." My laughter burst out like a sneeze.

"Claudia, to your room," Suze ordered, and I fled.

By my bedside stood a beloved old mosaic game with multicolored beads. When bored, I would design intricate patterns, always deeply satisfied by the geometric resolutions. How I loved placing that last bead. Whenever I moved about, the beads trembled and shimmered. Tonight I would make a star, each arm a different color.

When he knocked, the beads shook. He said "Anton," and as I walked toward the door I knew that my face must be as red as his had been at the table.

He looked at me, blond, babyfaced, and I did not avert my eyes. Instead of cloudy glass, I saw a shimmering brilliance, two precious blue stones.

Motorcycles? Chamberpots . . . frozen bleeding men . . . tears . . . No, I don't want this man in my room. I don't want him to touch my things, or me.

Standing firm in the doorway, I blocked his entrance.

"Claudiachen, what's the matter?" he asked.

I shook my head. "Go away," I mumbled. But his hand remained on the doorknob. What did he want? What else could I say? I wanted to close the door in his face. Instead, I watched him turn around and leave.

II

They had come from Czechoslovakia the previous June, crying: The Protectorate is a farce. . . . Czech rule is finished. . . . The Nazis are in Prague. . . . Jews fleeing by the thousands! I couldn't make much of that, although I rather liked the word "Protectorate." Found it comforting. But the fleeing Jews! *Flucht*, he had said in German. And I had imagined Jews obliterating the sun as they "flew" to safety. Uncle Paul and Tante Caro had landed in our guest room, and hardly a day passed without some sort of sisterly outburst.

"Yes, you stole soup cans, rice, my *Würstchen*," Suze cried.

"Ha, how dare you accuse me!" Tante Caro yelled back.

Franz and I were spellbound. When Max and Suze quarreled, it was always behind closed doors.

"Because you've suffered is no reason . . ." Suze shouted until, with a sigh, she stopped herself short. "Carochen," she said, trying to speak softly, "this is your home. Everything we have is yours but this food—these few provisions, which have been put away for an emergency, must not be touched. They are for us all. Who knows what lies ahead. We must be prepared and you—"

"What emergency?" Max interjected. "Don't you know that Hitler has guaranteed Belgian neutrality?"

"Never mind that," Suze snapped. "The Frau Doktor here has no business stuffing herself on the sly."

Frau Doktor. How the title rankled. Suze would never forgive her sister for having married a lawyer. Didn't she realize that here in pedestrian Antwerp such titles—Frau Doktor!—sounded ludicrous? This was not Vienna, not Prague.

"*Ach*," Tante Caro moaned, "you should have seen

my Meissen, my Beckstein, my Kokoschkas, my Bokharas. . . . That it should come to this, accused like a common thief!"

Franz and I sidled closer to Suze. I stared at a painted beauty mark dancing on Tante Caro's cheek as she worked her jaw in anger.

"She looks mad enough to kill," I whispered.

"And gobble Mutti up," Franz said, giving me a brotherly squeeze.

Suze always claimed that, as the youngest of five, she had missed out. In Jewish families, she complained, the oldest receives all the attention. Her handsome sister Caro had been sent to Vienna to study music, painting, and to acquire that fine Viennese veneer that would make her the belle of kaffeeklatsch society. Her father, my grandfather, a prosperous dry goods merchant in the Moravian town of Ostrau, was particularly delighted when, thanks to her newfound charms, she landed a husband. Married to Uncle Paul, Tante Caro exulted as Frau Doktor, the lawyer's wife. In those days, one had no identity without a title.

Suze knew that, despite its proximity to Vienna, Ostrau was a provincial town. And she had yearned for Vienna. She, too, wanted to talk about theater and opera, touch singers and actors, wear low-slung hats. But it was not to be. Under the Kaiser, the decade prior to World War I had been a good time to be prosperous and Jewish in the Austro-Hungarian Empire. But the war put an end to all that. In 1923, when Suze turned eighteen, her father did the best he could. He found her a husband who would show her the world.

Max wanted to cover her with diamonds.

He would bring home intricately folded envelopes from which would emerge stones of all sizes and hues. He would urge her to select the makings of rings, pins, neck-

11

laces, and bracelets; but Suze would demur. She knew that diamonds were not the way to impress the Jews of Antwerp. "Max," she said, "what Antwerp craves is a breath of chic." For that reason, she traveled to Paris twice a year just to see the collections.

Antwerp became a world diamond center with the arrival of jewelers from Russia and Poland in the 1880s. Some say that it was Antwerp's cold light that attracted the jewelers. Others that, as the main port for Jewish immigrants to America, Antwerp was the obvious place for the disposal of jewelry in order to buy ship passage.

But Max did not concern himself with any of this. For him, trading on the diamond exchange, even if the profession claimed to trace its honor code to the Talmud, was not what he had left Poland for. "I can't stand it," he would say. "I can't stand those wheelers and dealers, Hasids, *mazel und brucha* all day long, beards falling into their tea glasses, jewelers' loupes screwed into one eye, moistened forefingers picking up stones as if they were crumbs on a cake plate. Spare me that!"

His ambition was to frequent the homes of second- and third-generation Belgian Jews who had no direct knowledge of the Polish life he had left behind. Jews from Warsaw and Lodz were acceptable; from Odessa, too. Provided they carried themselves with westernized big city poise. When I asked about his childhood, he would refuse to discuss it. "It was awful," he would say. "Simply awful. We were so very poor."

At eighteen he had fled the draft and joined an emancipated brother who was a financier in Amsterdam. Although Max always referred to the business as banking, it dealt mostly in currency speculation and short-term loans against collateral. He caught on quickly and the "bank" prospered. In 1923, on the advice of a friend, he traveled to Ostrau to interview three possible wives. He chose Suze, who seemed to him a miracle of Austro-Hun-

garian delights. He never complained about having jour-
neyed so far to meet her, and all his life he would tell how
the friend had later sent him a bill requesting a match-
maker's fee and that he had gladly paid it.

My brothers were born in Amsterdam; by the time I
arrived, the bank had opened a branch in Berlin with Max
in charge. That is how, in October 1929, I happened to be
born in Germany. *Die kleine Claudia.* Until the age of three,
she lived fussed over by *Schwester* and *Kinderfraulein.* Was it
the astronomic inflation that brought such prosperity to
our house? Did Max foreclose on valuables, Rolls-Royces,
and jewels? He was never eager to discuss that side of
banking and, when the time came, he was not entirely
sorry to give it up.

In 1933, he left Germany for Antwerp. He said that
there would be no pogroms, no Reichstag fires, no Brown
Shirts in liberal Belgium, ever. Of that he was sure. His
ambition was to get out of the banking business and become an industrialist. He had his own capital now and he
wanted to be independent of his brother. He was still full
of hope.

He decided that zippers, which had just begun ap-
pearing on clothing, were the way to go. He found himself
a gentile Belgian partner, someone with a knack for machines. Together, they designed and built a factory. Soon
the zippers were being merchandised all over Europe and
Max began traveling to sales conferences and meetings. Always first class. Delighted, Suze quipped that he had con-
quered Europe like Napoleon. Her Napoleon. Occasionally, she would flaunt her *mitteleuropa* upbringing and
make it very clear that she had not come from Poland like
Max. He was not offended. In fact, he rather liked the
idea.

Parading fine wines and London tailors, Max did his
best to become a man of the world. Yes, his intestines suffered from the social leap and he found it necessary to

disappear here and there for cures that promised to "clean out and purify" his system. Afterward, puffing up his frame and smiling perhaps a little too eagerly, he might pronounce that the best, the only watering spot between Budapest and Berlin, was the Grand Hotel Pupp in Carlsbad. "Best medicinal waters by day. Best champagne by night."

And on Wednesdays, rubbing alcohol would permeate the air. Monsieur Max, I would be told, is being gone over by his masseur on the library table and the room is off limits, little girl.

My mother always dressed slowly, as if she savored the ritual. Nor did she mind the fittings, manicures, hairdressers, and beauty naps she considered necessary to bring about the final product. Every day culminated in an appearance, and she seemed to relish the preparation as much as the entrance when it finally came. "Antwerp, Schmantwerp," she would scoff, "after Berlin this town is barely a feather in my cap!"

This morning, she is standing on a pedestal, kneeling seamstresses at her feet. I plead to be allowed to help and, with the dedication of a page turner at a recital, I pass pins, one at a time, at the precise moment needed to hem and tuck her couture copies. She is standing so still that her reflection in the three-way mirror seems frozen. But her small brown eyes don't miss a trick.

III

Even at breakfast on the days she rose early enough to join us, her mouth would be glossed a bright red, her hair swept up with combs, and her couture robe firmly sashed. But this morning, disheveled and shiny with night cream, Suze was prepared to lead us up the narrow staircase to the roof where, for the first time, we would see puffs of antiaircraft smoke pose as clouds in defenseless blue skies.

Earlier, Franz had burst into my room waving arms and making machine-gun noises. "Get up! The Germans!" he had shrieked, his adolescent voice skipping more registers than usual. "We're going to the roof to watch the bombs drop."

I pushed into my slippers, my heart echoing his cry. Distant droning and the flak from antiaircraft guns confirmed his outburst. I felt no fear, only a terrible excitement. About time, I thought. After months of headlines, radio broadcasts, and frantic refugees, something was happening at last. Better than the Tour de Belgique, this would be just like the movies.

For me, the long forlorn afternoons with Mademoiselle in the lace-curtained apartment would now come to an end. I was ten, and for the past seven years we had lived on a high floor overlooking Avenue Isabelle in Antwerp. At dawn, on this May 10, 1940, a firecracker brightness had flashed through the lace. The date belongs forever to my list of personal anniversaries.

"To the roof? You're mad!" Max shouted, holding onto his leather armchair with both hands. "What about air-raid regulations?"

"Damn the regulations," Suze shot back.

But he persisted. "Let's stick to the radio where one can at least find out what's going on."

15

Could he be right? I recalled the long evenings spent around his precious Phillips radio. Yet now, *now* that he can finally see the war, he refuses to go.

"It's happening here, Max, under your nose," I heard Suze say. "No need for the radio. We're going up to have a look."

"It's perfectly safe," Pierre added. "They're after the port, and bridges and highways. Not this part of town at all."

"How do you know?"

"I know. I've read up on German tactics."

If Pierre goes, so do I. "Wait for me!" I called, and followed Suze into the limpid May dawn.

On the roof, I brushed past pajama-clad neighbors standing about like hospital patients out for an airing. Shouting, arguing, gesticulating, they were pronouncing on the fate of the world. Behind me, Pierre said: "Abandon us? Ridiculous. The English and the French will be absolutely loyal. One thousand percent."

The French, I thought tenderly. *Les magnifiques Français.* Although Belgium is bilingual, I had always attended the more fashionable French schools. The maid, the delivery boys spoke only *Flams,* while in our school we were made to memorize the fables of La Fontaine.

"Vive la France," I sang, skipping about, festive, giddy, secure in my immortality. Wave your feathered helmets, *Garde Républicaine!* I ran to the edge of the roof, hung over the cornice, and looked toward Avenue de Belgique, trolley-lined and tree-lined as always. There, on spring mornings just like this one, we would gather every year armed with folding chairs and picnic hampers to await the racing cyclists of the Tour de Belgique.

"Look up, idiot," Franz yelled.

"Over there, over there," someone shouted. "Near the port." A haze hung over the area. I tugged at Suze's sleeve. "The Steen," I asked. "Did they hit the Steen?" The old fort by the harbor with its dungeons and torture chambers . . . all those school trips . . . gone forever?

"What do I know? Get back."

"Tell me."

"Not now."

"Yes, now!" I insisted, but she was gone.

"You," I turned to Franz. "Did they hit the Steen?"

He pressed a pair of binoculars into my hands. "Look at the sky," he yelled, pointing a stubby, nailbitten finger at a specific spot. "It's a genuine Stuka JU-87 dive bomber!"

I looked but did not see.

Perfect day for an invasion, the German generals would report in their memoirs decades later. And it must have been for that reason—a truly flawless, crystal day— that the distant bombs, the explosions, the attack itself had such an air of unreality. For our neighbors, for ourselves, the war still belonged in Pathé newsreels. Suze alone declared herself ready to "get out."

I owe my life to her once and surely twice. Perhaps, under certain circumstances, the end does justify the means.

Buenas noches, muchacha. Whenever Don Estéban Martínez, the tall, bearded Salvadorian consul, visited us with his olive-skinned wife wrapped in her three layers of underwear, sweater, and fur coat, the greeting would caress me like the sound of a mother hushing her child. *Noche. Muchacha.*

Suze loved men like Don Estéban. Always paid her compliments. Filled the house with cigar smoke, but it didn't seem to matter. Wealthy, educated in Spain, he knew how to mix courtly manners with a modern spirit of adventure. He often dazzled us with a booty of masks and figures dug up, he said, on forays into the pre-Columbian jungle.

17

Suze would flutter like a hummingbird, showering him with snatches from *Die Fledermaus,* spreading her wings to reveal her gayest, most frivolous self. And Max would beam. No question that Suze had a knack for seeking out the right people. He knew that later, over cigars and cognac, he and Don Estéban would retire to the study to discuss politics and rare wines. Till then, let Suze have her fling. He enjoyed watching.

Don Estéban and his wife Doña Adela were expected for dinner on May 10, the day of the attack.

"Let's cancel," Max said immediately.

"Cancel? Not on your life. This is a perfect opportunity. Don't you see they might shed light on the situation. Not only are they not Jews, they're from over there, America, Latin America as they call it."

She sent me down to buy flowers. I felt light and free, as if I had shaken off the entire winter with my brown wool coat. The attack had ended hours before and a fresh spring brightness now seemed to bathe the avenue. Each wooden door radiated its own particular hue and the sky had returned to its untroubled state. I danced across the cobblestones to the florist. In Belgium, every sunny day is cherished. It seemed unbelievable that at this very moment, according to Foreign Minister Paul-Henri Spaak, bridges and roads were still being blown up a few hundred kilometers away. Hungry for the smell of spring, I chose tulips and lilies of the valley. Riding up in the elevator, I pressed the bouquet to my face.

Don Estéban did not fail to comment that the glaze baked into the *canard à l'orange* was exceptionally delicate. "Given the traumatic events of the day," he said, "that is no small accomplishment."

Suze accepted the compliment with her best Austro-Hungarian smile. "It was nothing, Don Estéban, the maid did it all."

18

Then Don Estéban got up and kissed Suze's hand. How gallant, I thought, half wishing his beard would tickle my hand too. Did Suze blush, or was it just carefully applied rouge that had been there all along?

"Tell me, Don Estéban, how long do you think it will be before the Germans march into Belgium?" Suze's voice sounded strained and high-pitched. I could see the vocal chords in her neck, but looked away lest she accuse me of staring.

"*Queridísima señora, estimada Suze,* never fear." Don Estéban's tone was almost tender. "Belgium has powerful allies and this Hitler will be stopped, must be stopped right now."

Max nodded. "Hitler has never met with real opposition. Now he will face two powerful armies, the British and the French." He smiled. "Three, if you count the Belgians."

"And don't forget the Maginot Line," Doña Adela said unexpectedly. We had become accustomed to her silences when her husband was in the room.

"But if they do succeed, where is one to go? We have no visas," Suze persisted. The tightness was still in her throat, but the question had a childlike lilt. She moved closer to Don Estéban on the green sofa and awaited his answer, her mouth, her beautiful mouth, parted as if she were hanging on his every word.

"Dear Suze," Don Estéban said, laughing, "you must not worry so much."

"King Leopold is not leaving either," Max said. "He is staying right here, in *la libre Belgique.*"

"That's not funny. He will probably welcome the Germans with open arms." Suze sounded bitter.

"Not fair," Franz, defender of kings, exclaimed. "If the Germans come, King Leopold will be the first to go into exile, or to prison. I'm sure of it." There was Franz, of all people, participating in the conversation like everybody else. While I, even though allowed to stay up later and later, seemed to know less than before.

Could Franz's grasp of the situation come from the coincidence that the king's son, Prince Baudouin, was his age and that Suze had always made sure Franz followed his example in dress and deportment? They would pore over the newspaper together, follow the prince's every move. Today, the prince played football. Yesterday, he spent the afternoon with his Latin tutor . . .

"Papi," I asked, "will I ever get to see the real Hitler?"

"Of course not," Max answered.

"Come here," Don Estéban called, pulling me onto his lap. "I will teach you a song." His wine and tobacco breath blew in my face as he began:

> La cucaracha, la cucaracha
> Ya no puede caminar
> Porque le falta, porque no tiene
> Marijuana que fumar.

Jibberish. I ran the words together, delighted with Don Estéban's attention, with his wine and tobacco breath.

After the Germans marched in, school reopened and we finished the year. During the summer, I saw singing soldiers, eagles and epaulettes, swastikas and shiny boots. I never failed to hang out the window in the early morning hours to watch the Wehrmacht step smartly along Avenue de Belgique on their way to work details. Could these soldiers, so clean-shaven, so radiant with victory, really wish us harm? They always smiled at me.

"Komm hier," crooked fingers called, as I went to and from school.

"Wo ist das Kino?" they might ask. "Cinema, ja?"

I could help them. *Kleine* Claudia, who can barely follow a conversation at home. And they—so grateful as they pulled photos of little blond girls out of their wallets. I reminded them of daughters and sisters back home!

Smiling and waving in turn, I skipped along, past the greenish-gray occupation colors that crowded the sidewalks, dodging military vehicles and Belgians on bicycles as I crossed the streets. If I never tell, the holiday, the topsy-turvy might go on forever.

It was my Uncle Paul, the lawyer from Prague, now overtaken here in Antwerp, who sometimes rescued me from Mademoiselle's determined grasp. Destitute without his work, he turned to me for companionship. Together, we would set out through Antwerp's old city on what he called either "mysterious surprises" or "terrible treasure hunts," although I could never see much difference between the two. His favorite haunt was the waterfront, where we would watch cargo ships unload. *"Ach,"* he would say, "if I were younger, I'd hop on one of those tomorrow." At other times, he took me to the zoo to see the one-eyed zebra. "I feel like the zebra," he confided. "Do you know what it means not to let a man practice his profession!" But ten-year-olds know nothing.

On special days, he would take me downtown to see the latest Shirley Temple or Walt Disney. "What is the shortest way to a little girl's heart?" he might ask. I would giggle, shrug my shoulders. "It is," he would whisper, "along the longest Van Houten chocolate bar in town."

Later, in the darkened theater, I could hear Uncle Paul nibbling beside me. I decided that he must love chocolate as much as I did or he wouldn't be eating it so slowly to make it last.

Suddenly, Hitler on the screen—flags and pomp. Uncle Paul's chocolate drops out of his hand. The Führer is standing by the Arc de Triomphe in Paris. He is saluting, smiling. Uncle Paul's breathing becomes shallow, it

21

whistles through his stained mustache. Hitler taps his riding crop against his breeches. Uncle Paul stands up. Seconds later, I have been dragged out of the theater. I plead with him to return. "We haven't seen the beginning of the film," I whine. "You've seen the devil," he replies. "That should be enough for one day!"

That night, Uncle Paul accused Max of being "blind."

"Calm down," Max said. "This is Belgium, not Poland. You've all let those Anton stories affect you too much. Poles hate the Jews, everyone knows that. The Germans simply gave them their blessing to do what they always wanted to do anyway. The Belgians won't allow it . . ."

"The Belgians won't allow it," Suze mimicked. "How childish you are! Who's going to listen to the Belgians?"

"Look around," Max insisted. "The worst is over. We have order and efficiency—Prussian discipline will do it every time! Street repairs, public works, rationing, signs everywhere with clear directions to the Kommandantur. It's a pleasure. This city never ran better. Even the black market seems under control!"

"Max," Uncle Paul said softly, "have you forgotten what happened to me in Prague?"

"But this is Belgium," Max insisted weakly. "This is my home, Paul, don't you understand that?"

This time I was on Max's side. Things were going just fine, in my opinion.

"And the rings under my eyes," Suze shrieked. "I can't sleep at night. We must get the children out of here."

She accused Max of dishonesty, of greed. He wanted to stay, she said, because he was now dealing in diamonds, and making too much money. "Damn you and your diamonds," she raged.

"How can one resist?" he replied. "With everyone scurrying to buy and sell, there's a fortune to be made.

Better than gold, diamonds can be hidden in the most inconspicuous places."

"Damn you and your diamond fever!" Suze cursed back at him.

"Try earning your own living for a change and see how it feels. Then perhaps you won't be as eager to turn down opportunities like this one."

"Next thing we'll hear you're trading with the Nazis like your friend Monsieur Mendelsohn."

"Don't be a fool."

"You're the fool, Max. We must get out of here. Didn't we learn our lesson in Berlin?"

"I will tell you again," Max said, straightening his back, "they won't try their dirty tricks in a liberal, tolerant country like Belgium. It wouldn't make any sense. They wouldn't get any cooperation, only sabotage. Didn't they pay Mendelsohn for the diamonds, didn't they?"

"So what. They can walk in tomorrow and freeze his assets if they so choose. I'm not going to let you get away with this."

Uncle Paul got up slowly. His reddened eyes drooped so heavily that I forgave him the aborted movie.

"I must go home and get some sleep," he said. "Tomorrow I want to be the first on line at the Brazilian Consulate."

IV

One October morning Suze came home and flung her hat on the hall chair. She asked whether Max had called, and when I told her that he was on his way, she seemed relieved. When he came, there were beads of perspiration over his lips. Pierre followed, slamming the front door.

"Have you seen the billboards?" he shouted. "German racial standards—grandparents on both sides!"

"Calm down, everybody," Max said. "It's only a registration order. We don't know what it means . . . "

"*I* know," Suze interrupted, "and so should you." She pointed an accusing finger at Max. The vein in her neck had swelled. "Are you living in some sort of wonderland? Once you place your name in their book, they've got you. They can do with you what they please. And we know what that will be. I've heard they're already setting up transports."

"Sometimes they pick you right off the street and send you away," Pierre said. Then, looking at me, he added, "Don't look so frightened, we'll figure something out."

"Do you agree that we have to get out now, immediately, if it isn't too late already?" Suze was glaring at Max.

"Mutti is right," Pierre said. Max often listened to Pierre when no one else could convince him.

"Let's get out of here. Hide out in Brussels," Pierre suggested. Max shrugged.

"No," Suze replied, suddenly very animated. "I have a better idea. I will go to the Kommandantur and speak to the Herr Colonel himself. I will request a registration postponement. It's been done. He could give us a document of some sort stating that our status is legitimate. That would allow us a little time to make plans."

"What if he makes you register right then and there? What about that?" Max sounded angry. He reached for a cigar and snipped the end off with his gold cutter.

"Make me? Ha, we'll see about that."

The next morning, in a gray silk suit and vaporous

24

Schiaparelli blouse, her sharp brown eyes softened by a smartly draped veil, Suze marched off to see the colonel.

"It can't hurt to look beautiful in a crisis," she had said, humming a favorite Dietrich hit from *The Blue Angel*.

Oh, but it does hurt. One look at her and the plainness of my gray flannels, my kneesocks, my God-awful brown shoes relegated me to a circle so inferior that I despaired of ever touching hers. How often had I clung to Suze as, resplendent and sweet-smelling, she had bent down to kiss me goodbye. Yes, I too dreamed of Rumanian kings, and of tea at the fashionable Century Hotel where she so often went to meet her friends. Over there, violinists played in the palm court and uniformed princes surely lurked behind every column. Was it surprising then that I made a scene this morning as well, this Schiaparelli beautiful morning, or that the farewells ended badly?

"Enough, Claudia," she said, irritated, impatient, as she freed herself of my embrace. "That's enough for now." And I had to let her go.

She returned triumphant, veil held high. "Always go to the top," she announced. Then she told us the whole story.

"I ordered the enlisted Wehrmacht soldier at the reception desk to announce me to the Kommandant, and you should have seen the look on his face! Dumbfounded but obedient. Imperiousness always works with these Germans." Bright patches had appeared on her cheeks. She was enormously excited. "Believe it or not, the colonel agrees to see me. He is sitting in a leather armchair by a coffee table, not behind a desk at all. He is about fifty, tall, already gray, pink-skinned, youngish face, not my type at all, but still rather handsome. He asks me to sit down and I let him have it."

"'What do you mean,' I say, 'by asking us to register? What is this all about?' I tell him I am from Moravia and speak in German, of course. Is his smile mocking, flirtatious, or condescending? Have I gone too far?" She pauses to heighten the drama. "No, not at all. He is amused by my fervor.

"'The registration is purely for administrative purposes,' he answers. Ha, I tell myself, the better to gobble us up, Mr. Wolf. 'Why single out the Jews?' I ask him that to embarrass him, but he is not ruffled in the least. 'It's just a system like any other,' he says. 'Cigarette?' He is still smiling, looking me over. Liar, monster, I think to myself. I am shaking inside, but refuse to show that I am frightened."

Gesticulating, lighting a cigarette, Suze seemed totally carried away by her story. "First I had to put him down," she continued, "now I decide to build him up. I plead with him like a child. 'Dear Herr Colonel,' I say, 'my husband is out of town, my children have the measles. Do grant us a postponement.' 'My pleasure,' he answers. Imagine that. 'My pleasure.' 'Come and register after the New Year if that suits you better.' I thanked him with all my heart and almost forgot to hate him for that moment. When I got to the street, I felt like dancing . . . "

Suze fell back exhausted. Max smiled, a twisted sort of smile. Perhaps he was relieved. As usual, he had been able to count on her. "Is it possible that the colonel felt compassion?" he asked.

"Who knows!" Suze shot back. "All *I* know is that I did it and that we have gained two whole months."

For Suze, the reprieve marked the beginning of an unrelenting passion to plot our escape. First off, she sent Max to sit in the crowded anterooms of Latin American consulates.

"Paraguay, Uraguay, Nicaraguay—do these countries really exist?" he cried.

"Offer them money," Suze said, "lots of it."

Visa and passport. Passport and visa. From then on, there was no other topic of conversation.

"Hurry, Max," Suze would order. "I hear there's a new Argentine consul in town."

"Line up, Max, get a number—the Dominicans are selling passports today."

Hurry.

"Show me your visa," I demanded one morning as Franz tried to enter my room.

"Idiot," he answered, "visas are nothing to joke about."

"Then stay out."

"Listen," he cajoled, "let's play occupation. I'll bring my soldiers and you can line up your dollhouses like a real street."

I was flattered by his invitation. He never asked me to play with him. The door to his room was always closed. At fourteen, he behaved as if eleven-year-old sisters were invisible.

I lined up my newest villa, the Swiss chalet from my tenth birthday, the shoemaker and baker shops from my ninth, and the Gothic church Mademoiselle and I had assembled from a paper model. Trees, traffic signs, automobiles, mothers with baby carriages, concierges with brooms—my town was soon ready for the invasion.

"All right," Franz pronounced. "This is Czechoslovakia and these two guys are S.S. men about to arrest Uncle Paul. Got that? They want to take him to a labor camp, but he's fighting back. Wham, bang, Uncle Paul pulls out a knife and stabs them. Then he runs into a bakery to steal some bread before escaping into the forest."

I stared at him in disbelief, but quickly nodded to show that I was following the plot.

"Sure," I said. "I'm in the bakery with Tante Caro and we try to stop the baker from calling the police. Tante Caro cries, 'They've already killed my son, now they want to kill my husband!'"

27

"Excellent." Franz was beaming. "Uncle Paul escapes through the back door, but now an entire company has been alerted to catch him. Here, help me line up these men. Give each one a rifle. They're aiming at Uncle Paul, but he's so fast, so agile, that they keep on missing."

"Uncle Paul? But he's such a fat . . . " I laughed.

"Silly goose," Franz mumbled.

"Look," I shrieked, "this baby's been hit by a stray bullet. Quick, call the ambulance." Franz was a genius at imitating sirens. The toy ambulance came screeching across the rug to pick up the wounded baby, while the concierge and the townspeople gathered around to comfort the mother. I noticed that the soldiers did not budge and seemed indifferent to the baby's fate.

"You be Tante Caro," Franz commanded.

"Baby, poor baby," I wailed. "You will die just like my own son." Then, in my own voice. "Quick, you be the doctor. Examine the baby."

"You be the baby," he said. "Lie down."

"You're crazy."

"No, I'm not. We're only playing."

He threw up my skirt and reached for my underpants.

"Let me go," I shouted.

"There it is," he burst out. "The wound."

"I'll never play with you again," I cried. "I'll tell Mutti."

"Go ahead. I didn't hurt you, did I?" He made a move as if to leave.

"Don't go," I called. "Let's finish . . . "

When Suze asked me to accompany her to the Palm Court at the Century Hotel, I was overjoyed. She rarely took time to be alone with me, and I could never get enough of her. My lot seemed such a miserable one compared to hers. Wherever she went, I knew that the grayness of Belgian winters would somehow be eclipsed by the brightness of her smile. Her teeth, strung symmetrically in their milky whiteness, brought to her face the glamour of a movie star. Smile for me, I would cry inwardly again and again.

"Wear the smocked dress," she said, "the one we bought in Brussels last year."

"It's so babyish."

"Never mind, just do as I say."

She looked preoccupied as we hailed a taxi, but I felt quite sure that it had little to do with me, and that once we arrived at the Palm Court, she would assume the vivacious public personality I so loved. I actually looked forward to being displayed in Suze's company among the murmur of voices at the Century, quietly content with, say, a *tarte aux fraises* that I would eat slowly and daintily so as to do Mademoiselle proud.

The doorman touched his cap and gave the revolving door a push. A semicircle later, we were enveloped by the rosy glow of the Century. China teacups from England, carts with pastries on crystal platters, violinists playing Kreisler tunes. German officers in snappy tunics. Everything as I had anticipated it.

Suze's eyes looked around the room until she found him.

"Don Estéban, what a surprise! Won't you join us?" My heart sank. I had thought it would be just the two of us.

Don Estéban stood up. "What a coincidence! Isn't Antwerp a small town," he said, and laughed. He was tall, graceful; his black beard, carefully trimmed, was majestic rather than menacing. He reminded me of the great explorers—Magellan and Vasco Da Gama.

But I refused to be seduced. I was angry, suspicious. I was convinced that Suze had known all along that he would be here and had not told me.

"For the young lady," Don Estéban said to the

waiter, "an enormous slice of chocolate cake."

I would not smile. "Make it a Napoleon," I said.

"She has a mind of her own that one, like Napoleon." Don Estéban was amused.

They chatted, Suze and her Don Estéban. The unexpectedness of this encounter; the coincidence. She put her arm around me. "Don't you like your Napoleon?" What do you care as long as you have Don Estéban to whisper in your ear and light your cigarettes.

She smiled. She smoked. He ordered cognac and called over a violinist.

"Wiener Blut," he requested, kissing Suze's hand. She looked into his eyes and, I was sure, held onto his hand for an extra instant. There was a girlish flush on her cheeks and I had never seen her look more beautiful.

I thought my heart would break. If only I could run home to Max. Where might he be? Where does he spend his days? The violinist was playing the waltz in my ear and I had the urge to rip the bow out of his hand. But, of course, I would not make a scene. Petites filles modèles don't make scenes, they have forgotten how.

"Goodbye," I heard Suze say.

"Not adiós," he said, "but hasta luego. It means we will soon meet again."

Down the carpeted stairs, past the uniformed doorman, through the glass doors and into the street where I recognized "l'heure bleu." Suze had often pointed it out to me. The melancholy hour, she called it. Everything bathed in burning blue. The Napoleon sat in my stomach like a stone. But Suze's step was light. She took my hand and said, "Let's skip together." I tore it from her, aghast at my boldness, unable to understand anything except the blueness in my heart.

"I always forget," Max was saying, "is San Salvador the capital and El Salvador the country, or is it the other way around?" We were in the library with Suze and Don Estéban.

"Make it your business to remember," Suze said harshly.

Her tone made my heart pound. Don't, I wanted to cry out, don't talk like that. But I stood by silently and watched Don Estéban, the impeccable diplomat, claim that he was breaking the rules by stamping a Salvadoran visa in Max's Polish passport. On the very library table where Max still received his masseur.

Then Don Estéban embraced Max and Suze, an arm around each one. "Treasure these visas, *queridos amigos*," he cautioned. "And use them only if you really must. I am not authorized to issue visas these days and my government would have my head if they knew. My great hope is that with a destination on your passport, you will find it easier to leave this unhappy land. Go to England, or Spain, and God bless you."

Max did not look blessed. He seemed, on the contrary, diminished by the formidable embrace. "Thank you, *amigo*," he said. His smile, I thought, looked like a grimace, for the lower lip was so taut that it would not give.

"Now we'll celebrate," Suze said, taking Don Estéban's arm and leading him into the dining room. Max followed with Doña Adela.

Three different wines, boeuf Wellington, braised endives, champagne with dessert—Suze wanted to make the farewell dinner unforgettable. Don Estéban sat on her right and I asked to sit next to him as well. How would he behave, with Max right there?

"*Como no, muchacha,*" he said, drawing me to him. "Like mother, like daughter." He winked at Suze.

"Don Estéban, talk to us about El Salvador," Suze said, laughing.

He looked across the table at Pierre and Franz. "Our señoritas are as luscious as the red mamey fruit, but

31

watch out for the chaperones—they are dragons." The boys gave him a self-conscious smile and Doña Adela, in black as always, fingered her napkin with hands as smooth and new as a young girl's.

"You, Estéban, were an expert St. George," she said.

We were ready for the third wine and Max rose to serve it. He had wedged himself between Suze and Don Estéban to pick up Suze's glass, which he proceeded to fill slowly, carefully. Then he just stood there, full glass in hand, murmuring something about a great wine year, unable to maneuver the brimming glass back to the table, for Don Estéban's and Suze's chairs were touching.

I looked up and met Max's trembling lower lip. His pallor made the gray eyes bulge more than usual and, lest they fix on me, I dropped the salt shaker I was holding in my hand. Pushing my chair away, I bent down to retrieve it. Don Estéban's leg was hard against Suze's and her intoxicated, beautiful laughter filtered down to the dark world under the table where I crouched looking for the missing shaker, murmuring, "I hate her, I hate her," until I felt the tears come.

It was time to pack and I did not mind. At last the family would always be together. Max, his affairs wound up, was home most of the day now and in Suze's way. Pierre found time to read me chapters from *Treasure Island* and Franz's tin soldiers remained intact in their boxes, the door to his room suddenly ajar and inviting. Mademoiselle had been dismissed for good.

Suze invited me to help her and we worked together like a real mother and daughter. I experienced the excitement I remembered from packing for summer vacations. In those days, Suze—organized and businesslike—would shoo the men out of the house and produce piles of bathing suits, cardigans, and beach towels that fitted perfectly into large, boxy suitcases. Helping her then had been a cherished yearly ritual. But now Max's presence complicated matters. He seemed inept and unsure. Unaccustomed to spending business hours at home, he roamed the apartment like a troublesome child.

"All right," Suze announced. "Everyone decide what is absolutely essential. You can't have it all."

"If I were to be stranded on a desert island, I would bring my Plato. I must have it," Pierre said.

"And my doll," I whined. "The one with the porcelain head and hand-painted eyes!"

Suze agreed to yet one more suitcase.

"Here, take this," Max said.

"This?" Suze looked at the large kitchen knife. "We're not fighting pirates, you know."

"Take it," he insisted. "It's a miracle of modern technology. Will never rust. Look," he addressed us all, "it's marked 'inoxidable.'"

"Get out of my hair," Suze said, "and let me pack."

"And this hatbox?" he shot back.

"I'm a drunkard about hats," Suze apologized and Max let it go.

V

The first-class compartment of the Brussels-Paris Express did not disappoint me. Once the access door closed and the train rolled out of the station, it would become, I knew, a cozy little world of plush, lace doilies, and flip-down tables. And before long, it would be time to investigate the contents of a wicker food hamper brazenly facing me on the empty seat across from mine.

There was another vacant seat in the compartment, by the window, for Max was not with us. Suze had decided that we should travel on the two o'clock and Max follow on the four because, she had said, he looked too Jewish and would get us all picked up. She had insisted that when traveling with false papers one can't be too careful. She had planned the journey with great care, but also with relish. "I will play the stylish matron bound for a Paris vacation with my children," she had plotted, fingering her expensive hand-stitched morocco luggage with such gusto that I had been fooled into believing that this might turn into a real pleasure trip after all.

But then, this morning, she had been tense and ill-tempered. Don't wrinkle your dress. Sit still. Comb your hair. Help me pack. She had barked orders until it was time to leave. And now, on the train at last, as I eyed the food hamper stuffed with sausage and fruit and chocolate, she said I should keep my hands to myself. And I hadn't even moved!

Train rides had always been the best part of vacations. Every summer, bound for Le Zoute on the North Sea, we would travel with hampers full of delicacies. Reaching for a nougat bar, trying to dislodge the sticky sugary candy from my teeth as the world rolled by was bliss. Traveling and eating in little train compartments felt like playing house.

Now I pressed my legs against the burgundy plush and tried to remain perfectly still. But the coarseness of the fabric made my calves itch and I had to bend down to scratch. "Stop fidgeting," Suze said, and I froze. No one spoke. Franz and Pierre, grunting over a chessboard, made no attempt to relieve the silence. I told myself that I should know better than to think of food at a time like this. Perhaps, if I moved away, the hamper would not tempt me so. I decided to risk another rebuff by switching to the window seat. Suze did not seem to notice, and I lost myself in a landscape of modest houses and small winter gardens that gave the impression that somewhere life was going on as usual.

Suddenly, there were shouts in the corridor. *Heil Hitler!* Pierre and Franz looked up. We stared at Suze. A vein throbbed in her neck as she braced herself for the border inspectors.

Before we left, Suze had quarreled with Max on the platform.

"No," I had heard her protest, "I won't."

"You must," he had insisted. "There's no time to argue. This last-minute deal was too good to turn down."

Suze's small eyes had begun to burn. "First you refuse to leave . . . threatened with deportation . . . and now, *now,*" she had shrieked, " . . . endangering us again . . . for a few diamonds!"

I had seen Max press a small packet into her hand and, to my amazement, she had begun to sob. She had mumbled, "No, no," but had made no attempt to return the packet to Max. He had embraced her, kissed her tears, whispered words of comfort. Then the whistle had blown. They seemed unwilling to let go of each other and I wondered whether it was possible that my mother and father loved each other after all.

Many years later, when "escape" stories seemed to pour out of her like perspiration after a fever, Suze would recount how greedy and foolhardy Max had seemed to her. "Our luggage," she would say, "already had false bottoms lined with diamonds and money. All we could possibly need. It was madness. I should have flushed that damn packet down the toilet. But then," and her face would light up, "all modesty aside, I came up with a genius of an idea." She always swaggered at this point. The memory of her craftiness would give her enormous pleasure for the rest of her life. "I read once that if you press a tiny object into an orange skin it will close again, heal itself, so to speak. And it did. And how! A German inspector even joked about taking one of our oranges along for his dinner."

Max met us in Paris as agreed. Terrified of being picked up, he had decided to risk all and install himself in a compartment filled with German officers. Because he had often been told that he bore a resemblance to Napoleon, he had attempted to pass as an Italian businessman—an industrialist, of course—and hopefully go unnoticed. His ruse had worked so well that he was not even asked to show his precious *laissez-passer*.

"So you see," he said to Suze defiantly, when we were reunited, "I, too, can be foxy when I want to."

The memory of that dismal winter in Paris sits in my mind like a long, dark corridor bordered by forbidden doors. Max rented an apartment in an obscure *arrondissement* and, so as not to arouse suspicion, enrolled Pierre, Franz, and me in a nearby school. I awoke in the dark and came home in the dark. I counted the cold days in the cavernous, severe school as if they constituted some sort of purgatory. I remember being briefly rescued by a case of *grippe*, of being allowed to stay in bed sipping camomile tea and reading my first Doctor Dolittle, a gift from Pierre.

Did I know then or did I hear later that the Germans were rounding up foreign Jews with the admirable cooperation of the French gendarmes? Did I overhear Max and Suze whispering in the dark about transit visas to Cuba or are these conversations the stuff of later nightmares? Did I see shadowy creatures sweep furtively through the apartment offering forged travel permits to Biarritz, St. Jean-de-Luz? Yes, they'd insist, the Spanish frontier, over the Pyrenees, yes, been done a hundred times.

January to May, four endless months. Or did they go by quickly? Why can't I feel it anymore? I sometimes wonder whether I perceived Max and Suze's terror so deeply that I have erased it from memory. I must have been frightened—we could have been found out, denounced at any moment. I must have wondered, how long can this go on; is it worth it even to try to fit in at school if you're only going to move on again? Better hold your breath, keep that Belgian accent low, and wait for the school bell that will release you to Dr. Dolittle and the enchanted world of the Comtesse de Ségur. Pretend you're not here, that this is not happening. Think "Après la Pluie le Beau Temps," my favorite story. Books can save your life.

And then it was spring and we picked up and left for St. Jean-de-Luz, on the Spanish border.

Max negotiated an "overpriced" villa high above the valleys and orchards of the Basque countryside. He complained that because Jews were considered high-risk tenants, he had been made to pay through the nose. Suze claimed to have no patience for such "details." Instead, she immediately began developing a plan of action to get us out of France. "I'll work the local Kommandantur," she said, "and you, Max, look around to see what else is being offered. The place is crawling with fishy characters promising illegal crossings over the mountains. Investigate."

But for me there was only June. June in a sunny landscape of wildflowers and country lanes. I could barely remember any signs of spring in Paris. Her budding trees must have been swallowed by mist and cold rain. But here, here in St. Jean-de-Luz, there were deeply green valleys and orchards heavy with cherries.

I have a vivid image of Franz and me walking into town in search of ripe cherries. At the greengrocer's we found, to our surprise, that the stands were bare. Inside, a heavy-set *marchande* pointed a conspiratorial finger toward the back of the store. I was fearful, but Franz gave me a push and together we followed the woman into a dimly lit storage room packed with cases of cherries.

"I won't sell to the *sales boches*," she spat as she heaped the precious fruit into our newspaper cones. We felt heroic as we walked home concealing our "goods." It was the first and maybe the only time I experienced a tinge of pride at being associated with the vanquished.

"I don't trust the Germans and I don't trust you!" Max was standing in the villa's square living room, pounding the table with his fist.

"All right, mister mountain goat," Suze yelled back, "get yourself tracked down by dogs, shot in the back as you mountaineer across the Pyrenees in the middle of the night. That's not for me nor for my children."

I put my hands over my ears. I hated to hear them quarrel. It was happening more frequently now and even my room offered no solace. The summer walls were so flimsy that I could hear every word. Suze was speaking again:

"Lieutenant Ducek, the young officer you malign so much, is Sudeten Czech. My *Landsman*. He cries, yes cries, every time we meet. He tells me that he feels personally responsible for the fate of the Jews. He wants to help us. And you? All you want to do is to flirt with danger. Escape over the Pyrenees! Pay off some dishonest guide who will ditch us halfway across! I have heard enough stories. *Non, merci.*"

"He breaks my heart, your Lieutenant Ducek." Max sounded angry, the words sputtered out as if his throat were completely dry. "How long did it take him to decide that he feels sorry for the Jews? How many visits to the Kommandantur by the beautiful Frau Suze?"

"How dare you! If I can convince him to give us a *laissez-passer* out of France, you can only be grateful. After all, everything's fair in love and war." Then she hummed a tune from *Die Fledermaus*:

> *Mein Herr Marquis, so ein Mann wie sie*
> *Der musste die Sache ja besser verstehn . . .*

After that, Lieutenant Ducek began spending his free evenings at the villa, drinking Max's wine, confiding his scheme for our escape. First, he said, he would convince his Kommandant that St. Jean-de-Luz was over-crowded with refugees. Then, he would suggest to the Kommandant that he, Lieutenant Ducek, be allowed the discretion of expelling a few "choice" friends. "To relieve the overcrowding, of course," he winked. "With your Salvadorian visas you will have no trouble being admitted into Spain, and that should make little Frau Suze here very happy, right?"

We were ordered out of France on twenty-four hours' notice, legally and by train, hand-stitched luggage, hatbox, and all. There would be no question of climbing the Pyrenees, of being tracked and shot at.

Before we left, Max declared that he wanted to give Lieutenant Ducek a token of his appreciation. Money, or jewelry perhaps.

Suze laughed in his face. "You must be joking," she said. "That won't be necessary at all."

"How does one know what is necessary and what isn't?" Max replied sadly. "Is life so dear that one must destroy what is most precious in order to survive? Once upon a time I knew what I wanted. Now, I feel like a beast. I have devoured myself. Was it to save my neck? Or the children's? Or yours, my beautiful Suze?"

I looked from one to the other. Suze seemed radiant. "We're going to live, Max, and that's what counts." He sighed.

A week later, Suze, Max, Franz, Pierre, and I were sailing on the modest liner *Magallanes* from Bilbao across the mined Atlantic toward Havana harbor and the New World.

In her book *The War Against the Jews, 1933–1945,* Lucy Dawidowicz outlines the fate of Jews who remained in Belgium as follows:

In October 1940, six months after German occupation, anti-Jewish policies began to be promulgated. . . . A decree issued on October 28, 1940, defined Jews according to German racial standards and ordered their registration. . . .

Economic measures against Jews and their property were enacted on May 31, 1941, setting in motion the "Aryanization" of Jewish property and the rapid impoverishment of the Jews. . . . By mid-1942, Jewish property was completely "Aryanized."

. . . As of December 31, 1941, Jewish children were excluded from the public schools. In the spring of 1942 decrees issued in Antwerp compelled Jews into forced-labor brigades. . . . On June 6, 1942, Jews were forced to wear the Star of David arm bands.

On November 25, 1941, the Germans ordered the organization of a Judenrat. . . . Its initial tasks were to provide social services and organize the education of Jewish children, but it soon was forced to transmit German orders. . . .

Early in 1942 deportations began. . . . According to German records, 25,437 Jews were deported to Auschwitz via the transit camp at Malines from mid-1942 through mid-1944. Several thousand were sent to Lodz and deported from there. Considerable numbers of Jews died in Belgium of hunger, disease, or overwork in labor and transit camps or as victims of random shootings and terror. In sum, about 40,000 of the 65,000 Jews who had remained in Belgium perished. . . .

VI

The *Magallanes*'s passengers,
mostly Jews from the four corners, had staked out terri-
tory for mid-morning bouillon as follows: Russians in the
salon, Poles on deck two, French forward promenade,
Dutch aft. Suze considered the German Jews, center promenade, her proper milieu, Max's Polish origins not withstanding.

"*Guten Morgen, guten Morgen.*"

A tall, plump man jumped up and offered Suze his
seat. "Heinrich Meyer, at your service," he said.

"Max Rossin, Tirette Éclair, Anvers," Max bowed
slightly. "My wife, Madame Rossin, our daughter Claudia."
He always gave Rossin a French pronunciation, ending it
in an "un" sound as if it had not been a castrated version
of Rossinski.

"Delighted," Heinrich said. "May I introduce my colossal wife Eva, eight months pregnant! This fine young
man in tennis shoes is Freddy Bauer and, of course, Herr
Rudi Getz." Heinrich nodded in the direction of an elderly
man who sat, drenched in tanning oil, his legs crossed.

"We're speculating about Havana," Eva said after
the introductions were over. "One thing we know for
sure—our beloved Berlin it won't be!" She tossed this off
with a contagious, toothy laugh that exposed the gap between her front teeth. "Freddylein, be a dear and see if
you can dig up a cup of bouillon. This body of mine ain't
what it used to be. I feel like an overworked machine. Next
time I am asked, babies anyone, I will politely refuse." This
was addressed to Heinrich, who shifted his weight.

"Just think, Eva," he said, "what a perfectly exotic
beginning for our little offspring, on a tropical island or,
perhaps, on the high seas."

She gave a mock gasp.

Suze relished irreverent people like Eva and Hein-

41

rich—older money, better educated, Jewish only by virtue of no longer being accepted as Germans. "Herr Freddy," she said to the youngish man with blond hair carefully parted and combed to one side, "a little bouillon for me, too."

Max cleared his throat. "I hear," he said, "that after the fiasco with the *St. Louis*—you will recall the boatload of refugees turned back in 1939—Cuba has been under considerable international pressure to open her doors . . . "

"Max is always optimistic," Suze interrupted. "The fact is that we don't have a Cuban visa. A Salvadoran one, yes, but who wants to go there? Even that visa is not entirely legitimate and so, we may end up faring no better than the passengers of the *St. Louis*."

"They would never turn you away, Frau Rossin," Getz said, pronouncing it like Rosen. "The *St. Louis* affair was a political situation, but the Cubans have an eye for the ladies, especially when their husbands can afford to pay. Money, money, money, makes the world go round . . . Just exactly what is Tirette Éclair, Herr Rossin?"

Max must have found Getz's lighthearted tone unsettling. They had been discussing matters of life and death and he could never step far enough from his troubles to joke about them. How he envied their assimilated aplomb. He really had little bearing in this Berliner world that suited Suze so well.

"Why, I am the president of my company. We manufacture a brand of zipper called Éclair. Exported all over Europe."

"Never heard of it."

Max must have wanted to run. How much more comfortable he would have felt on deck two, among the Poles, who would be impressed by his status, or perhaps in the salon, among the Russians, who took everything to heart. Still, he remained stoically at Suze's side, coughing nervously, clearing his nose. What a long and desperate struggle it had been! Financial success had brought him the trappings—fine car, fine clothes, fine children, a beautiful wife. And, of course, his beloved factory with its international sales meetings and subservient employees. All this had given his life the tempo of importance until moments such as this which left him squirming on a deck chair. The trouble was that he knew the Getz label. It was associated with film stars and socialites. "Herr Getz is probably miffed at having to sip his bouillon with the likes of me," he mumbled.

The agent in Bilbao had indicated that the *Magallanes* was fully booked. Still, after accepting an exorbitant fee, he had promised Max that he would find five berths somehow.

"Who cares where we sleep, as long as we get to America," Suze had said.

"In America," Max had explained to me, "there are no wars."

Built in the twenties and of uncertain origin, the *Magallanes* was without doubt a passenger ship and not a converted freighter as Max had feared. Her paneled dining room, hung with mirrors and chandeliers, would have been testimony enough, but there was a swimming pool as well, a token twenty by twenty, and a salon with a parquet dance floor and the obligatory wooden chaises on deck. Six notches on each chair. I could make it as flat as a bed or prop it, back up, so as to have a full view of the Atlantic.

I loved being aboard the *Magallanes*. Printed menus in the dining room: choice of chicken, *asado*, or *caldo gallego* for lunch. Swims and shuffleboard, bouillon and champagne, bridge and captain's dinners. For the children, Mickey Mouse and Donald Duck daily in the cabin-class salon. Suspended between two worlds, adrift between the old and the new, between war and peace, the two-week voyage proved long enough to cut everyone off from both shores. A pleasurable torpor settled on the ship. Was it the sun, gloriously high, tracing crisp shadows on the weathered boards of the promenade, was it the sun that burned through our dark European fears? Here on the *Magallanes,* life was being lived from meal to meal as in the most frivolous resort hotel, and even restless Suze seemed content to enjoy the limbo while it lasted.

Never before had I heard such a beat—three long and one short, over and over again. It spiraled down from the dance floor to my narrow upper berth where I lay on a thin mattress with a pillow over my head. Vibrations seeped through the pillow accompanied by the echo of an occasional giddy shriek. I imagined frenzied and twittering shenanigans in the salon. One, two, three—bang. One, two, three—bang. As if someone had trapped fine stones in a box and were shaking them. The whole ship seemed to be flapping like a fish in an aquarium. (Zigzag across the Atlantic to avoid submarines, Pierre had explained that morning.)

Zigzag, I pressed the pillow down and, in the darkness of my muffled world, a black dot seemed to be approaching, shooting straight and sharklike across the gray night waters, growing larger and larger, mean and black, elliptical now, a big black submarine about to crack my pounding heart. I tried to scream but could not make a sound. I wrenched the pillow away just as the blackness was about to rip into me, and awoke to the sound of the pillow's soft thud on the floor. The cabin was still except for the music from above and the voices I had to reach if I were to control my sobs.

Down the corridors, wrong turn after wrong turn, until at last I found the narrow steps that led to the promenade. I ran along the deck to the brightly lit salon windows behind which I found a chain of red-faced men and women holding each other by the waist, shaking and

44

laughing across the dance floor: one, two, three—bang. A handsome young purser, tall and dark, was leading the conga line, and there was Suze, hands on his waist, wiggling behind him. My eyes searched for Max whom I found at a ringside table in his finely tailored "smoking," once again very much man of the world, cigar in hand, foot tapping the beat of the wild maracas, watching Suze as intently as I was.

If I go in, Max might take me on his lap and caress the nightmare away. Perhaps I could even squeeze into the line and feel protectively enveloped by the panting dancers. But no, I would be asked too many questions. What's the matter. Why are you up? Are you sick? Better to stay outside wrapped in one of the ship's soft wool blankets and simply look in.

There's Pierre at a small back table with diminutive Dahlia, the pretty Dutch girl, in earnest conversation as usual, the intent look on his face curiously out of place amid all this hilarity and confusion. If only he would talk to me like that, but what could I add to his passionate discussions about poets like Rimbaud and Baudelaire? The music stopped, everyone sat down, and I watched Max call the waiter with an imperious snap of the fingers. Suze gave him an approving pat on the cheek and, when the champagne arrived, eagerly proffered her glass.

The conga line disbanded, I lost interest and switched to a deck chair that faced the night. I looked at the sparkling sky and was barely able to distinguish between it and the equally sparkling ocean. Was there really a horizon out there? I felt suspended in the middle of the universe and let the ship rock me back to sleep, comforted by the moving figures behind the window glass.

Geschichten aus dem Wiener Wald
Sind ewig jung und ewig alt
Die schoenste Geschichte die es gibt
Ist wenn ein Bursch ein Maderl liebt

I opened my eyes and turned around. Heinrich stood on a small platform, somewhat stiffly, an accordion strapped to his shoulder. Above him, on a table, stood Suze in her shimmering satin evening dress, legs slightly apart *à la* Marlene Dietrich. She was singing a waltz tune from *Tales from the Vienna Woods*.

I knew the waltz well. How many times had we told her, Franz and I, that with a voice like that she should be an opera star. But on the table! What was going on? I saw Max approach a tall, bony woman and invite her to dance. Round and round, the most beautiful tale in the world is when boy loves girl. Max's sense of rhythm was so good that soon they were circling across the entire floor. In his way, Max was as much an attraction tonight as Suze, who sang and sang in praise of spring and love while Heinrich swayed and pumped at the accordion in three-quarter time. Yes, at parties Max and Suze were a real team.

Someone threw her a red carnation. Max and the young purser reached for it but Suze was already pressing it to her chest. Flushed, her hairline slightly moist with perspiration, her smile sparkling like one of Max's diamonds, she hopped down, landing on both feet like a youngster playing hopscotch. I was dazzled.

Did Max love her as much as I did? Did he, too, yearn for those withheld smiles so abundantly lavished tonight? She was our star, exuberant, gay—who, alas, shone brightest for strangers. His wife. His hard-earned Suze, whose low-cut back was now turned to him, her iridescent smile for the young purser alone. With a bow to Max, he led her onto the dance floor, holding her closer and closer, his breath on her hair, their bodies touching, leaving Max, champagne-unhappy Max, behind.

At the next table, Getz whispered something in pregnant Eva's ear. She laughed a wicked, knowing laugh, got up, and began to shimmy on the dance floor like a mountain enduring an earthquake. Off in a dim corner, I detected Pierre and his Dahlia, fingers entwined, dancing cheek to cheek.

"Too much champagne?" I heard Max ask.

"Why?" Suze sounded defiant.

I shriveled into my deck chair praying for invisibility.

"You know why." Max's cigar was tracing hieroglyphs against the sky, his voice was shaking.

"From now on, what I do is my business. You have no right . . . "

"No right?"

"After all I've done for you, for this family, I will tolerate no reproach."

"I could see how much you were enjoying it. I didn't know exhibitionism was one of your . . . "

"We were dancing."

"For God's sake, the man was kissing your hair, fondling you . . . he's a purser, an employee, that's all."

"It just so happens that Señor Carlos was doing his job entertaining the guests—that is a purser's job, you know—and, yes, I found his company agreeable."

"You used to be only a flirt."

"Everything is changed, Max. We've been through so much, I need a little fun. Try to understand."

He moved closer to her. "I'll never understand," he whispered. "You of all people should have realized that. I'll never understand Don Estéban nor Lieutenant Ducek either."

"But you have all your diamonds . . . "

"How dare you!" he said, and I heard him swallow air as if it were a sob.

Suze recoiled and Max followed her back into the salon.

I huddled on the hard wooden chaise, pounded its

47

slats as I fought the captivity of this forest that was the ship.

The hand on my shoulder was Pierre's. "What's the matter," he asked, "why aren't you in bed?"

He let me cry. "Tell me," he repeated gently when I had calmed down.

"They were fighting," I pointed to Max and Suze. "They spoke as if they hated each other . . . "

"Oh that," he said, "It's not the first time. Listen, you're not to blame, so stop worrying."

Stop worrying! What a dumb thing to say. How could I stop worrying when I suddenly felt as abandoned, here in the middle of the ocean, as that orphan in the snow.

"What's going to happen to us?" I said.

"Nothing, silly, everything will go on as before. That's how grownups are. You'll see, in Havana you will never have to wear a winter coat again. Flowers bloom all the time. The sun always shines. You will be happy there. Now, dry your tears." He kissed me on the cheek and began walking back to the salon.

"And Don Estéban?" I called.

"What about Don Estéban?"

"You know."

"I don't know everything, and I don't think about things I can do nothing about."

I watched him return to the dance floor, with Dahlia in his arms. The most beautiful tale in the world is when boy loves girl. Damn, I'm only eleven. How long must I wait before I can join them in their Vienna Woods?

"Race ya!" I didn't stand a chance against Franz's muscular stroke and wasn't about to make a spectacle of myself in front of Suze's entourage. Freckled by the July sun, bleached even blonder by the salt spray, I had, more than ever, become the child of Max and Suze's fantasies.

48

"Forget it," I yelled back at Franz. Performance alone would define me, and I displayed myself twenty feet up and twenty feet down, breaststroke, butterfly, and crawl.

"Gotcha!" Franz had me by the foot and pulled me down. I struggled and surfaced seconds later. Furious, I chased after him around the little pool. We ran in circles until I stopped short without warning, turned around, and pushed him into the water before we had a chance to collide.

"Cut it out," Suze roared.

"Show us one of your fancy back flips," Max called. Very *soigné* as usual, he was draped in a finely tailored terry robe, padded at the shoulders, designed to elongate and trim pudgy bodies like his stunted by starchy childhood diets. Yes, I said to myself as I flexed my knees in preparation for the flip, I am special. All milk, red meat, fresh fruit, and green vegetables. A miraculous hybrid formed by dint of swimming lessons and arduous stretching at the ballet bar. Stroke, stroke, breathe in, breathe out, the pure joy of my weightlessness once again brought back that familiar feeling that I was somehow special. Yes, there must have been a mistake somewhere. Fair, long-limbed children like me do not get deported. They are offered sweets and smiles by dashing German officers . . .

"The odor of their damn olive oil permeates everything. What a barbaric way to cook." Lobster red, Freddy Bauer, heir to the vanished Bauer real estate empire, tennis shoes not withstanding, was once again complaining about the food.

"Do you remember how at the Hotel del Prado in Madrid they always asked how you wanted your dinner prepared, oil or butter?" Getz said.

"Of course, they even prepared schnitzel if you wished."

"Let's go down to the galley and have a word with

49

the chef. We have seven more days to go . . . "

"Please don't," I said. It seemed terribly important to stop them.

"What's that?" Suze asked, her tone an echo of the old speak-when-you're-spoken-to days.

"Señor Carlos, the purser, took me on a tour of the galley," I said. "They have drums of olive oil down there, but a very small supply of butter."

"Better stay where you are, Getz," Freddy said. "The chef might drown you in one of his drums."

"In that case, we'll send Señorita Claudia down to save Getz," Heinrich laughed. "She has special connections down there."

I blushed, feeling that I had somehow given myself away. I dove into the pool to regain my composure, then hopped out and spread myself on a large towel under the unwavering sun.

I loved uniforms. Bronzed Señor Carlos in his starched whites, his dress navy, gold buttons and braids. And at pool duty, wearing only a bathing suit and a religious medal. That morning, he had asked me in broken French whether I was enjoying the crossing.

"*Sí, sí, señor,*" I had replied, remembering Don Estéban's Spanish.

"*Muy bien,*" he had said, delighted with what he called my special gift for languages. "*Yo nací en Barcelona.*" He had pointed to himself when he had said "*Yo*" and enunciated the rest very slowly. A Spanish lesson.

"*Yo nací en Berlin,*" I had mimicked.

"*Entonces es alemana?*" Then you are German?

"No, no," I had protested. How could I explain to him that Max and Suze were, well, wanderers, that they settled here and there, never permanently? Five years in Germany, five in Holland before that, then seven in Belgium. I had never had a citizenship and, unless things

50

improved, I would be issued a Polish passport like Max's when I grew up.

"*Sí*," he insisted, "*es alemana. Una linda muchacha alemana.*" Slowly, clearly, A pretty German girl.

I had wanted to dispel the misunderstanding and say that I had left Berlin without memories when I was three, but it seemed too complicated. Smiling agreeably, German Fraulein that I was not, I had let him take me by the hand and lead me down on an inspection tour of the galley.

Will he seek me out again I now wondered, stretched on the moist, steaming towel. It was clear to me that I would gladly play Fraulein Claudia for Carlos any time. Another week and the voyage would be over. I would plead with Suze, I promised myself, to be allowed to attend just one of the evening parties, "Just for a little while," I will say. Then perhaps Señor Carlos will ask Fraulein Claudia for a waltz.

"Out of the question," Suze replied, when I finally mustered the courage to ask her. We were standing in my porthole-less cabin, getting ready for dinner, and Suze was fiddling with my hair. It was too short to sweep up like hers, so I asked Suze to let me wear it free, loose without the constricting "neat" hold of a barrette.

"Little girls must always look tidy and, when it's late, they belong in bed," she said. "Why, I didn't go to my first ball until I was eighteen, and that's how it should be. Everything in its own time."

"Carlos told me that in Spain children stay up until midnight."

"Carlos? Señor Carlos, you mean. Anyway, we are not Spaniards yet. I understand that in Cuba women run around in banana skirts like Josephine Baker," she said, clipping the hated barrettes firmly in my hair. "The streets are filled with screaming, leaping natives doing the monkey dance *à la Bakair*. Perhaps you would like that, too?"

"Yes," I mumbled.

"Excuse me? I hear, by the way, that you have been running all over the ship with Señor Carlos. Don't you know he's a busy man? The last thing in the world he needs is a little girl pestering him."

After Suze walked out, I pulled the hated barrettes out of my hair and shook my head until I looked wild. I examined my wardrobe of babyish dresses—loose-pleated cottons, smocked and shapeless. Young bodies must have freedom of movement, I could hear Suze say. But here was one with a sash around the waist that I could tighten to interrupt the desperate flatness of my pre-pubescent figure. I slipped it on and pulled in my stomach. I tossed my head from side to side as I walked toward the stairs that led to the dining room.

After dinner, Suze and Eva lingered over coffee.

"I'm very uneasy," I heard Suze whisper, "the man takes her God knows where . . . bowels of the ship . . . Spanish men . . . One can never be too careful."

"Nonsense," Eva laughed. "It's all very harmless. I could go for young Don Carlos myself if it weren't for this wretched condition of mine. Claudia has good taste."

Suze reddened, averted her face slightly. Composed, she replied: "Don't be silly, Eva. Claudia is only a child."

Child Claudia spent her last night aboard the *Magallanes* with her nose pressed to the glass window that looked into the salon. Her own farewell party, costume at that, had long since ended. This one, this New Year's Eve sort of affair, with funny hats and blowers, throbbed before her with desperate gaiety.

In Spain they say *Sí, Sí—* In France they say *Oui, Oui—* Every little Dutch girl says *Ja, Ja* . . . the story of her life. Trot, trot. Carlos was teaching Suze how to rumba, but she wasn't getting it. Lightfooted Max came over and cut in. Child Claudia held her breath, but there was no scene. Graceful Carlos danced on in the line of duty, titillating other game, the fat, slender, young, old ladies of the *Magallanes*. Pierre was getting it, swaying hips with his Dutch Dahlia. Franz, who had befriended the bandleader, was beating a small bongo, catching the beat. Only Suze's hips refused to loosen—no, she wasn't getting it, and asked Max to take her outside for some fresh air, where she ran smack into Fraulein Claudia's fresh face.

VII

Max tried to speak above the din of the docking maneuvers. "Maybe," he said almost timidly, "maybe Cuba is part of the United States after all. The United States is always called America, and isn't Cuba in America?" But when he saw the black musicians assembled on the dock to greet us, singing and beating their bongos, pounding the hard earth with bare feet, he feared that, not unlike Columbus, he had reached the wrong continent. "We're in Africa, in Africa, for God's sake! *Man hat uns verschlept.* We have been led astray."

"No, no," Pierre hastened to say. "This is Havana, the Paris of the Caribbean."

I could not see the connection. As the *Magallanes* slipped into Havana harbor, I had sniffed port smells of fried fish, tar, rotting fruit, and aromatic tobacco. Paris never smelled like this, nor did she ever gleam so white.

Paris never resounded to shrill whistles, boys yelling, peddlers, bottle music, and honking cars. And bongos.

I had seen my first Negro when I was five or six, a big black Congolese on an Antwerp street corner. His dark business suit and white shirt had looked like everybody else's but, as the news spread down the avenue, a crowd had gathered. And although I had sensed both his bravado and his pain, I had been unable to contain my excitement and had repeatedly pointed a finger at him as if he were a curiosity. Mademoiselle had been outraged, and I don't think I have ever pointed a finger at anyone since. Such images now flooded my mind as I tried to formulate my own vision of this land called Cuba, or Kubá, as I pronounced it then. The street-corner Negro? Little Black Sambo? Uncle Tom? My repertoire was unsatisfactory. Doctor Dolittle in Africa, then. No. Treasure Island, of course!

Across the gangplank, three men were singing and tapping bottles suspended from strings. *"Maniii . . ."* one of them sang out. *"Un poquitico de maniii . . ."* The sound lingered, reached my pulse. I felt Pierre's tap on the ship's railing beside me.

"Stevenson's Treasure Island is really out there," he said.

A flash of shame shot through me. Was I as transparent as all that? "Don't make fun of me."

"True," he said. "The book describes it perfectly and scholars have confirmed it. It is called Isla de Pinos and lies off Cuba's southwestern coast. Used to be a famous pirate haunt—one-eyed, one-legged pirates, you know, hobble, hobble."

I laughed. "Come on, Pierre."

"I'll take you there someday and you'll see. We'll find pirates, treasure, kit and caboodle."

I love you, Pierre, that's for sure. Because he was

54

seventeen and his face already had the angularity of an adult's—large fine nose, pointed cleft chin—I often thought of him more as a grownup than an equal. For me, being near Pierre always meant intense participation; yet because of the difference in our ages, he so rarely had time for me.

"It's a deal," I said.

"Por aquí, la piña dulce y madura!" The *turistas* of the *Magallanes* were being welcomed by the Havana Chamber of Commerce with fresh pineapples.

"Hey, mister," one of the Chamber of Commerce men called to Max in English. "Come here, mister."

"Merci." Max made his usual little bow and accepted a slice of pineapple. "Hm," he said, walking toward Pierre and me, pineapple juice oozing from his mouth. "Unbelievable. It beats the Canary Island pineapples and they are, as everybody knows, the best in the world."

I took a cautious bite. The fruit tasted sweet and silky, its juice filled my mouth, the enchanted aroma my nostrils. I could not believe that it had existed throughout my lifetime without my knowing about it.

"Manii." The song rang out once more. "Maniii," in the brightest of suns. Immigration officials, now settled at makeshift tables on deck, joked and smoked. Suze's eyes wandered past the brilliant waves lapping the sides of the Malecón wall, past the Morro Castle and La Cabaña fortress, symbols of imperial Spain, toward the apartment houses, trolley cars, and automobiles of the city. "They even have electricity!" she exclaimed only half in jest.

"What happens now?" she added to no one in particular. "Go up there, Max, and offer some money. Remember what Rudi Getz said—money really talks around here."

"What do you want me to do? Shove my wallet in

55

their faces? I can't speak the language. I think we should wait until we're called to the table. I'll take Pierre along then and he'll translate into English."

"This is crazy." She puffed hard on her cigarette. "To be at the mercy of this wretched-looking lot. I'll go talk to them, Max."

"Non, merci," he said.

"I know what to do . . . "

"No—Pierre, stand by me."

There they go again, I thought, right here in the middle of the morning, on deck, in front of everybody. Then, I heard our name.

"Rossín." The man pronounced it with a strong accent on the last syllable.

Max reached into his vest pocket and pulled out his Polish passport, slightly discolored from perspiration. He opened it to the page that held the Salvadorian visa. His hands shook slightly.

"San Salvador, *no,*" he said when he reached the table.

"El Salvador," Suze corrected.

Batista's chattering men rattled off a brief reply. Max, in turn, shrugged his shoulders, raising his hands toward heaven as an indication of helplessness. *"Anglais?"* he said in French. "English," he corrected himself.

"No English," the immigration official answered. "Spanish." He examined the passport. *"Tiene que pagar,"* he said.

"Pagar?" Max repeated. He looked at Pierre.

"Payer," Pierre said.

"Payer," Max smiled. *"Mais oui."*

Batista's men were patient and kind. They cupped their hands behind their ears to indicate their attentiveness. *"Payer."* They laughed. *"Mil pesos,"* they said, pointing at Max. Then, pointing at Suze, Pierre, Franz, and me, they said, *"Mil pesos"* four more times.

*　*　*

Pale beneath her fine tan, Eva was visibly shaken. "Pierre," she called, "how's your Spanish? They think we are spies and might send us back. Except me, because of my condition! They claim that the visas we purchased in Spain are invalid. Is this crazy?" She was very agitated, but not bereft of her usual irony. "They don't believe we are Jews—how's that! Haven't they heard of the famous Aryan test? With my big nose I can fail it with flying colors; and the men, well, all they have to do is pull their pants down, *Ja?* Please, Pierre, help us explain to these insolents that we're Jews and that Jews can't be spies, not in this war, anyway."

Pull their pants down. That's pretty funny. But Pierre would have no part of it. "No Spanish," he said. "Sorry. Give me a couple of weeks, Frau Eva."

The next morning, after countless Jewish-Cuban and American organizations had interceded, everyone was allowed to land. Those who had been unable to pay were sponsored by relief organizations, and the *Magallanes* eventually sailed back to Bilbao with a cargo of coffee and sugar, a handful of businessmen, and a couple of priests.

We finally disembarked, Suze and I, gracefully down the ramp in our flimsiest summer dresses and newly purchased fans. Max, Pierre, and Franz were in *guayaberas*—the loose, porous linen shirts, daintily pleated, sold by peddlers aboard the *Magallanes* the night before.

I watched porters and dockworkers, peddlers and taxi drivers point to hand and mouth and heart almost as if the spoken word were not enough and they needed sign language to convey meaning and feeling. What passionate things they must be saying! Punctuated with shrugs and gestures, they conveyed that sense of mystery only a language one does not understand can transmit.

As we crossed the gangplank under the brilliant sun, I remembered what Pierre had said about no more

57

winter coats. I believed him now. I felt that I had out-
grown the little brown coat with velvet collar a hundred
times. In later years, when Max and Suze would insist that
Cuba was just a stopover on the way to the United States, I
would disagree with passion. I embraced the alligator-
shaped island Cubans call "El Caimán" the moment we
stepped ashore.

VIII

========================= Shaded by hurricane-proof
ceiba trees, rimmed by blooming bougainvillea, the Hotel
de Apartamentos La Gardenia rose modern and seven stories high in Havana's oldest residential section, El Vedado.
Broken-down buses and trolley cars criss-crossed chaot-
ically on *calle veinte-y-tres,* two blocks away, while here, on
diecinueve, amid the walled old houses with their gardens
and verandas where sit mothers, grandmothers, and
maiden aunts who rock, flutter their fans, tend children,
and never go out, where maids slap-slap in wooden
chancletas, where fruit vendors compete with manic drivers
for the right of way, where a sudden rainstorm paralyzes
all street activity, where lottery vendors peddle a fraction
of a ticket and those who cannot afford even that play "fly
on the penny," here on *diecinueve,* where the air is as much
a mystery as it ever was in Egypt, the *Magallanes* refugees
able to afford it had settled at the three-star La Gardenia
to ponder the future.

Above us, in *apartamento seis B,* Mevrouw Groen, aft
promenade ex-*Magallanes,* her spick-and-span Netherland-

ish blood aroused, had once again declared *Blitzkrieg* on *las cucarachas,* tropical airborne variety. The thud of a shoe, the hard swat of a rolled-up newspaper augured an especially active dawn.

In *apartamento cinco B,* my own roaches fluttered and crawled up the walls under cover of night's waning shadows. Suddenly, a tremendous crash—Mevrouw Groen has lost her head!—and the gig is up. Mid-air collisions, frantic scurrying into cracks, the glistening insects' night prowl had been aborted by the rampage from above. As long as I live I'll never get out of bed until it's completely light.

An hour later, still cloistered under my mosquito net, sensing the brilliant sun beyond the shutters, I lifted the gauzelike material and slowly extended a foot onto the cool, tiled floor, looking down to see where I had stepped, what I might have disturbed. I opened the shutters and made a dash for the bathroom to wash off the night's sweat.

At breakfast, in the white-linen and mimosa-bedecked dining room, Mevrouw Groen wore her battle ribbons with pride.

"Ten," she announced. "Got ten this morning."

Franz leaned across the table toward me. "Ten what? Ten Nazis?" I giggled.

"Madame Groen, if you'll excuse me," Suze called in French, "but that *'Krach'* of yours every morning wakes my whole family." She had interjected the German word for noise because its guttural "ch" sound seemed more Dutch.

"And?" Mevrouw Groen shot back. "What am I supposed to do. Submit to the plague?"

"Mevrouw Groen," Pierre said, "cockroaches are prehistoric. They will inherit the world. You can't win."

"We'll see," she said. "If they're so ancient, then they must also be smart. They'll find out that *piso seis* is out of bounds."

"We would appreciate," Max mumbled, "a more

59

delicate method of extermination. Poison, perhaps."

"Just don't send them down to us." Pierre laughed.

Nothing, not even Mevrouw Groen, could spoil the astonishing breakfast at La Gardenia. We had been introduced to cornflakes the day before and I was now searching the dining room for the lithe waiter with the big white box.

"*Es americano*," the waiter had explained to Max, as if that said it all. Imported, expensive, *El Kellogg* symbolized high-class fare in Havana where, we would learn, anything American was considered chic.

"*Bastante, bastante*," Max said this morning, holding his hand up as the graceful waiter persisted in filling his bowl with flakes and milk.

"The word is *basta*," Pierre said.

"But I looked it up," Max defended himself.

"*Bastante* means both plenty and enough. *Basta* means enough and no more. *Basta*, with an 'a.' Can you remember that?"

Bewildered, Max repeated softly. "With an 'a.' Ah!" Then, changing his tone, he turned to me: "For God's sake, stop that crunching. You sound like a rabbit."

"But it's so good," I said. "Try it with sliced banana." How could I convey to him the pleasure of *El Kellogg's* amazing consistency, so crisp if you timed it right and did not let it sit a second too long in the ice-cold milk, the hard sweetness of the undissolved sugar mingling with the aromatic mush of the ripe banana. It seemed to blend perfectly with the magic sunshine, the glossy dark hair of the waiters, the twittering birds beyond the dining room's glass doors.

The miraculous abundance of strong coffee and sweet white bread pleased Max and Suze far more than the *gringo* delicacies I devoured with such relish. I watched Suze relinquish her dazzling Austro-Hungarian smile long enough to inhale an American cigarette with unabashed sensuality. Max waved at a fly, rolled a Vuelta Abajo cigar between thumb and index finger, and raised it toward his face till it almost touched the prominent nose.

"Take a whiff, go ahead," he said passing the cigar to Franz. "Nothing in the world like it."

I watched the smoke sputter out of Franz's mouth.

"Not like that," Max cried. "Look at me." He rolled the smoke on his tongue, tilted his head back, and blew tight white rings that encircled us like halos.

"Show-off," Franz teased.

It suddenly seemed as if everything had gone up in smoke: Nazi occupation, Nazi deportation, food shortages, the terrifying hassle for exit permits. *"Mas café, señor?"* Always plenty more of everything.

Max and Suze lingered over their coffee pondering the complexities of tropical existence with Eva, Heinrich, and Rudi Getz; poor tennis-shoes Freddy had not been able to afford La Gardenia and was rooming at a nearby pension. They smoked and sat around the fragrant center-pieces until the buzzing of flies and gnats made it clear that they had let the morning freshness slip by and that the sun had climbed so high it was too hot to go out.

"I can't think in this heat," Eva said, mopping her forehead.

"The coolest spot in town is the American Consulate," Heinrich said. "They have fans the size of airplane propellers."

"So what?" Max said. "I don't want to spend the rest of my days in waiting rooms. The Polish quota is light-years long and my passport is not worth the paper it's printed on." He recalled his years as a second-class citizen in Belgium where he had been subjected first to a white identity card and later, after years of clean living, to the coveted yellow card that had allowed him to own a business. "Belgian citizenship never!" he concluded.

"Ja, in America you automatically become a citizen after five years," Getz said.

"But you have to get in first," Suze replied.

"Cheer up," Eva said. "We won't stay here forever."

"Maybe you won't. The German quota reads like a welcome mat compared to ours," Suze said.

Max looked at Suze. "Guess whom I saw at the consulate yesterday?"

"Magda Lupescu."

"No, Mendelsohn, Mendelsohn from Antwerp."

"I don't believe it," Suze said.

"It wasn't his ghost." Max turned to the others. "The poor fellow," he explained, "sold diamonds to the Germans right after the Occupation, and when the Jewish community got wind of this, they trapped him on a street corner and beat him black and blue. His wife stopped speaking to him and he was ostracized by everyone. Even here, because too many people know the story, he dare not show his face. Maybe if he got into the United States, he could put all that behind him."

"Herr Rossin—'poor fellow'? What are you saying! The man deserves to be hanged." Nowadays, Eva's belly moved as she spoke and her words, as if blessed by the unseen baby, took on special significance.

"He told me that he has all his meals sent up to his room," Max remarked.

Suze's eyes narrowed as if she were about to pounce. "That's the least he could do," she said.

"Why, the man has children! He made a mistake and he's been punished. I'm ready to forget the whole thing," Max said.

"Herr Rossin," Heinrich said, "if he really traded with the Nazis as late as 1940 I, for one, do not wish to know him."

"Amen," said Rudi Getz.

"Quiet, here he comes now," Max said. I remembered Monsieur Mendelsohn's special friendship with Max before the war. Max always said that Mendelsohn knew everything about music there was to know. He had once

62

hummed a melody for me which, he said, Mendelsohn had composed. "Our Mendelsohn," he had joked. I saw the tall, bald, corpulent figure in baggy trousers get his key at the desk and disappear into the elevator.

"Max," Suze said, "you're crazy to show yourself in public with Mendelsohn!"

"I don't own the waiting room at the American Embassy," he answered. "Anyway, why be so hard on Mendelsohn? All is fair in love and war, remember?"

"Don't talk nonsense," she said, directing an embarrassed glance at Eva and Heinrich. "He did it for money."

"Not a bad reason, I would say," Max taunted.

"Herr Rossin, man does not live by bread alone," Getz said.

"Ah yes, Herr Getz, you are so wise," Max replied. "But where do you draw the line? Mendelsohn was acting as a broker for people who desperately needed to sell their diamonds. He just happens to have made a handsome profit along the way."

"There are things one doesn't do, regardless of the circumstances," Eva pronounced.

"Amen," Getz said again.

Suze lit a cigarette.

I jumped up from the table and ran outside to the jasmine- and gardenia-filled hotel garden. *"Linda, preciosa,"* the waiters whispered seductively as I passed by. I pretended not to hear and ran on to join the other refugee children in a game of hide-and-seek among the dwarf palms and giant hibiscus.

Shrewd, thin-lipped Madame Olivier maneuvered her car like a man—out of the city and into the newest suburb called Marianao which, in those days, was still partly populated with tin shanties.

"E'ta señora e' formidable," the Gardenia clerk had said, swallowing his s's for, so the story goes, he would

63

need them later to call "Psssst" after shapely young things. *"Habla francé'. E' inteligentísima."*

Superlatives, so readily lavished in Havana, meant little to Max. Pierre, who had acquired a working knowledge of Spanish during our six-week stay at La Gardenia, had explained that the woman in question was the widow of a French vice-consul. She dealt in real estate, and would help us find a more permanent home.

Huddled in a window seat, Max held tightly onto the strap as Madame's car veered past blurred images of vendors who screamed, laughed, pushed, thrust their wares through the window at every stop, crying food, hot and spicy. *"Tamales, tamales riquísimos,"* they said.

"What's tamales? What do they want from me?" Max cried.

"My mother makes 'em, I sell 'em, you eat 'em . . . " A hot tamale appeared under Max's nose. Madame stepped on the accelerator and the vendor yelped, *"Qué bruta!"*

"Look out!" Max screamed. Madame had barely missed an ice-cream wagon parked along the curb.

"They call their ice cream Hatuey," she volunteered as if this information might calm us down. "It's named after Cuba's only Indian hero, *El Indio Hatuey,* famous for having led a revolt against Velázquez before they all died of disease and overwork. Cubans honor him with what they love best—sweets."

"I like that," Pierre said. "What else do the Cubans love?"

Madame Olivier did not respond, she was all business again. "It is," she said, approaching the house, "a jewel."

I spotted it in the midst of an overgrown field. Its tiled red roof protruded beyond the brownish dried-out banana plants, all dead now after producing their single crop. The creeper-tangled field that had all but choked the banana's stalks had been forced to buckle under the power of stucco and concrete. The little house with its wide veranda had settled on this jungle-like environment like an enormous winged creature basking in the sun.

A house. Never before. I had always yearned to "go upstairs," or "run downstairs," or whatever it is that people in houses do. I had drawn childishly symmetrical houses with tulips in window boxes and a tree on either side. And now, at last, it was to come true. Mutti by the little stove, Papi in the best chair. Of course this one, with its pink shutters, dancing feather-like shadows, tiled floors still covered with plaster dust, this one that smelled so new, that had no history, this sunny house, far from the city, did not exactly conform to my European dreams. But no matter.

Before the war, I would occasionally spend an exceptional Saturday with Max. He would steer me through children's and toy stores urging me to choose anything I wanted. Max's little girl. Anything in the world is yours. Always free with money, on those Saturdays he seemed particularly eager to part with it and claim me with its power.

And I fed him my dreams. "There is a dollhouse, Papi, so real you wouldn't believe it" . . . Faster and faster, laughing as I pulled him along, we used to make our way through the toy section. "It has two stories and fireplaces in every room, and upholstered furniture in the salon and . . . " I would watch his face as it took this outburst and would see that all was well, for his often-taut lower lip was spread in a soft smile.

Later, over éclairs, ice cream, I would chat and giggle, high and free from all that indulgence. There will be two children, you see, and they will live upstairs with their dog, and the mother will use the tiny stove in the kitchen while the father smokes a cigar in the salon. He will have the best chair, *Papilein*—I would have switched from French to German by then to underscore the intimacy of our conversation. It was, in fact, my mother tongue. In a way. It was spoken to me during the first few years of my life, while we lived in Berlin. In Belgium, the language's development had been stunted. I used it with Max and Suze, who spoke it among themselves, but as I grew older, my brothers and I switched to the "real" world's French. We would never have a mother tongue; every language, no matter how well we spoke it, would always be a second language for us.

"Et bien, ça vous plait?" Madame spoke to Max abruptly, fingering her car keys as if to let him know that she had other more pressing business to attend to.

Max shifted his weight from foot to foot. He looked pained. Decision making outside the realm of business always baffled him. The back of his fresh *guayabera* was soaked. A perfect row of perspiration beads had appeared above his lips. The nose and forehead had begun to shine and the thinning black hair, so carefully brilliantined that morning, was beginning to curl.

"Excusez-moi," he said, with his usual little bow. "I must confer with my wife." Energized by Madame's aggressive demeanor, he felt emboldened to suggest to Suze: "How about it? Why not?"

Suze caught the wistfulness in his voice. "Ridiculous, Max! Can you imagine us here in the middle of the wilderness? You don't even know how to drive! How will the children get to school?"

Max capitulated. "You're right," he said, almost relieved. "Jews like us shouldn't buy houses. Can't stick 'em in a suitcase, that's for sure. We belong in apartments."

I wanted to scream. So close, I thought, we came so close, and then, pouf, all gone.

"Why," I asked, "why can't we live in a house like everybody else? There are school buses and Papi will learn how to drive."

"I'll drive," Pierre said.

66

"Me too," Franz added.

"Out of the question," Suze replied and called us over. "I don't trust this Madame Olivier," she whispered. "I suspect that there is something wrong with this house and that she wants to unload it. Look how isolated it is— you can barely see a neighbor. As for being the widow of a French diplomat, I don't believe a word of it. If you ask me, she looks as if she might be running a bordello or two. She's used to rich Americans, that one, Americans sent here by their fruit companies; refugees like us are not her cup of tea at all." She lowered her voice even more and we all leaned forward. "I'm sure she's anti-Semitic to boot."

Max nodded. She had said it all. He could not have expressed it better. I could not believe that I had heard Suze say what she did. Suze, always so sure of herself, always so arrogant, now seemed as vulnerable as Max.

They sidled over to Madame and Suze explained in no uncertain terms that houses were out. "Now listen here," she added, "we want to live in an apartment among civilized people."

Madame Olivier rattled her keys.

"Come on," Max said. "It's time to go."

IX

━━━━━━━━━━━━━━━━━━ The Negroes dropped the steamer trunk onto the slate path.

Madame had called the furnished apartment in residential Vedado wonderfully central. She had said that it was near everything: bustling *veinte-y-tres* down the block, bi-weekly *mercado* just two corners away on Paseo.

The workmen mopped sweat from their faces and lit cigarettes.

Max, morocco suitcases in hand, looked drained. *"Het moet vlugger gann,"* he complained. *"Niet so langzaam."* Whenever he was under pressure, he lapsed into Dutch. It was exasperating. He had once explained that he did this because Dutch was his first foreign language.

"Rápido," Pierre said to the workmen as he took the luggage from Max's hands.

"Rápido," Max repeated, and the men laughed in his face.

"No hay problema," one of them said, nudging his companion. They lifted the steamer trunk once again and groaned. *"Coño,"* they cursed when they felt its weight. It's the silver, I thought. Suze's *couvert* for twenty-four that would not be left behind.

A battered Paris hatbox over her arm, Suze followed the men, and I brought up the rear.

It wasn't a country house, but then it didn't feel like a city house either. Only three stories high, two apartments per floor, I liked the idea of living without an elevator. Lizards on hot stones, street shaded by giant ceibas, garden glowing with hibiscus which Cubans call *mar pacífico,* wild greenness cracking the sidewalk, gardenias, roses, wisteria trailing down terrace walls, a stray chicken, the cry of a pet parrot. Yes, I told myself, it will do.

How I treasured the instant gaiety of my sun-filled room. I would spend hours arranging knick-knacks on the cherrywood dresser . . . toy maracas, palm-decorated fans, mahogany dancing figures with African features, junk accumulated downtown. Maybe I should move this figure a little to the left. There, that's better. The dancers must frame the open fan exactly. And the maracas guard the dancers, of course. Over there, in the wardrobe, my dresses and skirts hung regimentally shipshape; on the bottom shelf, shoes, slippers, ruler straight. Everything had to be just right. This is my room, I would say to myself.

Nights were more problematical. The bed. Although I could not fall asleep unless it was absolutely smooth and tucked in at the sides, I needed to dismantle it every night before getting in. I had to shake out the sheets and examine the mattress in search of stray lizards and leathery cockroaches that could have slithered into my bedclothes and molted six times. Then, I would remake the bed and rest, satisfied at last that with the mosquito net tucked under, nothing could fall on me from the ceiling or crawl over me in the dark. Still, I might pop out of bed one more time for a quick last look underneath to make sure no one lurked there. You never know.

Exhausted, I would at last be ready for sleep. But no! Prayers. First a short German one learned from Suze. *Lieber Gott im Himmelszelt,* Dear God in your heavenly tent, *Lass mich sanft und sicher ruhen,* Let me rest gently and safely. And then the litany: God protect Mutti, Papi, Pierre, Franz, Roosevelt, Stalin, Churchill, the Allied troops—had I forgotten anyone? Ah yes, Tante Caro and Uncle Paul in Brazil, and Anton . . . Until that special day when the war will be over and Max will take his golden little girl out on the town to buy her anything she wants, anything at all in the world, he had said, for it would be that kind of day, when the war is over. Then I would sleep.

"Repetition, Max, repetition is the most fundamental principle in music." Monsieur Mendelsohn had squeezed himself into the largest of the four rocking chairs on our terrace. He accelerated the rocking, then slowed it down. "Variation, yes," he continued. "You can change the rhythm, the tempo, the key, but the basic melody is there if you pay attention."

69

"If you say so, Mendelsohn, I believe you. I can hear it in Mozart sometimes, but when it comes to Brahms, Chopin, and even Beethoven, I lose it. Other thoughts come into my head. Business schemes, for instance."

"Again, Max? Haven't you had your fill of business?"

"Look at the women, Mendelsohn, look how busy they are. Their work follows them wherever they go. Cooking, tending children, primping in front of the mirror and, if there's time left over, they join a committee or two. Hitler can't take from them what he took from us."

"What did he take from you?"

"What kind of a question is that?"

"I mean it."

Max straightened himself in the rocking chair as if he were reaching for the right words. He must have wanted to blurt it all out—his losses, his humiliations—but he was afraid of losing control. "First of all," he began slowly, "I lost my factory which had a worldwide reputation. I lost my routine, my tempo. I don't like variations, not big variation Mendelsohn."

"I do," Mendelsohn said, and laughed. "I'll be happy if I never have to do another business deal as long as I live. I expect to sit here and rock my troubles away until the war is over. This," he tapped the radio on a low table by his side, "is my best friend. Tonight there will be a live broadcast of the Havana Philharmonic, with Erich Kleiber conducting Beethoven's Seventh."

"Don't you wish you could attend?"

"I'm content, Max. I'm alive."

"Well, I've been thinking of starting something," Max said. "What with the United States so busy manufacturing war material, I believe a little Cuban zipper industry could do very well."

"And the machinery?"

"I brought the plans. I could have it built."

"Max, don't be crazy. It's diamonds the Americans want. People are opening polishing and cutting workshops right and left. Invest there if you insist on parting with your money. Don't start involving yourself in the building of complex machinery—you can't even speak the language."

"Excuse me," Max replied. "I mean no insult, but the less I have to do with diamonds, the better. It's not really my sort of thing.

"No, Mendelsohn," he continued, "I'm a zipper man. After the war, ask Van Velde, my gentile partner, about our international sales meetings, our foreign representatives. I used to travel . . . always the best hotels."

"But look at what diamonds did for us—we can both sit the war out in tropical splendor without lifting a finger."

"Is it because you have no choice, Mendelsohn? Is that why you appear so content?"

"Believe me, Max, exile is not the worst thing in the world. And I am exiled in more ways than one. My own wife . . . never mind. In the end, we are all alone, and the sooner you get used to it the better. My head is full of music and that's enough for me."

Max stood up. "Not for me," he declared.

"Can I come back next week?" Mendelsohn asked.

On Wednesdays *la señora francesa*—as Suze came to be known to the neighborhood merchants—went to the *mercado* with her red umbrella and her daughter in tow. She insisted that these expeditions were educational for me. The pitting of wits in the marketplace, which she remembered with relish from her own small-town childhood, taught one valuable lessons in how to manipulate people, she said. In Belgium, with its antiseptic grocery stores tiled in white, haggling had been as out of place as squeezing tomatoes. The market on calle Paseo struck me as a vulgar, dirty, naked place. But I was made to go.

"*Mire, mire, señora, la piña blanca, dulce, dulce, la fruta bomba madura, las naranjas de china, dieciseis por una peseta.*" Sixteen juice oranges for twenty cents!

"That's cheap," I said. "Isn't it?"

"Never cheap enough," Suze answered. "The asking price is never cheap enough. *Muy caro,* very expensive," she complained. Marketplace Spanish had come easily to her.

"*Ay, francesita,*" the miserable merchant cried, "*te doy un buen precio.*"

"No," Suze said. Her tenacity astounded me; it was as if her life depended on saving that penny or two. Heinrich had once told her that she would have made a terrific businesswoman. "Who, me?" she had replied with a girlish laugh. "Oh, no, never. I am what the French call *une femme d'intérieur.*"

The merchant finally gave in. "If she needs it more than I do, I say then let her have it." He announced this to the small crowd now gathered around us and everyone laughed. But the red umbrella did not care, and pressed every one of the sixteen oranges. Tomorrow our new Galician maid Concha would squeeze them by hand and serve us the slightly pulpy juice for breakfast, with an ice cube.

Tireless, Suze traveled from stall to stall, surrounded by a crowd of laughing, pushing boys vying to earn *un medio,* one nickel, for the privilege of carrying her purchases in a cardboard box on the head. She picked an eager little black face that would then follow us for the rest of the expedition, gibing and laughing with his barefoot and shirtless companions.

We were part of a caravan, trailing Suze. We stopped and moved at her whim; a squeeze, a haggle, *aquí,*

allá, here, there, wait, go. Get me out of here. Her box
filled up too slowly, mostly fruit, for she disdained the
starchy, fibrous roots called *yuca, ñame, malanga, boñiato*
that were Cuban staples.

"*Güter Himmel!*" she exclaimed at the sight of the
meat stall. "Steer's foot, pig's knuckle! Do they weigh the
flies, too? Oh but . . . goat meat, rabbit . . . " She was suddenly delighted.

The rabbits seethed in tightly packed cages.

"Rabbit," she murmured. "Haven't eaten *lapin* in
ages. I bet they would skin one for us if we asked."

Nausea bubbled into my mouth. "My God," I said,
"how can you say a thing like that!"

"That's what they're here for, isn't it?"

"You don't have to sound so happy about it."

"Wait till you taste it—*ragoût de lapin,* as the French
call it. Rabbit stew. *Un délice.*"

Nearby, a chicken's neck was being wrung and its
wild shrieks distracted Suze's attention. I tried to steer her
away. "I won't let anyone harm you," I whispered to the
caged rabbits before going.

I searched the wasteland that had been alive with human
cries and animal squeals only an hour before. Gone were
the collapsible stalls, the vendors and their wares. The
mercado had folded in a matter of minutes and the rabbits
were gone. Poor creatures, I murmured. I came back to
save you. A two-peso note lay moist and rumpled in my
tight fist. Above me, vultures with white underwings
soared and slid down the currents of air, then circled over
the field with bunched, ready claws. I felt the sweat trick-
ling between my new breasts. I had wanted so badly to take
one of those little rabbits in my arms. To cradle it and
reassure it. Nearby, claws and beaks locked, wings flapping, I watched a couple of vultures fight each other for

food. I closed my eyes and felt the sun exploding on my retina. The colors continued to flash after I reopened my eyes. I was filled with fear and nausea.

To my relief, I sensed another presence. A shabby white man was standing only ten yards away. I looked up apologetically. How can I explain my presence here on this deserted, dusty field? The man was pitifully thin. For all I know, he is competing with the vultures for scraps. But then I saw it. His pink, fleshy organ hung between the folds of his pants, strange guttural sounds emanated from his cavernous, toothless mouth. The vocal chords on his neck looked like ropes about to snap. He is a mute, I realized in a flash as the man stuck his finger up his nose to convey his intentions. I watched him walk toward me and knew that I should flee. But I could not move. Perhaps I was afraid that he would pursue me and overtake me from behind. When he was close, he grabbed my hand and placed it on his swollen organ. He moved it back and forth, all the while making those awful guttural sounds. The whitish liquid that oozed through my fingers drew rivulets on the back of my hand. I pulled away and began to run. The breeze I engendered wrapped my wet body in an icy sheet.

"*Hija*, look where you're going," Concha said as I collided with her at the kitchen door.

Sobbing, I fell into her arms. "Concha, *yo* . . . " but my Spanish was inadequate to explain what had happened. Concha stroked my hair and pressed me to her full figure. "*Ay, muchacha*," she said tenderly, "*el mercado no es para las niñas.*"

Niñash. I liked the way Concha's Galician *s*'s whistled through her teeth. Yes, I am just a little girl. I felt comforted by Concha's rippling body that smelled of kitchen soap. Her rough hands never seemed to shrink from touch.

"*Que pasó, niña?*" she asked, stroking my hair.

74

I desperately wanted to tell her. But how? The frustration redoubled my crying. "Concha," I got out, "*un homme* . . . " I stuck my finger up my nose to show what he had done.

"*Eso es muy feo,*" Concha said. That's very ugly.

"*Sí, sí,*" I insisted, pointing to my genitals.

Concha let out a shriek. "*Ave María purísima!*" she yelled and threw me down on the kitchen table. She pulled off my panties and examined me. Then, with a sigh of relief, she blessed the Virgin.

"*No hay problema,*" she said and pulled me up.

I felt that Concha had gone right to the heart of the matter. Yes, of course, the man could have raped me. No need to pretend anymore that I didn't know what that was. Concha knew that I knew and that was comforting.

Now, I thought, I won't have to tell Suze, who wouldn't understand anyway. I had just wanted one of those little rabbits for my very own.

X

Suze decided and Max agreed that our education should be in English. However long the wait, the United States, "America," was to be our final destination. Cuba was a stopover, nothing more. Therefore, Max and Suze never developed an interest in the land that took them in. Therefore, they never picked up *El Mundo* or *Diario de la Marina,* the leading Havana dailies, but read the German *Aufbau,* published in the United States, and the ridiculous *Havana Post,* published for the American community. And, in a flash of enthusiasm, they began taking English lessons twice a week, joined by Eva and Heinrich and Freddy Bauer. Rudi Getz had moved on to New York. Their teacher was an American expatriate called Mr. Hough, whose name they could not fathom. Three silent letters out of five, Eva said, was more than she had bargained for.

Pierre and Franz were enrolled at an American high school called Candler College and I was registered at St. George's, a so-called British school on Avenida de los Presidentes. I protested when I heard about this arrangement. "Listen," I said, "I want to go to a Cuban school with Cuban children." I could not understand why Pierre and Franz did not feel as I did.

As things turned out, St. George's attracted mostly upper-class Cuban girls whose parents wanted them to have Yankee manners—the proper preparation, they felt, for a life punctuated by shopping pilgrimages to the United States. For Cuban boys, such an education was considered inadequate, and they were sent either to the Jesuit Belén or to La Salle to do the more rigorous *bachillerato*.

Tight and bloated, my stomach would betray me on schoolday mornings by refusing to assimilate the beloved cornflakes and banana breakfast. The banana, in particular, would reassert itself all morning long, surfacing again and again, no matter how much air I swallowed. There is a Cuban saying that a well-assimilated person is *bien aplatanado*. Fully bananaed? I could see that I wasn't.

I dreamed of riding the navy blue school bus, as did so many of my Cuban classmates who lived in the affluent suburb of Miramar. Even some of the Vedado children rode. But Suze, in a surge of Old World stoicism, decided that I was "strong enough" to walk both ways. Under the young, low morning sun the walk along the well-tended flower mall and broad palms of Avenida de los Presidentes

76

was still bearable. But, coming home in the noontime swelter, it was dreadful. I would feel an unbearable lassitude that lodged itself in my head.

On a corner, near our calle B, an oasis loomed in the form of a shriveled Chinaman under a tree. He peddled, for a penny, cakes that dripped with sugar, cakes I craved to clear my head. These were symmetrically arranged in a glass box perched on a folding stool. Sitting cross-legged behind the box, the Chinaman was as immobile as his wares. Coconut, guava, custard—if I bought a cake a day for the five, six, seven years I lived there, I must have consumed thousands and we should have become quite friendly. But we never exchanged a word. Still, his taut, skeletal face peering out of the mandarin collar sits in my mind to this day. I know now that he was old enough to have been brought over as contract labor after the importation of African slaves stopped. Only men were brought in and they married black Cuban women. The offspring of such a union is the famous Cuban *chinita*. But my Chinaman, I had no doubt, was some sort of monk.

Actually, my main reason for wanting to ride the bus was not the weather at all. During the informality of pickups and deliveries, I had hoped to establish the beginnings of a Cuban friendship or two.

I hated having to huddle in the schoolyard during recess with the refugee children, the Cecile Edelsteins and Marianne Shapiros from Vienna and Rotterdam. I found their swollen, sun-reddened faces grotesque next to the blemishless, smooth-skinned *Cubanas,* who knew better than to let themselves be caught by the sun.

Why did our dresses look so desperately childish, Peter Pan collars and puff sleeves for heaven's sake, while their uniforms seemed the height of fashion? Why did our arms hang so stiffly at our sides while their hands danced in joyful pantomime? I wished I could change colors like the lizards that hopped across out hot sills. These days, my

77

hair would do well to be dark like everybody else's. I should have pierced ears, rings on my fingers, and fine gold chains with medals around my neck. I should have an assortment of fans, one for each day of the week. But first I should have a uniform. Suze had taken me to be measured at El Encanto department store, but it would be weeks before the precious things were ready.

When we lined up in the bare schoolyard early every morning, I stood at the end of the file because I was the tallest. God knows, I did not want to stand out in any way. To make matters worse, I had been placed in the fifth grade instead of the sixth until I mastered enough English and Spanish. Taller than the chattering heads of my Cuban companions, taller even than the occasional American student because I was old for my grade, I slouched, stuck my hip out, bent my knee, dropped my head. Nothing helped. I was the new girl in school.

"Hopscotch?" Marianne Shapiro proposed. She had drawn a chalk diagram on the ground. How foolhardy. How could she be sure this sort of game was appropriate here? Or didn't she care?

"Your turn," Cecile Edelstein screamed in my ear, but I had eyes only for my Cuban classmates. What hair, shoulder-length and permanently waved! Rose-painted fingernails! And what about the mysteriously scented whitish mist that covered their bodies—where does one buy it?

Ay chica. Rapid talk. Girlish laughter.

How come they don't perspire while we walk around with half-moons under our arms?

Qué bicho más raro—What a queer bird.

Who? Me?

Within six weeks, I was proficient enough to be promoted. I could now tremulously approach the beautiful, giddy Carmens and Margaritas during recess, figure out that girls call each other *chica,* that their parents are called *viejo* and *vieja,* that you point to your eyes when you use the verb "to see," and that the enigmatic white mist covering their bodies was Johnson & Johnson talc.

Miss Maple and Mrs. Vance, the so-called British headmistresses, were actually white Jamaican. Hard as they tried to give the school British tone (by finagling visits from British and Commonwealth dignitaries), its spirit was predominantly American. Yes, Canadian, Indian, Australian diplomats appeared at St. George assemblies and yes, we welcomed them with "God Save the King," by heart, all stanzas; but our textbooks were American and our teachers were mostly young, leftover tourists from the United States, whose childlike faces and quick smiles imparted spontaneity and exuberance to school life. They were not professional educators, but that did not seem to concern Miss Vance and Mrs. Maple.

Our teacher, Miss Harper, would perch on the edge of her desk, cross her legs, and expose her knees. She wore page-boy bangs and smoked cigarettes between classes. The Cuban students would jostle her and tell her anecdotes and jokes, and she would throw her head back and roar. I had been brought up to smile, and smile, but laughing like that, so loud, was unladylike. In Belgium we were expected to stammer when we spoke to the teacher. I loved the American informality.

There was no reason to worry then, even though I would soon be called to read in front of the class. Most of my schoolmates had been at St. George's since first grade and spoke English flawlessly, but I felt that they were kind and not out to mock me. And hadn't Miss Harper said only this morning that I was doing "splendidly"? I was surprised, then, that the lifelines in my palms were glistening with sweat, for in my heart I felt almost confident as I stood up, reader in hand, to face the class.

My voice sounded unusually strained. Still, I remembered to put my tongue between my teeth for the "th"

sound and not to accent the "ed" in words like "arrived."
Everything was going well. Miss Harper, who was dis-
creetly chewing gum, nodded encouragingly as I read on
until I came to the word "laughed." Here, I simply did not
make the connection between the "gh" sound and the "f"
sound. I read the word with a hard "g," my voice loud and
strong because the presentation had been going so well.
"Lauged." As soon as I said it, I knew it was wrong. There
were snickers. I thought of Mr. Hough—could it be that
the "gh" is silent after all? "Lou-ed," I corrected myself
softly.

"No, no, dear, the verb is to 'laff,'" Miss Harper
said.

Like in giraffe. How appropriate. A giraffe like me,
slinking clumsily down the aisle back to my seat. Where
had Max's little achiever gone? His number one girl. Good
God, where?

During recess that day, the Cuban circle looked
more forbidding than ever. When the girls dropped their
voices and drew together, I inched toward the edge and
eavesdropped.

"Oh that," I lied. "I started months ago."

"Real blood?" one of them asked snidely.

"Tons of it. Got it all over my sheets and had to
wash them out."

The circle opened a crack.

"Why the face?" Suze asked, still puffy from her afternoon
"beauty rest."

"You know why," I said, and pointed to the large
box on the sofa.

"For heaven's sake," she laughed after I had slipped
into my new uniform—navy jumper and white blouse—
"you look just like everybody else!"

"Wish I did," I said, "except that I don't." All alike.

80

How long had I been dreaming of this day? But the way things stood now, it was not to be. The cross of St. George, triumphantly red on a white shield—the school's emblem—lay in the El Encanto box amid the tissue paper instead of on my chest where it belonged. Although St. George's was a secular school and the emblem at best a symbol, many refugee parents had requested that their children be excused from wearing it. So, apparently, had Suze. I would never forgive her. The empty spot below the left shoulder smarted like a Jewish star.

"I want that emblem right here," I said, pointing to my budlike left breast.

"Nonsense, what will people say?" Suze was upset. "There's no satisfying you, really. We went to the best store and you're still complaining." Her breath had the staleness of sleep and too many cigarettes. Her face, without makeup, revealed its enlarged pores to me for the first time.

"I don't care."

"Don't use that tone with me. Now, take Marianne Shapiro, for instance . . . "

"She's stupid—and I wouldn't want to look like her if you paid me."

"Well then, tell me what the problem really is."

"It's the others. I want to look like *them*. Can't you understand that?"

"Of course I do. When I was young, I too wanted to be like everybody else . . . "

"And . . . ?"

"I remember wanting high-heeled shoes . . . "

"So there!"

"But this is different. It's a matter of principle. We can't pretend we're not Jews."

"But it's only an emblem. It means you are following school regulations and not making a fool of yourself by

81

announcing to the whole world—I'm a stupid Jew."

"Watch yourself." Suze lit a cigarette and inhaled deeply.

I pressed the emblem against my breast once more and, when I released my hand, it had gripped the fabric. "See how beautiful it looks?"

My appearance had always mattered a great deal to Suze. All those compliments about the smallness of my nose. "It even turns up a little." Miracle of miracles. Or the way she introduced me to her friends . . . Smile, Claudia, curtsy, Claudia, hang from the monkey bars. Back in Belgium, our wardrobes had been modeled on the royal houses of the day. Pierre and Franz dressed like the young Belgian princes, down to the last knicker. I, in flannels and tweeds and sashed party dresses, just like Princess Elizabeth and Margaret Rose. Shirley Temple had been too common for Suze.

I began to parade around the room, gingerly at first lest the tacked-on emblem fall off. I hummed "The Maple Leaf," a patriotic Canadian song I had learned in school, and visualized myself lost in the sea of uniforms at tomorrow's assembly. I grew bolder. St. George and the dragon. I charged around the room, sang "God Save the King" at the top of my voice. I was so excited I could feel red blotches appear on my face. Fair complexions always betray you. Everything shows.

"Stop that singing," Suze ordered.

"I hate being Jewish, I hate it!"

Suze raised her arm. "You don't know what you're saying."

"I do, I do," I taunted.

"Sit down," she said. She was fidgeting with the combs in her hair. "Now listen to me," she said. "If it means all that much to you, go ahead and wear the silly emblem. But let me warn you. It will never be up to you to decide whether you are Jewish or not. Your new little friends will tell you."

Not true. Not true. Not true.

"Quick, let's get needle and thread," I said. "And do you think I could try some nail polish one of these days . . . "

Cuban history was taught in Spanish by native teachers.

José Martí is the soul and spirit of Cuba. His words are quoted like Holy Writ. His aphorisms are learned early.

In class we repeat:

Ver en calma un crimen es cometerlo—To witness a crime in silence is to commit it.

Una mujer buena es como un perpetuo arco iris—A good woman is like an eternal rainbow.

Martí: poet, statesman, revolutionary, teacher, apostle.

Antonio Maceo, mulatto general who gave his life in the struggle for Cuban independence from Spain. His equestrian statue, of massive bronze like the color of his skin, stands mounted on a marble pedestral on Havana's Malecón.

Maceo—the Bronze Titan. Crazy, intrepid Mambí.

Mambí. I ran to the encyclopedia once more. Word of Bantu origin, imported from Santo Domingo. Refers to freedom-loving Cubans who took to the wilderness in the fight for independence.

Grito de Yara. The cry at Yara Plantation in 1868 that declared Cuba independent from Spain. Followed by a ten-year guerrilla struggle against Spain's finest. October 10. A school holiday. I have hung a small Cuban flag from our terrace.

El Apóstol. El Titán de Bronce. El Grito de Yara. Names learned at father's knee. Not my father's. Not Max's. It doesn't matter. I'll catch up. *Porque morir por la patria es vivir*— To die for the fatherland is to live. I think that I have never heard anything more beautiful than the Cuban anthem.

Tiny Cuba. Her history claimed all the grandeur of a Napoleonic epic. I applied myself to my studies as intently as any native daughter. Probably more so. Pierre laughed when I raved to him about the raids of the Mambí. "What a silly little revolution," he said.

When Suze suggested that I attend temple services on the holidays, I announced that I had an important history test that day.

I knew, of course, that it would be impossible to ignore the matter entirely, for the temple, Beth Israel, was situated in an old mansion along Avenida de los Presidentes, very near my school.

If only they had selected the Centro Israelita, an Ashkenazy synagogue in Old Havana founded by turn-of-the-century immigrants from Poland and Russia. Or, better yet, Temple Shevet Achima, located even further downtown (on Inquisitor Street!) and patronized by wild Sephardics called *los turcos* because they had come from Turkey in the nineteenth century. But no, with the exception of a few diehard Orthodox, the bulk of the refugee community had opted for the Reform American synagogue where page announcements were given in Spanish and services carried on in Hebrew and English. Even if I went to school, it would be impossible to avoid them completely.

"But it's Passover," Suze said.

"Oh, those dreary seders." Max sighed. "Why is religion so important all of a sudden?"

"It never used to matter," I added.

Suze flushed. "Things have changed. Too much has happened and we must affirm our survival. Right, Max?"

84

Max looked up, startled that she was consulting him. "Won't the WIZO do?" he said, referring to Suze's increasing involvement in the Women's International Zionist Organization.

Only last week she had come home, poured each of us a glass of wine, and asked that we toast the new president of the Vedado Chapter. She explained how, after the war had decimated the WIZO federations of Europe, nineteen new ones had sprung up in Latin America. "And little Havana has three chapters: the German-speaking refugees here in Vedado; the wives of American businessmen in Miramar; and the *señoras hebreas* of Old Havana, who speak such a charming mixture of Spanish and Yiddish. And I was in on it from the very beginning!" This was said with a sharp look in Max's direction. As usual, he did not fail to inpugn her zeal and imply that with her it was less a matter of social commitment than of social opportunism.

To my surprise, Suze countered Max's sarcasm with a calm explanation of how, as a young girl on visits to Prague, she had often come into contact with young Zionists. "In fact," she said, looking at us closely as if trying to decide whether we deserved the confidence, "in fact, I had a Zionist admirer who in 1922 left Prague for Jerusalem. He wanted me to go along as his bride and, for a while, I even studied Hebrew. Ah, if you knew the ardent discussions that went on! No one was religious, of course. We were all idealistic young people set on fire by the speeches of Theodor Herzl. Did you know that even Kafka yearned to go to Palestine toward the end of his life? Unfortunately, the poor thing did not make it. Anyway, I was tempted, I must admit, but I probably did not love my young man enough, or loved trips to Vienna more . . . and then Max came along and you know the rest."

"Yes," Max said with a sigh, "so I did. And how would you like to live in Palestine now?"

"Don't be silly. At my stage in life I need a certain

amount of comfort. But I promise you that I will pour all my energy into establishing a Jewish state for those who will be homeless when the war is over. I tell you," she said, squinting like a cunning cat, "if the Jews had had a country to call their own, Hitler would never have dared. And had he dared, everyone, including my dear brothers and sisters, would have been able to pick up and leave. We, you and I, Max, would not have had to wheel and deal . . . "

"Come on, did you really mind all that much?"

He had touched a nerve. Suze stopped short. She had been talking with disarming conviction and looked betrayed. "What's the use," she said, "of explaining anything to you?"

They both looked at me. I knew that they had lost interest in the issue of whether or not I went to school on the Jewish holidays.

"Synagogues," Max said sadly. "I've had enough to last me a lifetime. If you knew the long hours I spent in *cheder* as a child . . . how the teacher beat me if I so much as dozed for a second. Let her do what she wants."

School seemed different during the Jewish holidays. The Margaritas and Carmens were there, of course, but without the refugees, classes, small to begin with, were now intimate.

From the Parnassus of her desktop Miss Harper, knees exposed, decided to introduce us to Gilbert and Sullivan. She sang "Little Buttercup" with the sauciness of a music-hall tart. It was, I thought, the happiest song I had ever heard. I clapped longer and louder than anyone else.

"Call me Janie, kids," she said as she prepared for the next number.

Margarita nudged me. *"Es tremenda, no?"*

I managed to get out a tremulous *"Sí."*

During math, a stocky, cheerful girl called Marieta invited me to sit with her. She exuded that faint talcum

86

scent that, for me, would forever embody something essentially Cuban. I admired the velvet band that held her hair back and planned to obtain a similar one immediately. As we worked and chatted, I pretended that we were already best friends.

I glanced out the window and saw that temple services had broken and the congregation were promenading down the Avenida in their Sunday best. No, Saturday best would be more appropriate. The men, in black felt hats and dark suits, looked like angels of darkness on this bright sunny day. In their smart dresses and pillbox hats, echoes of Paris styles, the women seemed out of place on an ordinary weekday, or any day. They strolled back and forth, walking and talking in the European manner. I prayed for their disappearance by the time school let out.

"How about coming over to my house later on?" Marieta suggested. I spun away from the window to accept.

XI

I sat in my beloved yellow room savoring my secret. Take note, Leslie Howard, Errol Flynn, I am a *señorita*. For real this time. I am one of Diana's maidens. Order has entered my life.

If only these dreary people would leave so I could tell Suze. I looked down the hall and saw Mushka, the crippled manicurist, bend over Suze's nails. Dr. Vishinsky, the Polish dentist, sat by complaining, as usual, about her varicose veins. Typical afternoon on *calle veinte-y-cinco*.

"You see," Dr. Vishinsky was saying, "trouble is that electric drill is out of question for me. Don't have that kind of money. Mine must be pedaled like sewing machine. Downright primitive."

I wondered whether her short, clipped sentences were the German version of Polish speech. She talks like a telegram.

"Exhausting," she continued. "In this heat, at the end of day, legs swollen like watermelons. But old drill I had in Warsaw—what a marvel! German, of course. *Ach*, what's the use of complaining . . . "

One of Suze's hands lay in Mushka's palm across a small table covered with a white towel; the other was submerged in a sudsy bowl. Now that I am a proper woman, perhaps Suze would let me have a manicure, too. But not with Mushka. She was, I felt, some sort of dwarf. Hunched, partially lame, with a long, veined nose not unlike *Zverg Nase*, dwarf long-nose, the German fairy-tale character that had terrified me in childhood. Don't know what I'd do if she tried to touch me!

I placed myself in the living room hoping I could lure Suze away to ask her, very nonchalantly, for money to buy sanitary napkins. Señorita Claudia requests a moment of your time, I will say. She probably won't get it. Suze had often spoken to me about menstruation and her motherly concern had centered on the cosmetic aspects. "Always spend the day in bed," she had said. "It will prevent aging."

I had never felt better, or prouder. This was the culmination of months and months of waiting. I wanted to be congratulated.

"Mushka, Mushka, how are things?" Suze said, perhaps to discourage Dr. Vishinsky's litany.

"Bad," Mushka replied. "Bad." She snipped bits of loose skin from Suze's free hand. "My brother did not make it to Portugal, I am convinced."

88

Don't these people ever have good news?

"How do you know?" Suze asked.

"I would have heard by now."

"The mails are impossible . . . half the ships go down."

"Don't say that. He's supposed to come over."

"I didn't mean it."

"I have a contact in Portugal who promised to let me know one way or the other."

"Look at it this way," Dr. Vishinsky said. "No news is good news."

"Maybe, but how can one be cheerful in this furnace of a country? Don't the crickets keep you up? Every morning I wake up more tired than the night before. Then, the long lines at the Asociación Democrática de Refugiados Hebreos. These Cuban Jews," Mushka snorted, "are more disorganized than the *cubanos*. But I can't survive without their help. This," she said, kicking her basket filled with nail polish, creams, and acetones, "this barely buys dinner. And yet I'm busy. Can't complain. After you, the Shapiros. There the little girls get manicures too, you know." She shot me an indignant look.

"Claudia does her own," Suze said, laughing. "You ought to try Mushka," she called to me. "Her half-moons are a work of art."

I shuddered. Near-sighted Mushka. Her face, when she worked, almost touched the table. I would have to feel her breath on my hands. And her hands, holding mine . . . I tried not to make a face. She had been mistreated by the Poles even before the war. She was a true survivor. How I hated that word. On your knees, survivor! I belonged at the beauty parlors on *viente-y-tres* where vivacious girls smiled into oversized mirrors singing snatches of the latest *bolero*.

"No, thank you," I said, and watched Suze's other hand emerge from the soaking bowl, wrinkled, with

89

whitish rims around the nails. Mushka clipped the softened skin and reached for her assortment of colors. "What will it be? Coral, raspberry, deep pink?"

What if I stain before I manage to get the Kotex?

"Mr. Hough, how are you?" Freddy greeted the American with excessive cordiality.

"The class" had arrived just as Mushka and Dr. Vishinsky were leaving. "Mutti," I called, "I must talk to you."

"In a minute, a minute," she said.

"Very well, sank you and you," Eva sang.

Sank you and you, sank you and you, the others repeated in unison. They wanted to take advantage of every second of lesson time and always acted a little giddy at the prospect of being students.

"Mutti, *now!*"

"What is it, hurry up?"

I didn't want to tell anymore. Not like that, sandwiched between all her goings-on. "Nothing," I said. "I'll tell you later," but she was no longer attentive. Her *Mohnstrudel,* she screamed, was burning.

"I have a headache," Mr. Hough said.

"I have a headache," the students repeated.

"Kindly call the doctor."

"Kindly call the doctor."

"He will be right over."

"He will be right over."

Mr. Hough knew only English, like all Americans. The textbook, however, was in both English and German, and Heinrich had been placed in charge of reading the translations.

"Er kommt so fort," he said.

Ninety-nine and a half percent of the population of Havana speaks Spanish and *they* are studying English. It doesn't make sense, I thought for the hundredth time.

Last week, Pierre had explained to Max that we were not really welcome in the United States. Roosevelt was not a true friend. Nonsense, Max had replied, Roosevelt is a saint.

I pray for Roosevelt every night.

"Yes, yes, of course he hates Hitler and the Nazis as much as we do," Pierre had said to me, "but he still does not want us in his country. Nobody does."

"Why?"

"Because, little sister, Jews refuse to convert and become Christians like everybody else. It's as simple as that."

I'm a genius. Knew this all along. Why, then, must Max and Suze insist on making Havana just a stopover? "They want us here," I said. "Learn Spanish. *Rápido corren los carros del ferrocarril.* Try that." But nobody listened.

Of all the refugee friends, I tolerated the German bunch the best. They had a sense of humor and Eva's raucous laughter always cheered me up. I was tired of juggling Max and Suze all by myself. When we were home alone, the house seemed abnormally quiet. Boys, I thought, do not carry their share of the burden.

"Don't you sense it?" I would ask Franz.

"Sense what?"

"They only speak when it's absolutely necessary."

"Nonsense. They are just fighting less than usual."

Eva was laughing her toothy laugh again. The gap between her front teeth, she once said, was a mark of intelligence and good luck. "Tomorrow, I swear, I'll start my diet. But today it's too hot." Friedl, her little boy, had been born shortly after our arrival in Havana and now, more than two years later, she still looked pregnant.

At the sight of Suze's tea cart laden with Austro-Hungarian delicacies, including the *Mohnstrudel*, not burnt, Mr. Hough excused himself. "I have a headache," he said.

Swaying his rocking chair in a corner of the terrace, Max had barely uttered a word. The lessons always depressed him—he had terrible problems with grammar *and* vocabulary. "Anyway, I have other things on my mind," he would say as a way of excusing his poor performance. Now, having pierced his cigar with the gold cutter, he slid his chair closer to Heinrich.

"I have a worldwide patent, surely that's worth something?" he said as if continuing a thought.

Heinrich seemed to understand what Max was referring to. "You forget," he said, "that this is wartime and raw materials are scarce. Where will you get the brass?"

"I have thought that through. If I manufacture for the American armed forces, I'll get all the brass I need. I already have the applications on my desk." He pushed the rocking chair a couple of inches closer and leaned forward. "My machine is semi-automatic, you know." He tapped Heinrich on the knee as if he were about to divulge an important confidence. "The revolving drum has slits through which the zipper's teeth escape in one direction only. Rollers deposit the teeth on the cloth band and a whack with a hammer drives them in. Only the hammering operation is manual."

How he goes on and on and on. If only he knew my secret . . .

"I see." Heinrich began. "But take someone like Vitya Mazursky . . . "

Max's face twitched. He rubbed his eyes. "What about Vitya?"

"A man of the world if there ever was one. Reads Kierkegaard and collects art. Well, he's made a bundle with his diamond factory. Gets rough stones from South Africa via the United States. He knows a sure thing when he sees one."

Max looked up to Heinrich, I could tell, even though Heinrich now supplemented his income as an accordionist at refugee functions. He must have been somebody in Germany before the war, I thought.

"Diamonds, diamonds," Max was saying, "how I hate the useless things. Why do they persecute me? Sometimes I believe they have no function except to be traded. Back and forth, back and forth. Now a zipper, there's a thing of beauty—a perfect little machine, a tribute to man's ingenuity."

"How you exaggerate!" Suze burst out. "A zipper isn't something you show off, and I'm certainly not blinded by its beauty."

Is she going to start something here, now, in front of everybody? I'll put a stop to that. I'll just climb up on the table and na-na-na, I'll wave my bloody panties for everybody to admire . . .

But Max did not pick up on the provocative tone.

"Once upon a time, yes," he said, "you could wear a diamond and get some pleasure out of it. Now that's all changed. Thanks to the Communists, everybody is afraid to show wealth."

"When they take over the world, Max, you won't be any better off than the rest of us," Freddy Bauer said. "They really have it in for industrialists. That is what you call yourself, isn't it?"

"I'll show them my work-roughened hands," Max said, laughing at his own wit. I had not seen him this cheerful in a long time. The machines had recently been delivered and he hoped to go into production soon. "I feel like my old self," he had said at dinner the night before, and called for seconds of everything. Later, he had picked up the telephone and called Mendelsohn. "I'm all set to go," he had said. "And you are wrong. There's nothing like being out in the world."

"My workers," Max announced to Freddy, "address me as *el señor polaco*, the Polish gentleman, fancy that."

"That's nothing to boast about," Pierre said. He and Franz had just come in from school. "All Jews are called *polacos* here because Poles immigrated by the thousands after the turn of the century. Yiddish, believe it or not, is called *el idioma polaco,* the Polish language. How about that?"

"Wonderful!" Suze exclaimed. "Splendid. Serves the anti-Semitic Poles right."

"Amen," Eva said. "Have you heard that buttered German rolls are called *polaco con mantequilla?* I just love that."

"Hey, watch out, everybody," Pierre said. "Don't forget that I have a Polish passport. Canceled, of course."

"You?" Freddy said. He frowned.

"Do I have a Polish passport too?" I asked.

"No," Max said. "You have no passport yet. By the time you grow up, I hope you will have the best passport of all—American."

"Maybe Cuban." I said.

"Maybe," Max replied.

"I was born in Holland and have never set foot in Poland," Pierre said. "But the Dutch don't recognize the accident of birth and the Poles have disowned me." Pierre did not look the least bit concerned about his stateless condition. On the contrary, it was all a big joke to him.

When I was little, he used to entertain me by impersonating all the nationalities we were even remotely connected with. He would sing in Czech, pray in Polish, recite in German, argue in French, stutter in Dutch. He called himself the wizard of many tongues and pretended actually to clip on a new tongue as he switched languages.

"I think," Max said, "that these Cuban *polacos* are not smart enough. Yes, they are merchants, businessmen and all that. Calle Muralla is lined with their *tiendas mixtas* —clothing and shoes—and they do all right, prosperous middle class, you might say. But who owns the department stores, the grocery chains, the really big stuff? The Gallegos, of course. Here in Cuba the Spanish immigrants have out-Jewed the Jews. Something's definitely wrong."

Freddy Bauer glared and tapped his tennis-shoed foot.

"There's a saying here: thrifty like a Gallego," Pierre said, as if to bolster Max's argument.

"It should be shrewd like a Jew," Max quipped. He looked bright and alert and seemed unaware that he was irritating Freddy.

"That kind of talk is highly inappropriate, even in jest. Always gets the Jews into trouble." Freddy pronounced "the Jews" with special emphasis, as if the term did not include him. He stood up and asked for his coat, saying he had to be going.

I nudged Franz with my elbow. Look who's talking. We thought that Freddy's appearance—same pants, same shirt every day, and especially those tennis shoes—was so outrageous that it disqualified him from holding serious opinions. No one else walked around in tennis shoes in Havana; they were considered monstrously hot and made your feet smell. But Freddy, Herr silver-spoon Freddy, as Suze called him, wore his with dignity. His allowance from the Joint Relief Committee barely covered food and rent.

Suze jumped up. "Don't go," she said. "Please, Freddy." Her tone implied an apology. Max had somehow offended Freddy, but Suze would fix it, I knew. Why does she care what Freddy thinks?

Max's cigar had gone out and he was nervously shoveling strudel into his mouth.

"Be careful," Eva said. "That stuff is hard to digest."

Suze's face reddened under her tan.

"All I meant," Max's words came out slowly, painfully, "is that Jews could, if they wanted . . . I mean they should try harder, if you understand me."

Freddy stared and said nothing. His short-cropped hair coupled with the white tennis shoes gave him an athletic look. His body looked taut, as if he were about to leap—out the door? At Max?

95

But Max was determined to bring Freddy around.

"Well," he laughed, "come to think of it, met a man the other day, a Cuban Jew originally from Poland, who is, in fact, doing extremely well. He's in girdles, dresses, evening dresses, beachwear, you name it—represents important American manufacturers throughout the island. There's a success story! Has a mansion in Miramar, drives a Cadillac . . . "

"Enough!" Freddy stormed. "Keep your pushy Jews! They've gotten us into enough trouble. Has it ever occurred to you that the reason there is so little anti-Semitism in Cuba is precisely because the Jews who settled here fifty years ago have been content with modest accomplishments?"

Max was now totally bewildered. He had lost track of the argument and only wanted to placate Freddy. The worst thing that could happen would be to have Freddy leave in anger. Suze would never forgive him.

"Yes, yes," he mumbled. "Cuban Jews intermarry and stay out of politics and out of trouble. That's surely for the best."

At that moment, a lottery vendor's cry floated through the window. As it approached, I heard: *"El cuarenta-y-ocho, la sangre de gallo."* Rooster's blood, I knew, was used in witchcraft. Still, what a coincidence. If we won, I could credit my menstruation.

"Papi," I said. "Buy a lottery ticket, please."

"Why not?" he said. "This may be our lucky day. *Señor, señor,*" he yelled, leaning over the terrace wall.

"Herr Max," Freddy said, "is this how you propose to build your empire?"

"I believe in making an effort," Max said.

"But, Freddy," Heinrich said, "surely you know about Max's patent?"

Was he speaking in jest? I couldn't tell. I looked at Pierre for a clue and his preoccupied eyes told me that he was worried too.

"Aquí estoy," the vendor announced when Franz let him in. His clothes were tattered and he wore a house painter's cap.

"Entrez, entrez," Max said. What, French this time!

The man lowered the placard that displayed his numbers and walked toward us. His face and arms were covered with scabies, his lips looked parched, but his eyes, amazingly blue, were bright and playful. He did a little dance with the placard and pointed to a lottery ticket clipped near the top.

"I'll give you the whole number," he said using the familiar *te,* "all ten fractions for five pesos." He made a five with his hand.

Max jauntily put his hand in his pocket and reached for his wallet. He snapped the five-peso note between his fingers, then handed it to the man. The vendor tipped his cap.

"Here," Max said pulling out an extra peso, "for you." The man tipped his cap again. *"Sangre de gallo* is my hottest number."

The transaction over, the vendor looked toward us on the terrace, squinting into the light. The sores gave his face a grayish cast. He wore an old *guayabera* that had been laundered too many times. It was linen, though. His baggy pants, stopping as they did a little above the ankle, high-lighted his feet, which pointed out, Chaplin style. He wore freshly shined shoes.

When his eyes became accustomed to the light, they fixed on Freddy, looked him up and down, then stared at his tennis shoes. Freddy cleared his throat. As if to shake himself out of a reverie, the lottery vendor gave his placard a twirl. Then he reached for a ticket, unfolded it carefully, and tore off a fraction, which he handed to Freddy.

"For you, *amigo,*" he said. "You look as if you need it."

Freddy fumbled for some money.

97

"*No hay problema,*" the man said. "It's on me. If you win, you can buy yourself a pair of proper shoes."

Freddy looked around to see who else had heard. Then he stuffed the ticket deep into his pocket. "*Gracias,*" he mumbled.

"*Muchas gracias,*" Max said loud and clear. He made his usual little courtesy bow and offered to escort the vendor to the door.

When he came back, he sat down next to me, all smiles. "Claudia," he said, "there's something different about you today. You look like such a young lady. How old are you, anyway?"

"Oh Papi, you know. Almost thirteen."

"Then I can't ask you to sit on my lap, can I? But when our lucky number comes in, I promise to take you dancing."

XII

She must have heard the door open, for she raised her head and attempted to focus through the gauze. Stretched out under the fine mosquito netting she looked like a huge child in a draped cradle.

"Who is it?"

"Get up," I said. "It's three o'clock."

"Claudia, for God's sake! Marching in here like a stormtrooper with those heavy convent-school shoes of yours!"

"Well, Mutti," I said. "Are you awake?"

She stared at me. I tugged at my school jumper, for

I knew what she was thinking. *Ein Backfisch*—Neither fish nor fowl. She's said it often enough. No waistline now that you're thirteen. Riding and ballet is what you need. Plenty of it.

"Don't forget about tonight," I said.

"Tonight?"

"Yes, Marieta's party."

"Oh, that. We'll see."

"What do you mean, 'We'll see'? You know I can't go without you."

Do her friends laugh when she tells them that she's expected to chaperone me, that she must sit in a circle of rocking chairs surrounded by ample Cuban ladies in black who snap their fans open and shut as if they were making important pronouncements?

"*Ach*, Claudia," she said, "you don't want to go to those parties. Do you really expect me to crane my neck and clear my throat if your partner tries to do the cheek-to-cheek with you? Frankly, you look terrified, as you should considering your age. Crazy land. By the time they're fifteen, they think of marriage. Really, these dances are highly inappropriate. When I was growing up . . . "

"Come on, not that again. Let me have some fun."

"I happen to have other plans for tonight. I'll ask poor Concha . . . "

"Servants are not acceptable, and you know it. That's the way it is here. An aunt maybe, but I don't have any."

"Hush, don't say that. You have three."

"They're not here. They don't count."

"You're not going to cry, are you? You either shriek or cry these days. One whiff of tropical air and you've sprouted into a full-blown adolescent. Just pray that your bust doesn't keep growing."

I looked down. She was right. I could no longer walk around without a bra, and at this rate . . .

"And you used to be so sweet and demure. Anyway, I could get someone to drop you off at the party, how's that? I'll explain to Doña Mercedes. Marieta's mother will understand."

"No! Not this time. I'm tired of being different."

"We'll see, we'll see. You're making me late for an important appointment. I must get dressed. We'll talk when I get back."

She pushed herself off the bed and went to the dressing table. She scrutinized her face in the mirror. "Just look at this! What a mess!" she cried.

I watched her soak a small piece of cotton with astringent lotion and guide it under the eyes, along the nose, down toward the chin. She seemed pleased with the effect of her tightened skin and reached for a lipstick. Quickly, she applied color to the upper lip and pressed it down to make an imprint on the lower.

"The sun," she said, perhaps to me, "the sun is the best makeup artist of them all." She adjusted a white turban-like hat that set off her apricot tan.

Her silk print dress was tight at the waist and broad at the shoulders. It accentuated her buttocks. She stepped back, away from the mirror, then turned around and looked over her shoulders. She winked at herself. "Hope the bus conductor doesn't pinch me again today," she laughed. "Crazy people, crazy land," she sang as she applied a dab of Arpège behind each ear.

"Goodbye," she called. "Don't forget about your homework."

"Don't worry."

"We're not going to stay in this happy-go-lucky land forever, you know. Someday, we'll go to America and then, my dear, you will need an education. At your age, you should have your head buried in a book."

"All right. Goodbye."

*   *   *

I flicked on the radio, looking for a soap opera. *"La última noche que pasé contigo . . . "* crooned a seductive male voice, *"quisiera olvidarla pero no he podido . . . "* I sang along. Tonight, slowly, gently, a schoolboy would press his cheek against mine, his warm breath would be on my ear for a three-minute song. I turned the dial, ah, here, Tchaikovsky—the theme song. *La Novela del Aire* is about to begin. Would Alfredo propose today? Would Graciela accept? I slipped into a world lived for love alone.

Had Max and Suze ever loved like that?

Pass the salt.

Pass the pepper.

Some nights, dinner was unbearable. They barely spoke. Except to question Pierre, Franz, or me about school.

Pass the salt.

Pass the pepper.

It pained them to say even that much. Max fidgeted in his chair, uncomfortable in his own home. Suze seemed eager to end the meal so she could grab one of her cigarettes.

Graciela solo desea lo que yo deseo.

Estás seguro?

Si. Me ama.

Pass the salt.

Pass the pepper.

Graciela wants whatever I want. She loves me.

Are you sure?

Are you sure?

Alfredo will not propose today. He is not sure.

Tchaikovsky flows from the radio in rivers of violet. I can't wait for tonight.

Suze has acquired a triptych mirror just like the one she had in Antwerp. I can see myself three ways. I think I've stopped growing. Thank God. And my hair—how the humidity makes it curl. But it's still very light. *Rubia preciosa,* the men call as I walk along the street. I peek again. Pssst. Pull in your stomach, tilt your head up. Hey, that's a nice profile. Get out of that uniform. Take a little rouge, lipstick, perfume.

I reach into a drawer and pull out one of Suze's brassieres. Lace and silk, all hand made. I almost fill it, all right. Flesh-colored panties to match. Not bad, smelling of Arpège like Suze. *Ay, ay, la ola marina . . .*

I began to shake my hips and wave my arms—I knew all the latest hits. I bleed now and know all the secrets. Happens to everybody, Suze had said. On those days, you must get plenty of rest and let yourself be pampered. Women need to be pampered, she had repeated. Well, Max had pampered her, and where did it get him?

I reached into the drawer again, but this time the contact was not silky. It was paper, a letter: "My darling, without you life is . . . " Just like the soap opera!

I knew, and suddenly felt that I had known all along, that Suze had a lover, a man, not Max, who made her glow and primp and smell good. I held the letter high, wishing someone would walk into the room and surprise me. "I don't want to know," I murmured, "I don't." The signature glared at me.

I stuffed letter and underwear back into the drawer, ran into the bathroom to wash off rouge and lipstick. Quick, my uniform!

All the glow from the soap opera, the fantasies about tonight were gone. I felt nothing. I went into the kitchen and picked at a mango. The peach of the Caribbean. Everything is the something of the Caribbean. The Paris of the Caribbean. The whore of the Caribbean. I knew Uncle Vitya and liked him. Family friends were always "Uncle" to the children to bridge the gap between the formality of mister and the familiarity of first names. He dined with us sometimes. Always brought wine and candy.

Sang melancholy Russian songs. The kind of man Suze would like. Where do they go when they meet? Do they, like Cuban lovers I've seen, walk along the Malecón holding hands as they watch the misty spray appear over the big wall that contains the sea?

The yearning returned. A boy's warm breath on my ear. Out of the chaperone's sight, on a lantern-lit veranda, I would turn supple, press my body against his. Scandal proof with my mother in attendance.

"And Uncle Vitya?" I asked point-blank when she got home.

"Uncle Vitya? What about him?"

"How is he? Haven't seen him in a while."

"As far as I know, fine."

Her eyes shifted, but I refused to release her. I stared as hard as I could.

"Say hello for me next time you meet him."

"What time is that party of yours?" she asked, pulling off her gloves one finger at a time.

"Eight o'clock."

"So early!"

"I've been waiting all day."

"No sense my getting undressed, is there, if I have to run out again in a little while?"

"That's right, Mutti. I'm glad you agree that I, too, am entitled to some fun."

XIII

Sitting in his damn chair, walled off by the newspaper, Max cleared his nose at regular intervals. The mannerism drove me up the wall and I would play games with myself to see how long I could manage to stay in the same room with him. I rarely lasted more than seven or eight minutes, but tonight he had seemed so down that I decided to stick it out a while longer.

The tropical sun had not been kind to him. Brown patches speckled his face and his bulging gray eyes were often bloodshot. The hair, still black, was thinning. Where had the old resemblance to Napoleon gone? Instead of short and erect, I saw him burdened, bent.

I wished Pierre and Franz would stay home more so that I would not feel the weight of Max's despair as much as I did. But Franz had become a tennis fanatic and, dinner over, he would dash off to play the night courts of the Vedado Tennis. The club had become his refuge from home—he swam there every afternoon and baked his strong, muscular body into a bronze tan. Nicknamed *El Belga,* he paraded his exotic person for the girls to admire. That his studies suffered seemed irrelevant to me. Joining a club was my heart's desire as well, but so far the closest I had come were occasional visits to the exclusive Havana Yacht Club as Marieta's guest.

And Pierre? He had fallen in love with a young Austrian poetess and spent every evening with her. During the day, when not in school, he hid in a corner of the terrace and read. He spoke of going on to law school and I feared that I would have even less of him then.

I'll stay with Max until Suze gets home, not a second more. Out three, four nights a week to attend her meetings, Suze must be taking her presidency of the Vedado

WIZO very seriously . . . unless she is seeing Uncle Vitya on the sly.

"What's doing at the *fábrica?*" I asked.

"Don't ask. For a while things were going along fine. We got the required permits to import brass and we filled our zipper orders. Including the U.S. Army and a Cuban Woolworth chain! But now we're waiting for new permits. Without raw materials, how can we produce?" He cleared his nose twice. "And those workers." He sighed. "I walk up to one to give him a piece of my mind and Dutch flies out. When I'm excited, I lose control . . . "

I've heard that before, I thought. All that business about how no one will listen to him, how the workers are always kidding around, how he can't act the boss.

"Can't Uncle Heinrich help? His Spanish is so good."

"Yes, yes, he can help, of course, but it's not the same. I have to be able to give orders. We're selling zippers hand over fist, thanks, in part, to Heinrich, and now we've just got to get cracking so we can meet the demand."

I should comfort him in some way. Put my arms around him or something, but I don't. He used to come home from the Turkish baths glowing with life. Or the barber, or the tailor. I was six, seven, and he was quite a dandy then. Smelling of expensive cologne, he would take me by the hand and we would buy up the town. Business was always "up" in those days. And now? *Merde,* he can't even speak a language properly. Not German, nor French, nor Spanish, not even Yiddish for all I know.

I flicked the radio on. Ah, here was the Tchaikovsky theme song I knew so well—could it be a rebroadcast of the *Novela del Aire?* No, just the regular piano concerto. Max lowered his paper. "Ta taaaa ta ta ta ta," he hummed. "Leave it, leave it," he said as I reached for the dial, "it's Tchaikovsky."

We were the homebodies then, Max and I, although

he, at least, could occasionally slip out to sit in the Viennese *Konditorei* on *viente-y-tres* to drink their big coffees with whipped cream. *Señoritas* like me have no place to go in the evening. We sit home and wait for the phone to ring. Marieta had already called. So had Margarita. We had joked and laughed. Why can't Max appreciate Cuban humor? His workers are only after a few harmless laughs. Why doesn't he drink black coffee, like everybody else here?

Now, the phone had stopped ringing and it was too quiet. That certain someone—Pepe this week, Rafael the week before, had not called. I heard Concha grumbling in the kitchen, exhausted as usual. Up late every night chaperoning a marriageable daughter and her *novio,* she gets hardly any sleep.

That's what I need, a *novio* of my own, someone who would come and visit every night, sit on the chintz-covered sofa and hold my hand. Full moon and empty arms. If that's Tchaikovsky, I think it's sublime . . .

I lay in bed and listened to Suze's breathing. I had not heard her come in but now, awakened by cricket, moth, or dream, I felt an unbearable hatred for the body in the next bed. I hated myself too for pretending that nothing had changed in my life, for accepting the fraud about the room that had once been mine, that still gave the appearance of being mine, but wasn't.

On its bright yellow walls I had tacked new idols: Tyrone Power, trimly sashed for *Blood and Sand;* Leslie Howard, frail, romantic Leslie, *Intermezzo*'s violin poised to caress me to sleep; and Robert Taylor, whose kisses in the misty London darkness of *Waterloo Bridge* had brushed against my lips many a night. My cherrywood dresser was filled with fans, velvet bands, and hand-embroidered handkerchiefs; my closet stood spick and span as ever, my schoolbooks neatly stacked on the small desk by the window which had been hung with voile curtains at my request. Eva had called the look very *"jeune fille."*

What was *jeune fille* doing in Mother's room, then, inhaling Mother's perfume, watching her toss and turn?

Max slept in my room now. Come nighttime, we both turned into pumpkins. Max amid the voile curtains. I in the twin nuptial bed near Suze. During the day, "my" room was still officially mine to entertain friends in, to talk on the telephone in, to do homework, play radio, play teenager or pampered *señorita* in. But I would always detect Max's odor, sniff out the scent of his cigar as I walked in the morning after to dress in front of the gaping, unmade bed. By then, Max had showered and was busily attacking a papaya in the dining room.

Whose idea had it been, this sophisticated arrangement at my expense? As if I didn't know.

Gimme back my room! Gimme back my room! I had howled every day for a week till my swollen eyes had refused to open. To no avail. They had stood embarrassed but firm. Max snores. Keeps Suze awake.

Try earplugs, a chin strap, I had pleaded like a fool.

We have, they said. Nothing works.

XIV

━━━━━━━━━━━ Forgive me, father, for I have sinned.

How old are you, child?

Fourteen.

Then you are a woman?

Yes, father.

Name your sins.

Deception, fraud, jealousy . . .

What, no sexual transgressions!

That, too, father, of course.

Describe them.

If you let me peek under your cassock . . .

Marieta let out a shriek. "Why, you . . . " she began.

I got up from my kneeling position at her side shaken by equal spasms of laughter.

"Let me, let me," I cried, pulling at her skirt. She fell off the chair and we rolled across the floor, hugging and laughing as if this adolescent friendship were the sweetest thing we would ever know.

I could have avoided the foolishness, the embarrassment, and the anxiety had I only been a little less greedy, a little less hungry. One afternoon without Marieta should not have mattered so much. One afternoon away from the beautiful pink stucco house in Miramar would have made little difference in the long run. Our friendship, which had begun two years before when we shared confidences about our changing bodies, was certainly constant and true. But at our age, assumptions needed to be reaffirmed again and again.

It had become a habit to leave school three, four times a week in Marieta's chauffeur-driven car to spend the afternoon in the bedroom with leaded windows.

To get there, we would pass miles of stately homes representing every architectural style—verandaed houses set in gardens, marble mansions, and stark ultra-modern Bauhaus affairs. Although I did not know it at the time, had I but looked beyond this facade, I would have seen rows of sad-looking shacks built of old boards, tin cans, and palm slabs—windowless, gardenless hovels perched below the hill that was Miramar. Yes, I had heard people complain that the shacks, veritable slums, they said, were spreading and encroaching on the "good" neighborhoods. Where was my sense of compassion, I wonder today, when I heard that they had neither light nor water nor sanitation; neither schools nor doctors nor nurses? Feverish adolescent that I was, my own world was all that existed. In the bedroom with leaded-glass windows, Marieta and I would do homework, and talk, talk, talk.

I learned things from her that were far more important to me than anything I was taught at home. She was my link with the big Catholic world that permeated our lives. In it, time moved according to the Church calendar: saint's day, Christmas Day, Lent, Assumption, confession, absolution, communion.

"And if," I had once asked Marieta, as we were sitting on her bed munching *pastelitos de coco,* "if you repeat a sin, then what?"

"It always depends on the sin," she had replied. "A little venial one, *chiquitico, chiquitico,* like wearing cap sleeves, just means another set of Hail Marys. But Padre Marcelo is really down on, you know, petting. When I told him that Gustavo had touched me there . . . "

Shivers. Kneeling by the confessional, lips pressed to the grilled opening. Oh, to divulge a heady secret to Padre Marcelo and to be "punished" for it. The Lord's Prayer, which we recited in school every morning, was ecumenically tame compared to a Hail Mary so full of grace. Oh, how it made my temples throb! At fourteen we lived, Marieta and I, in a state of sexual obsession.

"Tell me more."

"Padre Marcelo wants us to save ourselves for the men we marry. He preaches abstinence and tells us how we should hold ourselves on the dance floor. Last spring, during retreat, he drew diagrams of dancing couples. Six inches between partners, he cautioned, not a fraction less. Who's got that kind of willpower?"

If Marieta ever wondered why I did not attend retreat like everybody else, she never said. She and my precious Carmens and Margaritas were, I now realize, innocents raised in an Eden-like environment in which the only stranger was the pink-faced *gringo*. At best, Jews were dim biblical characters; at worst, they had killed Christ. But all that was ancient history, and the ten to twelve thousand *hebreos* on the island attracted too little attention to become an issue. But I did not know that then.

"Here, look, this is how he drew it," Marieta had said. Across her notebook, alongside her round and serene handwriting, she drew a boy and a girl holding each other in dance position. The boy's member was erect.

"Not like that!" I had gasped, delighted.

"Of course not, *boba*, but he's no fool. We all knew what he was talking about."

"What does he look like?"

Marieta had leaned forward. "People say he took vows because of an unhappy love affair and I believe it. He is lean and swarthy, always seems to need a shave. You know the type. Tyrone Power, *mas o menos*." Giggles. Give me Padre Marcelo, lean and hard under the flowing Dominican cassock.

Beyond the window, beyond the pink oleander, Marieta's two brothers whizzed by on their bikes. The deep blue of their Jesuit school uniforms seemed but a sky-colored blur. Then, the high-pitched voices approached and the boys came into the room and devoured every last *pastelito de coco*. Marieta screamed, shooed them out. They implored my mercy.

"Go," I said laughing, "we have homework to do."

"Sure, sure," Pepe the older, aged twelve, said. "Yak, yak, yak about boys."

There is no place I would rather be than in this house among these people.

* * *

The mistake lay in involving Suze. I had asked her to pick me up because Marieta's chauffeur was having a day off, which was very unusual for Cuba. Although I tried to keep my life as separate as possible, Suze had met Doña Mercedes before, at the various parties she had reluctantly chaperoned. Now, she was grumbling again.

"In Europe," she said, "a girl your age travels alone, but here, even an old hen like me has to be careful." When she called herself an old hen, I knew that she was in one of her "down to earth" moods and that I should be wary.

Doña Mercedes had insisted that Suze come for *merienda,* the mid-afternoon snack that's as much an institution in Cuba as English tea or French *goûter.* Later, while Marieta and I did our homework, she had promised "Señora Suza" a good chat to compare notes "on our *pepillas.*"

Doña Mercedes welcomed Suze at the door with the typical Cuban greeting, *Mi case es su casa*—My house is your house. She cooed over Suze's silk dress.

"My dress is your dress," Suze replied. "Really," she continued, unzipping it at the waist, "I mean it. It will look wonderful on you."

I reached out to stop her. "It's only a saying, you're not supposed to mean it."

"Ach, Claudiachen. It will be most becoming. These chubby Cuban bellies could use a little streamlining."

"No German," I hissed. Why did she, with her scarce eyebrows and small, squinting eyes, think she knew so much about style? "If you did not stick so much to your own kind," I whispered, "maybe you would appreciate Cuban standards of beauty a little better."

"Oh quiet. Don't take it all so seriously."

Doña Mercedes, round and pale from a life spent indoors, looked distressed. She watched us and occasionally fanned her armpits. I knew that she would not refuse

Suze for fear of offending her. There was no such word as "No" in Cuba.

"Come, come, *señora,* a little courage," Suze said, pulling her dress off. "It will fit. It is amply cut. I'm not such a slender creature myself, you know."

Now you joke about it, but I've seen you poring over the bathroom scale.

How it irritated me to have Suze so full of zest and mischief. She could barely speak the language, yet here she was, undaunted, determined to charm and dazzle. Well, she had come to the wrong place.

Marieta echoed Suze's enthusiasm. "Try it on, Mami, do. You will look glamorous, like an American."

Marieta, you fool, you don't know what you're saying.

Doña Mercedes uttered a meek *"Bueno,* Suza, if you really wish it."

We were in the living room, for God's sake, of the house I thought the most beautiful in the world. Here where Marieta and I shared so many adolescent confidences, here where slip-slapping servant girls brought us trays of dainty rimless sandwiches and hand-pressed fruit juice, here in this very house which I indeed wished were mine, Suze's shenanigans intruded like the shrillness of a blackbird's caw on a still afternoon.

"That's the spirit," Suze twinkled. "We'll turn your Mami into a glamour girl."

"No," I said. "We will not."

Where did she get the nerve? I, forever balancing my tightrope act, needed to proceed with so much caution. Not fair. She felt quite at home here, more so than I. "Our house in Ostrava," she had once told me, "rambled on and on into the most wonderful attic filled with wooden trunks. My sisters and I would disappear there to dress up in costumes fit for Franz Josef's court." Was I the only one destined never to live in a real house?

Suze put her arm around me. *"Kätzchen"*—little kitten—"come join the fun."

Don't touch.

Stripped to her corset, tugging here and there to keep it in place, Doña Mercedes was ready for the farce.

In my eyes, Doña Mercedes could do no wrong. She knew how to wear the unchic clothes required of a proper Havana matron: baggy rayon prints over corsets, sleeves and high necklines that spoke of Catholic modesty, clothes my Suze would disdain. April to November, Doña Mercedes wore the regulation white pumps and matching handbag. Come "winter," she switched to black patent.

"But it's always summer here," Suze would insist, when I begged her to conform. She sported platform shoes, turbans, dresses cut on the bias, dresses that delineated the contour of her breasts, dresses whose folds followed the movement of her body. The *Vogue* patterns she and her *modista* studied with such care were, in my opinion, passports to a treacherous identity. I despised them.

Doña Mercedes was shimmying into the silk dress. Suze stood by, in her flesh-colored slip, ready to pull and tuck. Finally, it was on.

"Élégante, élégante," Suze exclaimed in French. "You look like a *Parisienne.*" She dragged Doña Mercedes to the mirror. Her face lit up at the sight of her compressed body.

"Caramba," she said, "not bad." She turned sideways and looked over her shoulder. Her ample rear was bulging. She was every Cuban male's ideal. *"Muchachas,* what do you think?".

Before we could answer, the left seam gave way and the dress split.

"Ave María," Doña Mercedes screamed. *"Qué cosa, qué cosa!"* She was puffing and fanning her armpits nervously. "Suza," she cried, *"perdóneme. Ay Dios mío, qué cosa."* She looked as if she might burst into tears, but didn't. The

heat of the language had taken care of her emotions. *"Vamos a arreglar eso,"*—We'll fix it—she said as she led Suze to the bedroom.

"Doña Mercedes," Suze answered. *"No hay problema!"*

Marieta walked over to the baby grand and began playing a Chopin mazurka. I could not tell whether the set look on her face came from anger or concentration. Was she annoyed that her mother had been placed in such a foolish position? Was that why the mazurka's notes flew around the room so aggressively? Was she thinking—how these *polacos* get out of hand! I wanted to tell her that her beloved Chopin was a *polaco* too, but that would be cheating. What I really wanted was to get Suze out of here. Give her a piece of my mind. I tried to feel out Marieta's mood.

"Listen," I said, as soon as she stopped playing, "I'm sorry. My mother, you know, gets carried away."

"I'm the one who should apologize," she replied. "We tore your mother's beautiful dress, but the expression on Mami's face was priceless!" She laughed and began to hum the mazurka's melody.

I felt so relieved that I grabbed her hands and began a coltish dance. "Oh Marieta, Oh Marieta, ta, ta, ta." I sang. How could I have doubted you?

Then the maid announced that *merienda* was ready . . .

"Ay, chica," Doña Mercedes complained to the maid, "these sandwiches look anemic. Take them back and let's have lots of cheese, guava, and ham. Don Andrés will be here any minute."

Don Andrés! Marieta's father was never home at this hour. I could see that the little tea with Suze was turning into a social occasion. I considered faking a stomachache.

Vigorous, resplendent in his starched white suit and black cravat, Don Andrés joined us among the potted

114

shrubs and rubber plants on the flagstone patio. His physique spoke of tennis and golf and he always wore that fresh, scrubbed look people in hot climates strive for. He belonged to one of Havana's "forty families" whose clannishness excluded even the President. Men brought up the way he had been usually owed their jobs to a *botella,* political patronage, but Don Andrés was different. His position as head of a leading utility company was the result of ambition and hard work. Cuba, he used to complain, is being developed not by Cubans but by *gallegos* and *americanos.* My people, he would add, are like unruly children—full of rebellion but little followthrough. He wondered whether Cuba would ever actually shake off Spanish and American influence. We are too playful, or too greedy, he would say.

Suze looked mortified to be introduced to this handsome man dressed in Doña Mercedes's rayon. She looked shapeless and lost in the big dress. Catholic modesty did not become her and I felt a surge of tenderness for her waiflike appearance. She crossed her legs and pulled the hem up slightly. She smiled, but remained cautiously quiet. I was relieved.

*"Fulano de tal'*s blue Cadillac arrived yesterday; *fulana de tal* lost the tennis tournament. My sister's migraines are not improving, your father's gout is acting up . . . " Doña Mercedes was bringing her husband up to date. Illness and gossip was my idea of civilized conversation and I missed not getting it at home.

But Don Andrés looked restless and tried to engage Suze in conversation. How long, he asked, had she been in Cuba, and did she like it here?

"To the first question, I must answer four years. To the second, I must answer that I think your country is the most beautiful in the world."

What! Could she be flirting?

Don Andrés laughed and leaned forward. "I am

happy to hear it. I hope you will stay with us a long, long time. Our girls are such good friends." He gave me an affectionate look, which I returned a thousandfold. "Your husband," he continued, "is some sort of industrialist. Are you here on business?"

"We are here," Suze bristled, "because over there, across the ocean, there is a great big war."

Take it easy.

"Oh yes, of course." Don Andrés gave an embarrassed laugh.

My stomach was actually hurting now but I needed to stay and check on what Suze might come up with next.

"Let me tell you," she said, grabbing Don Andrés by the arm, "about the lucky breaks we had, which is how we happen to be here today."

At home, the war talk rarely abated. How many times can one listen to the telling and retelling of the same "escape" stories? They were, it seemed, eternally fresh to Suze. Never tired of them. Now, God help me, she was going to inflict one on Don Andrés and Doña Mercedes. War stories belong in the movies, I wanted to shout, not on Quinta Avenida among the royal palms!

"I want to go home," I said, tears stinging my eyes.

All conversation stopped. "What's the matter," Suze asked, "not feeling well?"

"The child looks flushed," Doña Mercedes said. "Maybe a fever." She placed her hand on my brow. *"Ave María,* she's burning up. Come, lie down for a bit."

"No, no," I said, "it's nothing like that. I forgot to feed my canary this morning and I'm worried about him."

They laughed. "Silly girl," Suze said. "Run and call Concha, she'll take care of your bird for you. Then we can stay a little longer and enjoy your wonderful friends."

"But Concha is off today, Mutti."

"No, we switched it around because her daughter is getting married, or some such thing."

Wretched Concha, wretched daughter. I got up to make the call. Behind me, I heard Suze begin: "The Germans, you see, had required us to register so that when the time came to get rid of us, they would have a nice handy list. Well, I decided to trick them and, dressed in my best Schiaparelli . . . "

Yes, she had gotten us out. She had saved our lives, and yet her pride in retelling these stories infuriated me. I, who had all these years so delicately trod the fine line between deception and candor, to the point of even deceiving myself, would now be crassly unmasked by my mother the storyteller. Marieta, help me! But how could I tell her that we had fled, diamond-lined suitcases in hand, because we were Jews decreed for extermination? How could I tell her if I would not tell even myself!

Marieta showed little interest in Suze's story and suggested we go to her room to work. I thanked my guardian angel. We were deciphering the *Iliad* when Don Andrés came in and looked over our shoulders.

> *Achilles' wrath, to Greece the direful spring*
> *Of woes unnumber'd, heavenly goddess sing!*

He took a mock bow.

"*Ay, Papi, por Díos,*" Marieta said, smiling. "Calm down."

"Hey, I'm not simply a tired businessman," he said. "Once upon a time, when I was young, which you two *pepillas* surely doubt, I had a passion for the classics, especially Homer."

"Don't call us *pepillas!* We're as serious as you ever were," Marieta protested.

He doesn't look troubled, I thought. A good sign. Maybe Suze cut the story short.

"You know, of course, that the Greeks read Homer the way we do our Bible," he said.

117

The Bible? Which Bible?

"For example," he continued earnestly, for he had that very special Cuban quality of living intensely in the present, "take the reconciliation of Achilles and Priam. Achilles felt compassion for the old man even though he was the enemy. The Greeks were being taught a lesson similar to what our Bible teaches us. Compassion and forgiveness are, as you know, the very essence of Christianity. Interesting, isn't it?" He was looking directly at me. What could Suze have said? Raging against the Germans, bemoaning the plight of the Jews? How much did he know?

I had recently begun studying the New Testament and was not totally unprepared. Don Andrés was looking at me still and seemed about to say something. I wanted to cut him off before he asked me the question I did not want to hear.

"Isn't it in Matthew that we are taught to love our enemies?" I said, my voice so faint I wasn't sure Don Andrés would hear me. I wanted to take the "we" back as soon as I had uttered it. Stop trembling. It's just one little word, a pronoun at that.

"Claro," he said. "Matthew and Luke. There you have it—the morality of the Greeks is not always so alien from ours. Remember that as you read on, muchachas. And Claudia," he said, turning to me, "your mother is a very charming and interesting lady."

As if I didn't know.

XV

When Margarita Sáenz y Tamayo, only daughter, only child, turns fifteen, all Havana will hear about it. *El Diario de la Marina* will describe this "rose-colored" moment in Margarita's life with the aplomb of a Homer. The rotogravure will display sepia photographs of the debutante dancing the first waltz on her father's arm. Later, baby-faced young men in white tuxedo jackets will step forward and lead Margarita through the erotic gyrations of the *guaracha* and the romantic melancholy of a *bolero* on the lantern-lit terrace of the Havana Yacht Club. As flashbulbs explode, nubile Margarita will cut the tiered cake that celebrates her budding womanhood. When the picture appears in the newspaper, my smiling face will be among the guests. You can count on that.

It had not been easy, wangling an evening dress out of Suze. I realize now that she, who considered herself in the prime of life, must have found it painful to see me in a sexual role at fifteen. Crowded into our hot bedroom, we slept side by side, charged, restless, our romantic fantasies so populating the room that it must have swelled and groaned from the pressure. Did we speak? She would say: "At your age, I was reading *Anna Karenina*. Cheap love stories were for servant girls."

Don't speak about my age, don't think about it, I wanted to answer. Don't touch anything of mine. I could not bear to brush against her, to watch her eat—her appetites frightened me.

"Like this," she commanded the *modista* with gusto, gathering the silky white tulle of the evening dress around my waist.

I gave an involuntary quiver. Like this, she probably said as she guided Uncle Vitya's hand when they made love.

Once in a while, she would make a stab at patching things up. Mothers and daughters should be friends, she would say, tell each other everything. But, in the end, it must have suited her that we were not such good friends. God knows, she was busy enough with her own affairs.

Most of the time, it suited me, too. Gone was the childhood ache to touch and hold her. I breathed and lived the Cuban sun now. No fall. No winter. No end. No death. Just warmth and sun, and skies without clouds. Under the gaze of the innocent hibiscus, by the club's pool, I would allow the sun to promise me shelter and constancy. Modestly wrapped in a terry robe, of course. Sunbathing was only for *gringos* and the European refugees at third-class clubs. At the Havana Yacht, only the men were allowed to parade their physiques on the beach.

Standing on a raised platform, the Orquesta Hermanos Castro blares *mambo* and *merengue* across the ballroom and toward the calm waters of the Gulf of Mexico. Ruffled shirts and satin pants are okay if you play for the *turistas* at the Tropicana, but for this night, on the occasion of Margarita's *Quince*—the rite that stands between her first communion and her wedding day—they have worn black tie.

It is that sort of party. Señora Tamayo de Sáenz in black lace, a bejeweled comb in her hair, echoes of old Spain, is leading a brigade of long-gowned chaperones, a reluctant Suze among them, to a round table on the edge of the dance floor. For this night belongs to them also. They have brought their charges this far unblemished, and it is now time for redoubled efforts to make sure they toe the line until matrimony. Then the fun will be over; but no one has time to think about that.

Across the room, I catch a glimpse of Franz in a dinner jacket that barely fits now that he lifts weights in addition to playing tennis. He waves but does not come over, for he is being attentive to Graciela, a classmate from

St. George's who is usually not invited to society parties. She is a professional dancer.

Together they step onto the dance floor and I envy Graciela her easy grace. She has bangs and heavy black hair that, unlike mine, holds its shape when she moves. She does not throw herself around like the rest of us; on the contrary, her torso is always erect, and legs, shoulders, and arms seem to move independently. Thick-necked Franz, fair and stocky, enhances her ethereal qualities—they are a well-matched pair. Sometimes I overhear Graciela in the schoolyard telling an eager group of girls about her devotion to the Alonsos, her teachers. Alicia, Fernando, and Albertico, she coos. My family. The girls show a mixture of fascination and disdain for Graciela's stories of rehearsals that drag into the night, of flowers received from secret admirers, of invitations to champagne *tête-à-têtes* that she says she refuses. Is it worth being a ballerina, even a prima, if you are going to be excluded from the everyday world? Now that I had cracked the inner circle, I wouldn't dream of giving that up.

I decide that Franz, alias Francisco, Paco, Paquito, looks quite *aplatanado* out there, weaving the *guaracha* into an homage to his lady love. My brother who shuttles every day from school to gym to tennis court seems to fit in much more effortlessly than either Pierre or I. Perhaps it is his physicality that makes a warm-weather country like Cuba a natural habitat for him.

I watch other couples join them on the dance floor. Surely, this is the best moment of all, pure anticipation, everything to come. Bold, shy, I stand near the large silver punchbowl where I can feign activity. I drink one, then another. Is the punch really spiked as Margarita had promised? After the third, I no longer mind being taller than half the boys, and I soon feel more beautiful, more desirable than anyone else. Who's that winking at me? Could it be? Yes, it is Harry Medina, eighteen, very worldly, Cuba Libre in hand. He's had a few, I bet. Wonderful Harry! And not too short. He twirls his index finger, pointing at the dance floor. I accept.

The music pounds louder and faster, the bongo player is dripping sweat, a delicate flutist picks up the melody. Harry undoes his bow tie, shakes his body this way and that, exquisitely loose, exquisitely rhythmical. My ruffled dress flutters as I shake my shoulders and wiggle as best I can.

"*Ándale, la belga,*" Harry says. That's me, the Belgian girl.

"*Qué loco eres,*" I reply, hair flying as we shimmy across the floor.

How easily, how painlessly, I had fallen into the shams that had brought me here. Sitting on my desk was a boxful of passes, little pink cards, given to me by the Marietas and Carmens in my life, passes that allowed me to cross beyond the Havana Yacht's flower beds, through the gate and, very casually, past the uniformed doorman any time I chose. But always as a guest. Not unlike poor Batista who, everyone knew, had been denied membership because of his mixed blood. *Juntos pero no revueltos*—together but not mixed. The color line in Cuba was social rather than political.

I no longer yearned for dark hair, dark eyes. My Cubans had displayed a hankering for the blond, the fair, like the rest of the world. And my eyes. Why, I had only to believe half of what they said.

"Your eyes," Harry Medina murmurs when the music stops, "are as green, as deep as Gustavo Béquer's *Ojos Verdes.*"

There.

I saw Dieter come toward me as the band began a *bolero,* the slow, melodic dance without hip movement so dear to Cuban lovers. My hand in his, our bodies almost touching, his cheek brushing mine, I wondered about this fair, un-usual-looking boy who had appeared so unexpectedly. I could not place him and felt flustered because the *bolero* is the most intimate of all dances, so slow every heartbeat, every breath is revealed. I was afraid to move back, look up, say anything. Had he crashed? No. Hundreds had been invited and I couldn't expect to know them all. Yet I had the feeling that I had seen him somewhere before, especially the blond, heavy hair that fell on the forehead like a schoolboy's, the broad shoulders that seemed deli-cately graceful all the same. And the face . . . I simply had to have another look. I tried to pull away, but he wouldn't let me. The hand on my back had the assurance of a man's.

The music stopped. He said, "I'm Dieter Müller, how do you do." Might as well have clicked his heels! And such a German name. He *is* German. I could sense it by the way he moved. More rigid somehow than the Cubans, whose gait fits the looseness of their *guayaberas*.

"Too hot in here, don't you think?" He took my arm. "Let's go outside."

He spoke typically slurred Spanish, like a native. A Prussian accent would have surprised me less. I followed him to the terrace knowing that, under an unspoken agreement, the chaperones would allow us ten, fifteen minutes outside. Someone at the round table was keeping an eye on the clock.

Dieter was smiling at me as he picked a hibiscus near the pool and placed it in my hair.

"A little blond Gauguin girl," he whispered.

The sort of thing Pierre might have said. I looked up, enchanted.

"And you . . . " I began. In his white dinner jacket, his face burnt by the alien tropical sun, Dieter's propor-tions were heroic. Especially in this land of lithe, small men. Siegfried. Of course! On the cover of Max's *Gotter-*

dämmerung album. Wagner, Max had often said, transported him into faraway worlds. You remind me of Siegfried, I wanted to say, but realized how foolish that would sound. Might as well call him Prince Charming.

He had been born in Havana, he said, and his father, now a professor at the university, used to be headmaster of the German School that had closed in 1942.

"And you? Let me guess. Scandinavian."

It would have suited me to be Scandinavian. Anything except what I was. Born here, raised there, parents from here and there. Five languages. The usual panic was beginning. If you are born in Germany, then you are German, *Fraulein*. Couldn't Señor Carlos have been right?

"I'm from Berlin," I said.

"Unbelievable!" Dieter's blue eyes looked me up and down. He put his arm around my waist and we began to dance. "We are the perfect pair," he whispered.

Perfect features mean perfect minds. Who said that, Goebbels? A crooner began a slow "Poinciana," Sinatra's phrasing with a Latino lilt. Dieter led me across the moonlit terrace, kissing me softly on the ear.

A tap on the shoulder made me turn around. It was Suze.

"I've been trying to catch your eye," she said. There was an amused look on her face. "The ladies at the round table are getting restless. Better come back inside."

XVI

━━━━━━━━━━━━━━━━━━━━━━ Seen from below, Helmut
Dantine's dark eyes had a fanatic gleam that thrilled me.
The black and white glossy of the star in full German re-
galia, which Hollywood had sent, fanned my daydreams
from the wall above my bed. Dieter, I thought, would have
been too young. But no. They might be drafting them at
fifteen and sixteen now that things are going badly.

In an interview published by *Aufbau* and read aloud
by Suze, Helmut Dantine had declared that he was tired of
Nazi roles and looked forward to playing Crown Prince
Rudolf in the movie version of *Mayerling*.

"That would be something to see," Suze had said
wistfully. She was sentimental about everything connected
with the reign of Emperor Franz Josef, Rudolf's father. It
brought back memories of her Czech childhood. "Those
were the days when gallantry reigned," she would say.

"Those were the days," Pierre had teased, "when
you needed two heads. One to satisfy your wife, and another for your mistress."

"Hush, Pierre, don't say things like that, not about
one of the world's great romantic tragedies. Imagine," she
had said, turning to me, "Crown Prince Rudolf of Austro-
Hungary! Trapped into an unhappy marriage. Went to
the royal hunting lodge at Mayerling to kill himself and his
seventeen-year-old mistress. She died with a rose in her
hand."

"You don't believe that stuff, do you?" Pierre had
laughed.

"Most certainly do."

Suze fingered her Magda Lupescu earrings. Prince
Carol, another old favorite.

"I believe it, too," I had said. Stories about star-
crossed lovers suited me well.

If only Pierre were not so—factual. Or better yet, if

I could stop asking so many questions. But it was too late. He had already explained too much. Last night, when I had casually inquired about Nazi activities outside Europe, he had said that right here, in this very Havana during the thirties, there had existed a great deal of Nazi intrigue. It was even rumored that during the Spanish Civil War the legation had controlled a Fascist spy network for all the Americas! Havana had seen sumptuous banquets displaying Nazi and Falange flags in support of Franco. And now? I had asked. Pierre shrugged his shoulders. Nothing to worry about.

Just where did the headmaster of the German School fit into all this? How patriotic was Professor Müller? Not enough, thank God, to return to the fatherland in its hour of need. Or did he serve it otherwise? With luck, he was the intellectual type, absent-minded, not an activist. Perhaps, just remotely perhaps, the war had not touched Dieter very much. Living here, on the other side of the world, his family might not have concerned itself all that much with Europe. If you question me, Dieter, I'm prepared to lie and lie. I've never been happier than with this first love. My father, I say, is an industrialist, a zipper tycoon with factories all over the world. We have always traveled. I am a linguist but not a Jew.

Padre Marcelo had, of course, been absolutely right. If to slip a hand under the blouse is a venial sin, to touch the nipple must be mortal. Say yes, Dieter had pleaded. Be my *novia* or I'll die. They all say that, but I had believed him anyway. We'll die together, Dieter.

I rolled over, away from Helmut Dantine. Clammy bed. I fumbled for my fan. On the night table my fingers touched ashes. Max's burnt-out cigar, left over from his night visit. Black and blue, Max had said. They beat Monsieur Mendelsohn black and blue. And Suze?

In St. Jean-de-Luz, the smartly cologned German Lieutenant Ducek had visited almost daily, a bouquet of roses in hand. He had seemed young enough to be Max's son. Blond hair straight as a doll's wig. Shoulders as broad as, well, an Olympic swimmer . . .

After a few glasses of wine, Max's wine, Ducek would shed his stiff tunic, unbutton his shirt collar, pass his fingers through his hair time and time again. Suze would gaze at him, leaning forward, mouth soft, eyes alert, and encourage his youthful avowals. Like the perpetual roses on the table, she had been in full bloom that summer, her thirty-sixth.

"*Ach, liebe Frau Suze,*" Lieutenant Ducek had murmured. "This is just like home. No, better than home. You are the most beautiful," he had kissed her fingertips, "and Herr Max here is the kindest . . . "

I had glanced at Herr Max and wondered why he didn't throw Lieutenant Ducek out of the house.

But instead Max walked over to the small, cheap radio provided by the villa's owner and ran the tuner up and down. He could not find what he wanted.

"Damn these *chansonniers* and their *chansons*," he had raged. "*Parlez-moi d'amour* from morning till night. They call that music!"

Pierre had mumbled something to the effect that the masses are also entitled to their entertainment.

"You have an explanation for everything, Pierre," Max had replied sadly.

At the table, Suze and Ducek clinked glasses and spoke softly. Were they rubbing legs under the table as well? I just hope, I remember thinking, I just hope that I never catch them kissing, long slow kisses, like the German soldiers and diminutive French girls who held hands and embraced at café tables in town. I began to sing: "*Alouette, gentille alouette, Alouette, je te plumerai. Je te plumerai la tête, je te plumerai la tête, et la tête, et la tête . . .* "

"Claudia," Suze had stormed, "Lieutenant Ducek and I are trying to talk."

"Let her sing," Lieutenant Ducek had said, tipsy and tolerant.

And I continued, louder and louder, *la tête, le bec, le nez* . . . until the sting of Suze's hand across my mouth had made me stop.

"Once, when I was small," I said to Dieter, "my brother Pierre took me ice skating. We were living in Belgium then. My feet got so cold, so cold mind you, that he had to take off my skates and socks, and rub the feet to restore circulation. I can't imagine anymore what it feels like to be cold like that."

Hand in hand with Dieter, the ten-block walk home from school seemed much too short. Blond and freckled, Dieter was undiluted while I, succulent willowy hybrid that I was, passed as his equal. People turned around to look at us. *Gringos,* they sometimes murmured. If only they knew.

"And Christmas in Germany," Dieter said. "How about that! We used to go every year until the war. My grandfather's tree, with real candles, gingerbread and marzipan. Have you ever . . . ?"

"Marzipan, oh yes. And nougat."

"When I got older, I liked it less. German kids are, how shall I describe it, different. Do you know what I mean?"

"Of course."

"They are more defiant, I guess. Always busy with silly pranks. That's because they're brought up so strictly. Were you?"

"Not particularly. I was mostly ignored, I think. When I wasn't in school, I was sent to the park with a governess we called Mademoiselle. She pretended to be high-class but in fact met her gentleman friend in the park, rain or shine. Naturally, she'd insist that we never miss a day of 'fresh air.' What a bore, and I was too dumb to complain to my mother."

"Fresh air was good for you." Dieter ran the back of his hand along my cheek. "Such beautiful skin," he said.

128

Dieter's gentleness surprised me. On Sunday afternoons, in the darkened Auditorium movie theater on calle
Linea, amidst *pepillos* and chaperones, he would hold me
so hard that I wanted to cry out. When he kissed me, he
bit my mouth, my neck, so that I had to run to the ladies'
room for cold-water compresses before going out into the
Sunday sun. Later, at El Carmelo, the Americanized café
where we would order cokes and sit at large, round tables
with our friends, he would assert his proprietorship by
keeping his arm around my chair. On my right, Marieta
would give me sly looks that said, I saw you, and I would
give her a knowing smile back. The next day, in school, I
would take her aside to display the black and blue marks
on my neck.

We were almost home now. Concha would have
prepared a hot Cuban lunch: pot roast perhaps, with *moros
y cristianos* and a large bowl of papaya and mango salad,
Max's favorite. I didn't want Dieter to meet Max, I know
that now. I knew then, too.

A proper Cuban *novio* not only has the obligation to
walk his girl home from school, but he is also expected to
visit her every day. I encouraged Dieter to come in the late
afternoon, when Max was at the *fábrica*. I told myself that
it was best I get homework and piano lessons out of the
way first. We would sit among the cacti on the terrace or
on the chintz-covered living room couch, holding hands
and kissing until Concha rattled the dishes or decided that
this was the moment to mop the living room floor. She was
sharp, our Concha. By seven, Suze would breeze in and
chat with Dieter in German. She liked him. He was so po-
lite and handsome, she said. By eight, when Max arrived
for dinner, tired and dejected, Dieter was gone.

We were a block from the house when I noticed
Max's black sedan pulling up in front of the driveway.
Why so early today? Damn. If we kept on walking we
would reach the house before he had a chance to disap-

pear inside. Without thinking, I pushed Dieter toward the Chinaman who was standing at his usual post under the tree.

"Look," I said. "Look at this."

"What?"

"The pastries," I said. "Like a work of art, don't you think? Each one different and so beautifully, so geometrically arranged."

"Want one?"

The Chinaman had lifted the glass lid, expressionless as usual.

"Yes, no I think. I'm about to have lunch."

"It would be a shame to disturb the arrangement," Dieter said and laughed. "But let's do it anyway. *Dos,*" he said picking out one yolk-colored and one cherry cake.

The Chinaman placed each on a tissue square and Dieter paid the two pennies.

I looked up the street. Max and the car were gone. What luck!

Dieter handed me one of the cakes. It tasted less sweet than usual.

XVII

Dieter pouts like a true Cuban male, even though I swear that I have not batted that eyelash the way he insists I have . . .

"You," I say, "are allowed to leer at every shapely female going by."

"But," he replies, "you know that I hold all other women in contempt and detestation."

"No," I say, "I won't smile . . ."

We quarrel like typical Cuban lovers. Senseless, silly squabbles. It is expected of us. We are jealous, suspicious, we probe each other's glances, want to penetrate beneath each other's skin. Later, we make up and promise each other eternity. For reassurance, we touch as we walk, he the back of my neck, I an arm around his waist. I like feeling his waist. While his shoulders dazzle, even frighten me, for swimming, rowing, tennis have made them exceptionally broad, his waist, which seems small in comparison, implies hidden strength. It feels hard yet fluid when we walk, and it is this revelation that makes me yearn to caress him and move my hand along the widening line of his torso though we are on the street. I don't, of course. Not on the street. I grab his hand instead and listen for his pulse with my glistening palm.

George Sand once wrote that at nineteen one needs to love, love exclusively. Everything must relate to the beloved. One wants to be graceful and talented for him alone. I am fifteen, Dieter seventeen. This is the tropics and we are precocious. There is another side, though.

"You," he says, "look like a Memling Madonna."

"Hitler," he says, "was theater and art."

"When I was little," I say, "about eight or nine, I used to dream of being chosen to present flowers to the Führer, in newsreels of course." (I never say to myself, I am not a little girl anymore. I know all about Hitler. I know what's going on.)

"My cousins were Hitler Youth," he says. "I attended one of their campfires and it was magical. The circle must have been fifty feet in diameter. There was not just one fire, but dozens blazing mysterious signals into the night sky. When we sang, it was as if all were suddenly right with the world. Know what I mean?"

I am slightly embarrassed by this display of awe. But yes, I knew what he meant. And yes, I belonged there with him, cross-legged on the grass, because, by telling me, he had chosen to include me and to aryanize me in his image.

"My father," he adds, "prizes German culture above all others. In the old days, in the German School, history was my best subject. That made my father very proud. I was brought up to read Goethe and Schiller, too. Sometimes, *Liebchen*," he smiles, "I wish you were less attainable so that I could pine for you like a sorrowful Werther."

Included again. I thrill at the sound of his *Liebchen*. We rarely speak German for we are too immersed in our Cuban ways. But when we do, it is a private signal, a mating call, a clue to remind us of our special affinity.

"Werther in Havana, that's pretty funny," I say.

"Werther along the Malecón," he says.

"Werther eating mangoes?" We laugh.

"Have you ever heard Hitler speak?" he asks.

"Have I ever!"

I watch Dieter climb on a chair, push his hair across his forehead, place two fingers above his upper lip.

"Die Juden sind unser Unglück," he shrieks, fist in the air. "The Jews are our misfortune. Long live natural selection! And I select *you*."

He jumps down and whirls me around the room.

"How was that?" he asks.

He has never confronted me this way before. I had half expected his "Hitler" to defend the war that was being lost. Germany was on the brink of collapse, the Siegfried Line had been breached only a few days before. Rant about Cologne, Dieter, and insist that it will not fall. But no. He leaves me standing in the middle of an open field with no place to hide. *Die Juden sind unser Unglück*. My misfortune. Handwriting on the wall. It was just a joke, I tell myself. Laugh. And I do. Awkwardly at first, then harder, like a guilty child whose transgressions have gone undetected. "You're as mad as Hitler," I say.

*   *   *

See you at mass, midnight mass.

Misa de Gallo on Christmas Eve is the social event of the season.

See you there, my friends call.

Shall I be ill?

Nonsense. Suze, of all people, encourages me to go, out of curiosity, she says, like a tourist. If she knew, what would she say? But she doesn't seem all that interested. No time. She's been named president of the Vedado WIZO and, if she's still carrying on with Uncle Vitya, she must have her hands full.

"Here," she says with unaccustomed female camaraderie, "wear this *mantilla*. Your young man will find you irresistible." She likes Dieter. Appreciates his good manners. He speaks to her in German and is less strange than the Pepes and Marios I used to bring home.

See you at mass, midnight mass. I'm frightened. It is one thing to be dishonest through silence; another to go to mass and actually act out the ritual. I play with the *mantilla*. Angelic madonna. If I were really a Jew, wouldn't I get some sort of sign? Wouldn't the face in the mirror insist?

The baroque cathedral exudes flowers and song, Bach and processions. *O exultate,* the organ cries. I file past relics in the side chapels, past sacred toes and fingers. I see women weep and pray.

Candles and incense have made me lightheaded as Dieter and I kneel side by side. But my heart beats like a hammer.

I fix on Marieta and Doña Mercedes on my left and, when the moment comes, I move to make the sign of the cross as they do. I tap the forehead, touch between the breasts, and then let my hand fall. Didn't complete the motion. Will I be saved or damned?

We spill onto the arcaded cobblestone square, hand in hand, singing "Silent Night" at the top of our voices.

133

The Three Kings have been assassinated by the *gringo* Santa Claus, newspaper editorials bemoan. "O Little Town of Bethlehem," we sing, words fresh from a Christmas pageant at St. George's. Still, traditional noisemakers do roam the streets and the aroma of *lechón asado* permeates the air in the Spanish tradition. So, what's all the fuss about? Best of both worlds. I wouldn't miss this for anything. Oh Pandora, how easily you shove your shame into a box!

It is almost morning when Marieta's chauffeur brings me home. I slip into the house and fall on the bed. Restless night, unholy night. The *Obersturmbannführer* is kicking the furniture around. Get out, he screams, get out of this room! My poor old room. Its butter yellow walls have lost their gaiety. They sweat and breed mildew like a northern cellar. The *Obersturmbannführer* towers over me. His boots creak. I realize that of course he's been hiding under the bed all these years. I'm almost relieved that he has decided to show himself. Butter-haired *Obersturmbannführer*. I crawl out of the room on all fours, down the hall toward the parental moss green bedroom. He kicks me. Move along, he says, and I scream. The pain, I say, the pain. Hush, he murmurs, I will make it go away. He gathers me up as if I were a small frail child and cradles me in his arms. I love you, he says . . . then I wake up.

Love me. Love me. Dieter has become the bearer of all bliss. Max and Suze have receded into a soft-focused world. She seems less abrasive, he less needy. I barely notice them. Even Pierre and Franz, whose comings and goings used to intrigue me so, hold little interest. My childhood has ended and taken with it the remnants of family life.

"But I am your brother," Pierre said one afternoon after I had complained about his barging into my room with barely a knock. He sat down and beckoned to me. "I need to talk to you," he said.

His usual bemused, slightly detached look was missing. He was frowning and seemed to be searching for the right words. The hesitation made me uncomfortable. Pierre at a loss? If he's roused himself out of his world to come into mine, he's too late. I don't care what he thinks anymore.

"I'm troubled by your consuming interest in Herr Dieter," he began.

I resented the sarcasm and didn't answer. He had never paid much attention to Dieter and me, considered us kids, I suppose. Why the sudden interest?

"I have nothing against Dieter, of course," he continued, "if only he wouldn't play up this Germanic superman thing so much. Those shoulders, that carriage, that shock of hair—it's too much! Have I imagined him whistling the Horst Wessel song, or does he actually . . . ?"

I bristled. "Leave Dieter alone." Pierre, all skin and bones, must be jealous. I knew that he had contempt for athletics. Even pooh-poohed Franz's interest in tennis. Said it was the best Franz could do to get out of the house. Mindless stuff, he called it. But I loved Pierre. I had never thought of him as physically weak; yet at this moment, seeing him pale and bony before me, I felt a certain distaste.

"I will leave Dieter alone," he said. "It's you I won't leave alone. The way you look at him. Damn it, next thing you'll be wearing braids to seduce him. I overheard the damndest conversation between you two—I mean daydreams of presenting flowers to the Führer, about Hitler Youth campfires, for God's sake. Unbelievable! Have you forgotten what's going on? Who you are? How can you play these little games?"

I flushed. How dare he eavesdrop! "I don't know what you're driving at. What little games? I'm not going against the war effort, am I? You can't blame Dieter for what's going on three thousand miles away!"

"Do you ever think about what Hitler and the Germans are doing?"

"Of course."

"Tell me, then."

"Well, they're fighting against the Allies . . ."

"That's nonsense. Tell me really."

"They want to conquer the world."

"So did Napoleon, and he was not that sort of monster."

"They have broken treaties . . ."

"Come on, Claudia, cut it out. Say it."

"Say what?"

"You know."

"They've accused the Jews of wanting to take over Germany . . ."

"Go on."

I wanted to cry. "Tell *me*," I said.

"No, I want to hear you say it."

"I can't."

"How about murder, genocide, and extermination!" he shouted. "Oh, how they would have loved to get their hands on Papi, and on me, and even you, pigtails and all . . ."

"It's not true," I cried, "and get out of my room!"

I got up, walked toward the window, my back to Pierre. Then, without willing it, I turned around and threw myself into his arms, crying.

"He may be all right, your Dieter guy," Pierre murmured. "I know you're stuck on him, I understand that. Of course he's not to blame. I just sensed something—oh, Claudia," he pulled out a dirty handkerchief and began to wipe my face, "you're a smart girl, think . . ."

"You don't like him because he's athletic. But it's precisely that quality, how can I explain it? If a lion came charging out of the forest, I know that Dieter would stand his ground and kill . . . not with a gun but with a sword . . ."

"A lion charging out of the jungle! Now there's a likely situation! I, of course, would retreat to the highest tree and yell for help."

"You would be afraid," I whispered.

"Why not? But my chances of survival, let me point out, would be a thousand times better."

"Dieter would not want to run away, he would welcome the chance to kill and it's that—oh, it sounds silly, forget it."

"You're expressing admiration for physical prowess, very natural for your age . . ."

"Don't give me that 'natural for my age' stuff," I shouted. He had missed the point. "I admire the mind just as much. Dieter is brilliant. His courage would be a thing of the mind."

"Watch out, Claudia, or you'll make him into a *Supermensch* and that's dangerous. They don't exist, and even your Dieter can crack."

"Never. You should see him row. He can make his canoe fly on the water."

"Oh là là, love, my little sister, is blinding you."

"Why'd you start all this if you aren't going to take me seriously?"

"I do but, you see, I want you to realize something else, though maybe you are still too young. No offense meant. I consider myself a citizen of the world. I have no nationality, Man with a capital M is my idol, but somewhere, somehow, I know where I come from, who my people are, and that's important. I can move away and out only after I know what it means to be a Jew born in Holland of Polish and Czech parents. But you, you want to disguise yourself as a Rhine maiden . . ."

"What's a Rhine maiden?"

"Oh, you're hopeless. Love him. He's okay, your

Dieter, I guess. Just don't forget why we are in Cuba."

Pierre gave me a long look that was meant to be intense. Might as well have shaken his finger at me. I couldn't see the point in all this examination of motives. You're in Cuba because circumstances put you there. That's all. Of course I loved Pierre and all his complexities, but today he had gone too far. I did not question him about a certain Austrian poetess, did I? And if he chose to spend his life with his nose in books, I let him be.

In season, on a white-hot Saturday afternoon, I would dig out a little pink card and head for the Havana Yacht to cheer Dieter as he crewed the winning team. Later, on the club's terrace, amid the elderly, noisy domino players, he would reappear, radiantly broad-shouldered, slightly out of breath.

As we sipped lemonade so sweet one would think we had an obligation to consume the national crop, the boys at our table would tell stories and the girls would giggle. The Cuban male's gift for *choteo* (banter) is learned at a tender age, and sharp, barbed anecdotes vied for female admiration.

At times, a rainstorm would interrupt us. But when it was over, after only fifteen minutes perhaps, newborn shafts of sunlight would curve around the umbrellas and we would bring our drinks back out, wipe the dripping chairs, and resume our talk.

> *Quiero un sombrero*
> *De guano una bandera*
> *Quiero una guayabera*
> *Y un són para bailar.*

The whole table was singing.

Sombrero de guano is the unfinished straw hat worn by the Mambí. That much I knew. But not the words to the song, which seemed to go on and on, verse in, verse out. Wretched folksong. Had cut me off, taken me out of the warm circle.

Someone began tapping a glass with a spoon, someone else clapped hands flamenco style. It all seemed so easy, so natural. But I had to remain silent, at best mouth the words. How can I explain what it felt like to sit there, mute, in the face of all that exuberance? I tried clapping but somehow didn't cup my hands properly and the sound came out hollow, the beat way off. Plastic plant in a tropical forest.

What kind of songs did I know? *Malbrouk s'en va-t-en guerre* . . . there's one. I could sing it for them. French is chic here. I could teach them the words. How does the second line go, and the third? Where had I learned it, anyway? In kindergarten in Antwerp? Had it been sung at home? Forget it. The truth is, I don't know it at all.

My joints felt stiff; the back of my neck gave off a dull ache.

"What's the matter?" Dieter asked disapprovingly.

The uneasy expression on my face annoyed him. He, Dieter, excelled at everything—sports, academics, social grace—and he expects me to keep up with him. I should be a *pollo* (sexy Cuban chick) one minute, virginal Nordic maiden the next. Look at him, beating time with his fingers against the table, head bobbing like some sort of crazed African.

> *Luna, lunera*
> *Cascabelera*
> *Dile a mi chiquita*
> *Por Dios que me quiera*
> *Dile que me muero*
> *Que tenga compasión*
> *Dile que se apiade de mi corazón.*

"*No puedo* . . . I can't sing," I said on the verge of tears. Even this song, a popular hit, drew a blank. I swallowed hard and took a sip of lemonade. It went into my windpipe, and I began to cough.

"No need to make a scene," Dieter muttered and, without warning, pulled me up and led me toward the beach. I felt the fine sand seep into my sandals; when the coughing abated, I said: "Look, I wasn't born here, I don't know all the songs."

Dieter grabbed me by the wrist and pulled me toward him, slowly twisting my arm behind my back. The unyielding hardness of his body seemed to define the softness of mine. I wanted to tell him that he was hurting me, but he began to kiss me, harshly, I thought, my lips between his teeth. I was afraid that he would make them bleed and swell, and tried to pull away.

"There," he said releasing his grasp, "that should make you feel better."

"You're mad," I said, rubbing my mouth, "why should that make me feel better?"

"Pain drowns out all other feelings, especially self-pity." He laughed and looked boyish and unthreatening again.

"Where did you pick that up?"

"When I was small, I used to have a *manejadora*, nursemaid, involved with the occult. *Ay, mijita*, let me tell you that she used to keep a rag doll in my room, which she pricked whenever I was naughty or scared. At some point, I realized that the rag doll bore a resemblance to me, stringy straw hair, blooming cheeks. I don't know when or how I got the idea of pricking myself whenever I could not endure something. At first, it was mostly to increase my tolerance in sports, but later it spread to other things as well."

"Thanks very much, *chico*, but that's crazy. You are just replacing one pain with another."

"Yes, but the second is self-inflicted, and you can control it. My only limit, then, is my will."

140

"But *you* did it to *me*."

"That was just a demonstration. Anyway, it is almost the same thing since it was done by choice."

"Not mine."

"But mine . . ."

"I can't follow you," I said. I tried to smile. "Just don't forget that your Memling Madonna is fragile."

"That's a laugh. You loved it. Come on, you feel better. Admit it."

He began shuffling back to our table, singing:

> *Memling madonna, Memling madonna,*
> *Dile a mi chiquita por Dios que me quiera . . .*

past the gossiping chaperones gesticulating in the dining room. We dared more, I sometimes think, under their watchful eye than the *americanas* with all their independence.

Back at the table Dieter, with his usual good manners, held a garden chair for me. He pushed it in and its metal edge jammed against my knees. Had he pushed it too far on purpose. Why?

"*Muchacho*, what's gotten into you?" I whispered. "Sure you haven't been seeing too many Humphrey Bogart movies lately?"

He did not like that at all. Gave me a black look.

"How can you even imply that I am influenced by childish American films!"

"Sorry," I said. "Only kidding."

When Dieter acts offended, when he stares into space as he is doing now, I would be willing to rearrange the spheres to bring him back. His was the only order I craved. I recalled the harsh kiss on the beach. Given in anger, it had also been full of passion. It stung on my lips now as I joined the singers around the table, and the words came as if by a miracle.

Dieter's kiss, I realized to my dismay, had been an infusion. I leaned against the hard back of the chair secure in the knowledge that his possessive arm would be encircling it, and me.

XVIII

I was so consumed by my own affairs, I did not know how deeply Pierre had become involved in politics. I had grown accustomed to seeing him on our terrace, philosophy book in hand, low in the corner wicker chair, near the cluster of cacti Suze had chosen because they required little care. Then, last fall, after enrolling at the *universidad,* he had broken with his Austrian poetess and begun carrying Marx and Engels under his arm. He spent less and less time at home and, when he did show up, he would bombard us with statistics picked up from fellow law students:

Only 4 percent of rural families eat meat, 35 percent suffer from intestinal parasites, 43 percent are illiterate, 66 percent live in houses with dirt floors . . .

"The idea," he lectured one Saturday as I returned from the Havana Yacht, freshly powdered, my hair still wet, "the very idea that it should be my sister's ambition to appear in the *Crónica Habanera,* one more debutante amid the rotogravures of canasta parties, fashion shows, *Quince* extravaganzas . . . Pardon me if I gag. How *do* you stand all that clubby chatting, eating, drinking, gossiping?"

Only a few weeks ago, he had badgered me about Dieter. Now it was the clubs. I yearned for the old Pierre with his head in the clouds. Sometimes I wished he had never gone near the *universidad*.

"Leave me alone," I said. "We're not hurting anybody."

"There's nothing more decadent than a country club. Acres of manicured, groomed land, every blade snipped daily so the precious few can putt and holler 'birdie.'"

I groped for a rebuttal and the best I could come up with was Marieta's father. "What about Don Andrés?" I said. "He's earned his right to play golf, hasn't he? He's no *botellero,* he works hard all week."

"My dear child, Don Andrés is no exception. Who do you think owns the utility company he is vice-president of? El Tío Sam, of course. The Compañía Cubana de Electricidad is not Cubana at all. What people like Don Andrés need is a little enlightenment. He is cultivated and understands something about technology; he's the kind of man we should have on our side, working for Cuba, not for the Americans."

"We, Pierre? What are you up to?"

"Nothing. Just keeping my eyes open. We've been here for years. Doesn't it bother you to see little kids knock each other down scrambling for pennies, begging when they should be in school? About time we felt responsible for what's going on, no? Alejandro has convinced me to work with Eddy Chibás."

Yes, I would be happy to talk about Alejandro and get Pierre off my back. Politics didn't interest me, but Alejandro did. He came to the house often and, of late, had begun noticing me. It was impossible to ignore him. Alejandro not only filled the living room with his bearlike bulk, but his voice and movement carried through closed doors to the back of the house, until I couldn't not come out and listen to what he had to say. Of course, everybody knew about Eddy Chibás. His radio harangues were famous. Pierre and Alejandro had joined his new Ortodoxo Party, which wanted to oust the current President, Ramón Grau San Martín. Batista had stepped down earlier this year and permitted democratic elections, but Chibás believed that the new *presidente* was no less a gangster than his predecessor. He had founded a people's party and declared all-out war.

"You're crazy to get involved with Chibás. Batista and Grau are out to get him—it's in all the papers."

Pierre only laughed. "There are those who dream and there are those who act. Don't ask me to hide behind books all my life. Did you know that Batista's regular cut on public funds was thirty-five percent? Things are hardly better now."

I should listen. Maybe he's right. How often had Pierre chided me for doting too exclusively on Dieter? "Your life's too narrow," he had said. "There's a big world out there."

A few days later, Suze dragged us to the Hotel Nacional for an evening of drinking and dancing with some rich Americans she had met through the WIZO. "God bless them," she had said. "They sign petitions and checks like movie stars distributing autographs. Without them we will never have our Jewish state."

She had tried to entice Pierre with all the wrong arguments. "Mr. Goodstein is the King of Swimwear. Bigger than Catalina! His daughter Daisy is eighteen and beautiful. Why not make the 'sacrifice'? Where's the harm?"

Pierre pleaded a stomachache. Said he loathed the Nacional. "I can't stand to think about that jewel of a hotel perched on the edge of the Malecón, filled with Cuban peons at the beck and call of brash Americans. And now that the United States is using it to house soldiers, ten horses couldn't drag me there."

But Suze never listens. She harped on the need for

a Jewish state, on the wonderful business contact this could be for Max, on the desirability of Miss Daisy. In the end, Pierre went because Suze does not accept no for an answer.

"Look," Pierre said, giving me a shove. "Peon number one." I watched Max slip the uniformed carhop a folded peso note. "Smell," he said, as we entered the darkened hotel lobby. "Smell the invader." Perfume and leather oozed out of the gift shops that lined the *galería*. Max and Suze led us past a large neon sign that read POOLSIDE BAR, and there, at a table near the swimming pool, we found the Goodstein trio.

The King of Swimwear wore a wrinkled striped cotton suit, the seersucker type Americans use back home when it gets hot. Cubans wouldn't be caught dead in such an outfit. "Why," Pierre whispered to me, "why must Americans chew their cigars instead of smoking them?" The senior Goodsteins were short and fat; Mrs. Goodstein was bright blond to his bald. Miss Goodstein, the gorgeous Daisy, chewed gum. The only mouth at rest was Mrs. Goodstein's, but her arms, which seemed disproportionately short, were hung with loud charm bracelets. "Ridiculous," Pierre muttered again. "How can a powerful country like the United States be represented by people who look like that!"

Snapping her fingers and giving her head an occasional shake, Mrs. Goodstein was singing:

> *I got the sun in the mornin'*
> *And the moon at night . . .*

"Hello, hello," she called. "I'm so glad to be here. What a beautiful country! What a beautiful day. Ho. Ho. Ho." She laughed with her mouth pursed into an "O" shape. Suze later explained that she did this to avoid getting laugh lines.

145

Young Daisy smiled demurely and had the good sense to get rid of her gum. She would be fat someday, but the firmness of her young flesh as it burst out of tight shoes and a girdled behind had its charms. She was not unaware that the American servicemen at the bar were leering at her.

Max strode forward with outstretched hands. He didn't meet a fashion tycoon like Mr. Goodstein every day!

From the swimming pool, which is built on a cliff, I could look toward the Gulf of Mexico while, immediately below us, the curved wall of the Malecón kept the waves from spilling onto the highway. At dusk, headlights along the drive are shimmering extensions of the water. It is perhaps the most exquisite spot in all Havana.

Mr. Goodstein ordered frozen daiquiris all around. He included me and I was flattered to be considered old enough. This would be my first taste of the famous ball of crushed ice flavored with rum and lime juice. But Pierre waved his hand. "Not for me, thanks," he said.

"A Cuba Libre perhaps?" Mr. Goodstein inquired solicitously.

"Rum on the rocks," Pierre grumbled. "Without Coca-Cola."

Mrs. Goodstein resumed her chattering and even Suze seemed taken aback by the barrage. "Met this darling croupier at the casino . . . offered to show us the town, in his own car . . . The most fabulous drinks, papaya punches, out of this world . . . Tomorrow we're after handbags, alligator and snake . . ."

Mr. Goodstein took Max aside and I could see his hands working as he tried to explain the subtleties of promoting swimwear. "Every year," he said, "you have to come up with something new: a color, a style, a new fabric, enough to drive you crazy. But we do it and, thank goodness, it works."

Max nodded. He was cautious about his English. Eager to promote his wares, he suggested a zippered suit. Mr. Goodstein waved him away. "Nah!" he said. "They'll get their flesh caught . . ."

Pierre turned to Miss Daisy.

"I'm off to college after this jaunt," she said.

What would she study there?

"Literature, art, perhaps. I really don't know for sure." She giggled, fingered her hair and twisted her rings. Pierre smiled softly. He seemed taken by her ingenuousness. Or was it the baby softness of her features? Would she firm up with age? Some American faces, judging by the tourists I had seen, never show character.

Suze was regaling the Goodsteins with stories about her WIZO partners. In proud English she told them that the *hebreos,* though fiercely inbred, had succumbed to Cuban mannerisms and values. "Generous and willing, yes. But excitable." She raised both hands to indicate what she had to put up with.

Miss Daisy asked Pierre whether he was a Zionist, too.

"Who, me? I can see enough problems right here not to concern myself with what's happening thousands of miles away."

"But it's a Jewish issue," she insisted weakly.

"Think of me as a citizen of the world," Pierre said. "Did you realize that in Cuba only four percent of rural families eat meat?" And off he went. She leaned forward; she seemed interested. As an American, Pierre told her, she should understand her country's role in Cuba. "Your U.S.A. cares more about its investments than about putting food in a child's stomach."

"My country . . ." she said, "we do care. Why we're fighting right now to protect democracy."

"Very nice," he replied. "All that's very nice. But this is an entirely different matter. Americans own more than a third of all Cuban sugar mills, ninety percent of the

147

utilities. They send their people to run things and don't even try to know the Cubans. They teach their servants how to cook hamburgers because they know *arroz con frijoles* is an inadequate diet. They make us drink Coca-Cola and buy their cars so we can spend our hard-earned pesos on American products. Very convenient, of course, which is why they make sure our corrupt leaders stay in power."

She seemed genuinely confused. Poor Miss Daisy. Pierre could be a handful. She had not bargained for this. There was a tea-dance of sorts going on behind us and Pierre became aware of an expectant look on her face. "Ah, of course," he said, "you've come to the Pearl of the Antilles to rumba and samba, not to blemish your clear young skin with the pimples of poverty and malnutrition."

They did the box step to the band's "Begin the Beguine," and she followed obediently. When it was over, he held her for an extra moment.

"Listen," Pierre said, as they returned to the table, "when you get back to your country, tell them about us, tell them it isn't right." She moved her head closer to his and whispered, "I will. I promise." He was beginning to like her in spite of himself, I could tell. I felt left out. The band began to play "Poinciana" and I yearned for Dieter. It was our song . . .

The young servicemen at the bar were punching each other playfully. Were their faces red from liquor or sun? "Hey, Mac, this round's on me," one of them said. His biceps bulged under the starched tropical khakis. His blond crew cut pointed skyward. "Drink up, everybody," he bellowed.

Pierre looked up and spat. I saw the ball of saliva hit the side of a chair. Where had he learned that? I glanced at Suze, but she was engrossed with the Goodsteins and Max was leaning forward, listening. Only Miss Daisy's eyes widened. Should I apologize for Pierre? Or make a joke?

I turned around. Someone else had been watching.

I had sensed it. A small, fastidiously groomed hotel employee, his slick black hair very shiny against his pale skin,
stood a few feet away grinning at Pierre. *"Son animales,"* he
said of the soldiers.

"Bah," Pierre said to Miss Daisy and me, "a bunch
of barbarians. Enlisted men from one of the American
bases. Shouldn't let them out."

The G.I.s were off their bar stools now, jostling each
other harder than before. One of them was pushed out of
the group. His blond crew cut glistened under the pool
lights as he approached us. His comrades were watching
and laughing. My hands felt cold. Was he coming over to
ask me to dance? What would he smell like? Would he try
to hold me close?

But it was Miss Daisy he wanted. Before she could
accept or refuse, the hotel employee stepped forward and
put his hand between them. He explained, in Spanish, that
enlisted men were not allowed beyond the bar.

"What's going on here?" the soldier asked, hitching
up his pants. Miss Daisy gave him a coy smile.

"Oiga," the hotel man said, tugging at his royal blue
lapels which bore the hotel crest, *"aquí no hay baile para los
soldados americanos."*

"What's going on here?" the young soldier repeated.
He moved closer to Miss Daisy and the Goodsteins.
"What's all this about ballet?"

Miss Daisy batted her eyelashes and looked back
and forth. Did she believe the men were arguing about
her? Mr. Goodstein leaned over and nudged her. "Watch
your purse," he said.

The hotel man addressed the soldier in a slow, deliberate voice: *"Bar,* okay, *baile no* okay, *pisina no* okay." As
he spoke, he pointed to the bar, the dance floor, and the
pool.

"Piss what?" the soldier asked.

For the first time, Mrs. Goodstein lost her smile.

Suze suggested calling the manager. "He'll know English," she reassured her.

Without glancing in Pierre's direction, Miss Daisy got up and let the young soldier take her arm. "He's welcome to her," Pierre hissed. The hotel employee cursed under his breath and picked at his finely defined mustache. With a giant stride, the little man intercepted the couple. He twirled his index finger, pointing down, and shook his head like a parent admonishing a child.

"He don't want me to dance?" the serviceman asked, dropping Daisy's arm. He looked toward the bar, but his buddies had lost interest and were facing in the other direction.

"Poor bastard," Pierre said. "He really does not know which end is up."

"To hell with him," the soldier said, pointing to the hotel man. "He don't even speak English."

"Neither do you," Pierre murmured loud enough to be heard. The soldier gave him a black look. But before he could say anything, the hotel man had latched onto the soldier's arm and attempted to lead him back to the bar. The soldier yanked himself free.

"What's keeping the manager?" Suze cried. "Pierre, do something!"

Miss Daisy seemed on the verge of tears.

"Keep your hands to yourself, nigger," the soldier shouted to the hotel man.

Pierre trembled. "Sir," he said to the soldier, "kindly come with me. I will explain to you exactly what is going on." But the soldier brushed him aside. He had eyes only for the little hotel man. He grabbed him by the lapels and shook him. "You're full of sour chicken shit," he roared.

The bar, the pool, came to a standstill. Only the tea-dance continued undisturbed. The hotel manager came running, but too late. The serviceman had punched the hotel employee in the jaw and toppled him into the pool. A lifeguard dove in after him. The soldier, his tropical khakis drenched with sweat and pool water, continued to shout: "Full of sour chicken shit . . . full . . ."

Pierre stepped forward and, to my horror, covered the soldier's mouth with his hand; his face was contorted with rage. My gentle brother! "Shut up, you bastard!" Pierre yelled. The soldier, all hard, muscular basic training, took aim and hit Pierre in the face, in the groin . . . I watched them wrestle, roll on the grass. "Somebody do something," I yelled. "The brute will kill him!"

Finally, military police and hotel security pulled them apart. The soldier was shipped back to his base. Pierre, bloody but intact, was given a not so gentle warning by the *policía*. He was told that under no circumstances is the peace of the Hotel Nacional to be disturbed, ever.

When we got home, Suze applied ice bags to Pierre's swollen face. Max paced up and down and I sat by his side holding his hand. Dearest Pierre, if anything happened to you . . .

I have found out that he writes pamphlets for radical organizations and I'm scared. Pierre once told me that if civilization is measured by restraint, then Cuba, where political assassinations are part of the way of life, exists in the Dark Ages. Oh, Pierre, how could I have doubted your courage?

XIX

"Concha!" Suze called. *"Diez cafés con mucha crema!"*

As Vedado president, she had been selected to chair a WIZO meeting at which the three local chapters would be asked to merge. Now, as I watched her orchestrate the seating arrangements, she confided to me that she was a bit nervous.

"I'm keeping my fingers crossed," she said, "that the German ladies of my Vedado Chapter will be too well bred to show their disdain for the Yiddish-speaking *señoras hebreas* from downtown. And the Americans from Miramar, I just hope they'll be patient with the bureaucratic Europeans—*quelle affaire!* I'm relying on strudel and *café mit Schlag* to sweeten the whole lot."

A woman called Sarita was pointing to a cheap novelty vase and I half expected Suze to burst out as Tante Caro had years ago: *Ach,* you should have seen my Baccarat, my Shiraz, my Flemish oils. But instead she smoothed her dress, patted her hair, and told the women she hoped they would be comfortable in her modest home.

Madame la presidente! Look at her unfaltering smile. How does she do it? Always rises to the occasion. Would I too preside at such meetings someday? I certainly did not want to go to Palestine or send anyone else there. A land of Jews. I couldn't begin to imagine Jews who are not outsiders speaking the wrong language.

She seated the women in a diplomatic circle—this one next to a friend, that one on a particularly comfortable chair—and prepared to take the floor. The women, still overcome from the exertion of travel in a tropical climate, were fanning themselves and dabbing necks and faces with embroidered handkerchiefs. If we stayed here, could I end up like the *señoras hebreas* and sport ruffles, permanent waves, thick ankles, and massive forearms? Wouldn't I prefer to be "chic" like Suze? Even today, with the temperature way up, she had chosen a dark striped rayon with a demure white collar and three-quarter sleeves.

"Yes," Suze was saying, "I know. One never gets used to it. Let me turn on the electric fan. Señoras, please, I am trying to talk. A task force to organize the merger. I need a task force. *Man darf sein still,*" she admonished the agitated *señoras hebreas* in Yiddish. "Ah, here we go. I see a hand. Frau Bunschaft, you will represent the Vedado Chapter, Frau Ratner the *señoras hebreas,* and Mrs. Howard Miramar . . . Ladies, please! The baby home in Safed depends on us!"

The cry for the baby home, which the WIZO was supporting, was said with such urgency that the chattering finally stopped. Suze had turned the meeting around and the women settled down to work. After the merger, they would publish a trilingual newsletter and, after much discussion (a tombola proposed by the *señoras hebreas* having been shouted down), Suze settled the issue of fundraising by announcing that she had obtained from Restaurante Moishe Pipik, Havana's foremost and only Jewish restaurant, a promise to cater a fashion show "at no cost whatsoever."

"Bravo, Señora Rossin," Señora Ratner shouted.

Had she also won over dour Frau Bunschaft? I looked and found her nodding and smiling. Bravo Suze.

Blowing strudel crumbs down the front of her prim black-and-white-checked dress, Frau Bunschaft was venting her anger at the British for refusing to get out of Palestine. "I spit *pfui* on them," she told the women sitting on either side of her. "I propose a WIZO boycott. No more Bundles for Britain."

Suze handed her a napkin. "*Ach,* Sophie," she said, "cut it out. The WIZO is nonpolitical."

I asked why the British were against giving Palestine to the Jews.

"Remember this," Frau Bunschaft replied, directing her blue-green watery eyes at me. "Nobody ever gives up control without a fight. The British are there and naturally they refuse to get out. It's human nature."

"But does it belong to the Jews?"

"Of course it does. Read your Bible."

"Wus soll man tin?" Señora Ratner asked, beating her fan against her enormous bosom.

"I'll tell you what to do all right," Frau Bunschaft replied, forgetting to snub everything Yiddish. "You take two British and knock their heads together, that's what. And if that doesn't work, you light a fuse and explode it you know where."

Concha appeared with the coffees and the women threw themselves on her. *"Ave María! Sagrado Corazón!"* she cried as I grabbed the tray just in time.

Accelerating the tempo of her fan, Señora Ratner leaned forward. "Did you know," she whispered between sips, "that at Moishe Pipik's daughter's wedding last year the bridegroom didn't show? They found his pants, his socks and shoes at the edge of the sea. Poor thing, didn't want to get his clothes wet! And the feast that didn't get eaten—you won't believe. Herring, six varieties, salmon, corned beef, *arroz con pollo, queso con guayaba,* a mountain of *smetana*—even strudel from that new *Konditorei* on Calzada . . ."

Sarita interrupted. "You call *that* strudel!" Turning to Suze, she added, "They skimp on the nuts and the dough is like lead."

How does one drown oneself in the sea? With lead weights? He must have kept his underwear on in case he washed ashore. Why didn't he simply say, No, leave me alone, I won't marry her?

The story had excited everyone and the fans went in all directions, open and shut with flamenco zap, giving the room a feeling of agitation and movement. Suze was doing her best to call the meeting back to order as Concha, varicose legs weaving in and out, began clearing the debris.

"I mean it," Frau Bunschaft repeated. "A nice short fuse . . ."

The front door opened at that moment and Pierre

154

walked in. He smiled awkwardly and motioned to Suze, who waved him away. "Later," she called. "Later. Can't you see I'm busy?" He tried to communicate across the room, over the ten heads. "I need to talk to you!"

She stood up and her eyes were so bright that they looked feverish. "This," she announced, "is my son Pierre. A very hardworking young man. In a couple of years he will receive his doctorate in law and then he will tell us how to get the British out of Palestine for good." Turning to Pierre, she called: "Come in then and have a piece of cake. *Concha, otro café!*"

Pierre glanced at me. I can't help you, I grinned. Better accept the cake. He snaked his way through the circle until he stood next to Suze in the archway that led to the terrace. The late afternoon sun silhouetted his nervous figure bent over Suze's chair. In that golden Cuban glow, even the cactus seemed lush, especially now that it had sprouted an extravagant pink blossom. Yes, I could understand Pierre's allegiance to Cuba better than Suze's to Palestine.

The doorbell rang. I opened the door and saw two men holding a third whose face was the color of slate. "Alejandro!" Pierre leaped across the room. His eyes filled with tears as he took in his friend's blood-soaked sleeve.

Suze marched toward the door. "What's this?" she cried, staring at the wounded man. Before anyone could answer, she motioned to three señoras on the chintz sofa. "Put him there," she ordered. The señoras simply stared, their fans silenced. Only Pierre and his friends spoke in rapid whispers. "For God's sake," Suze interrupted, "will somebody tell me what is going on? What has happened to Alejandro?" She looked toward the three dumbfounded women on the sofa. "Get up," she commanded again. "Come on, get moving." And she waved the three men into the living room.

The WIZO ladies were babbling all at once now:

Was ist den los . . . qué pasó? . . . Wus soll man tin . . . pobrecito
. . . he's really out. But Pierre ignored them and took Suze
aside. "I tried to warn you," he said. "Just get everybody
out of here. There's been trouble, this is a political matter.
Alejandro has been shot, but the bullet just grazed his
arm."

I got down on my knees and peered into Alejandro's face, felt his pulse. "He's in shock," I said.

"I'm calling an ambulance," Suze said.

"First get *them* out of here," Pierre pleaded. He
looked at the two young men with Alejandro and made a
gesture of helplessness.

Suze tried to make herself heard above the women's
voices. "Señoras, there has been a motorcycle accident. We
must take care of this young man. Please excuse us. Yes, a
fellow student—young people today! Please, let us ad-
journ. I will call each and every one of you in the morning,
I promise . . . goodbye. . . . Thank you for being so understanding."

They filed out, all except Frau Bunschaft, who
stopped Suze at the door. "Where did it happen?" she
asked.

"Sophie, please. I'll tell you the whole story tomorrow."

"He doesn't look as if he's had a fall," Frau Bunschaft insisted. But Suze pushed her out, grumbling about
German insensitivity. She turned toward the living room,
which had lost the sunlight and now held only empty
chairs. Her makeup had worn off and she had not had a
chance to repair it. She began moving the chairs to one
side.

"You know Alejandro of course, and these are
Wichito and Sergio, two classmates active in Alejandro's
campaign," Pierre said.

"Campaign?"

"What do you think we've been talking about all

these weeks? Alejandro is running for the vice-presidency of the law students' association."

I looked at Wichito and couldn't understand how he had been able to support Alejandro, who was over six feet tall and corpulent. Wichito, a foot shorter, was either undernourished or one of those individuals who burn up food as fast as they eat it. He showed Suze a piece of paper on which was printed the message: JUSTICE IS SLOW BUT SURE.

"That's the note they left. Some justice!" And he spat.

"But why? What has he done?"

"He's standing in the gangsters' way, that's what. They want all the power at the university and are willing to kill to get it. Alejandro is Chibás's man, and that's enough to make him a target."

Will Pierre be next?

"*Furchtbar!*" How dreadful, Suze exclaimed. "But the wound. It needs proper dressing. Let's get him to a hospital."

"We must keep Alejandro out of sight. Anyway," Wichito said, trying to look cheerful, "look at him. His color is coming back. He's been fixed up with a tourniquet and we've sedated him. He'll sleep now, and then he'll be all right."

Yes, Alejandro looked more normal now. He had perspired a great deal and his curls were wet, but his face was peaceful as he slept in our midst. I was relieved. Of all of Pierre's friends, Alejandro was my favorite.

"Young man, you don't know what you are talking about. There's danger of infection, gangrene." Suze picked at Alejandro's arm and saw that under the bloody shirtsleeve, there was a clean but bloodstained bandage. "I'll call Dr. Schnitzler then. He's one of us . . . he won't give you away."

"But tell him to come late, when it's really dark," Wichito said.

Suze looked alarmed. "Why the precautions?'

"I don't think we were being followed," Sergio reassured her.

"Are you implying that they could come here, to this apartment and look for Alejandro? And what would they do with the rest of us?" She turned to Pierre. "Did you mastermind this? Have you forgotten what we have been through? For this? To be pushed around by gangsters!"

"Stop it," Pierre shouted.

Does she own us because she saved our lives? Will we always have to account to her?

"If you must have a cause, why not choose Zionism?"

"Don't talk about things you know nothing about!" Pierre's face was red and I marveled how in only one year he had shed so much of his quizzical nature.

"Maybe your mother is right," Sergio said. "You really have to be a *cubano* to understand our intrigues. Now that the war is ending, you will be able to go back to your homeland and become a big *jefe* over there."

"Sergio, sometimes I think you are as naive as my mother. Homeland? Don't know the animal. Jews travel, speak many languages, assimilate countless cultures, which is what makes them free. I have chosen Cuba, freely; please don't take that away from me." He stopped, then added softly: "I need to do this."

Pierre asked me to run into the kitchen for some beer. I also brought back a moist cloth which I placed on Alejandro's forehead. How strange to see him lying there like that. He who never kept still. "Never, *nunca*," he would argue, "we won't allow it, we must, we will . . ."

"The university is just a stepping stone for political power. Its autonomy is a mockery," he had cried only yesterday on this very terrace, flinging his index finger in the air to mark his point. "Our beloved President makes sure his man's at the head of the student federation. *Dulces para todos . . . la cubania es amor.* What garbage!"

Max always insisted that Alejandro had Jewish blood. "It's in the eyes," he would say. "Brown, sad, deep, can't you see it? Not to speak of the nose, the sensuous mouth, the curl in the hair. Way back somewhere . . . converts during the Inquisition, I'm positive."

I began to suspect that the need to figure out who did and did not have Jewish blood was not restricted to the Nazis.

Alejandro would laugh and salute Max as a *compadre*. "Sure hope so," he would say, lighting a cigar. "Sure could use some of that Jewish tenaciousness."

"You? You have enough tenaciousness for five Jews," Pierre said.

Sometimes I thought that Alejandro brushed against me on purpose.

"*Oye*, come join us." He would take my arm.

"Leave her alone," Pierre would say, laughing. "She's sixteen and she's got a *novio*."

When I stood next to Alejandro, I felt small and frail. A large man like that could crush you. Lie on your ribs and pant in your ears. Moisten your body with the sweat of his passion. If I wanted to, I know I could get him so excited that he would swear to be mine forever. When Sergio began explaining to Suze and me what had happened, I pulled my chair forward so I could hear Alejandro's heavy, regular breathing.

"Our university's an arsenal," Sergio said, glancing toward the kitchen door.

"It's okay," Pierre said. "The *criada* has left for the day."

"It's a nest of rival gangs who fight for the franchise to sell illegal diplomas, exam questions, student federation posts—you name it. And they know that Alejandro is obsessed with the idea of change. *Coño*, he was shot on his own doorstep. He won't survive unless we get him out of the country."

"You must admit that sometimes he overdoes it," Pierre said. Turning to Suze, he explained that only the week before two policemen had stood listening while Alejandro addressed a street-corner crowd. Looking them straight in the eyes, Alejandro had shouted: "I'll fight, I'll kill if I have to, I'm no St. Francis, I'm neither meek nor gentle nor guileless." It was a miracle the cops did not arrest him on the spot.

Suze took a long slug of beer. "Well, isn't that nice! A real provocateur! And you've brought him to our very doorstep." She narrowed her eyes and focused them on Wichito and Sergio. "My son will no longer be a part of this madness. Get Alejandro out. Out!" she screamed.

"Your son will not what?" Pierre yelled back.

"You heard me. Out. I said out!" She was fingering her beer glass, turning it around and around.

"You don't mean that. If anything happens to Alejandro—he has all that energy, he's crazy—he thinks he *is* Cuba. When I'm with him, I believe we can move mountains. I know that sounds trite, but you'll see, he will."

She picked up the glass as if to drink from it, then slammed it on the table. Some of the beer spilled out and made a puddle which she did not wipe up. "You've put me in an intolerable position," she cried. "Of course I don't want to chase a sick man out of my house, yet how can I allow my family to become endangered, perhaps massacred by the police? You have brought him here, I suppose, because you felt Jewish refugees would not be suspect. How naive you are! Jews are always suspect—in Vienna, in New York, in Addis Ababa!"

I couldn't believe that she would even consider turning Alejandro away. "Why," I shouted, "why are you always obsessed with this Jewish thing? Pierre and I want to be free of that." It felt good to say "Pierre and I."

160

"Grow up first!" she cried. "I'm calling Papi and Franz and telling them not to come home, and I'm ordering you to leave the house as well. I don't want you here when the police decide to raid this apartment."

I started to protest, but Suze held up her hand. "I have the final say," she said. "We'll keep Alejandro until Dr. Schnitzler arrives to clean out the wound. After that, you'd better get him out post haste."

Wichito murmured that I should obey my mother, but Pierre waved him aside. "It's good for her to be here," he said. Suze got up to make her phone calls.

When she came back, Pierre was standing between Sergio and Wichito. "Mutti," he said, "if the persecution we suffered during the war taught me anything at all, it is not to remain uninvolved when I see injustice."

"*Ach*," Suze interrupted, "don't talk to me about injustice. You can't hang everything on Batista and that man Grau. Things are the way they are here because the people allow it. It's the climate, Pierre. They barely need a roof over their heads, nor much in the way of clothing. The soil, I am told, is so rich that if you stick your finger in, something will grow. Nobody is starving. That is why they are so undisciplined. And it won't change."

Sergio made a movement as if to reply, but Pierre waved him aside.

"How I despise what you're saying," he shouted. "How you disgust me! You and your *Kaffeehaus* philosophy. Try traveling sometime and you'll see how wrong you are. Or just open your eyes next time you go to your *mercado*. Don't you realize that those children who fight over the right to carry your packages, by the time they're five or six have plied a dozen trades—scavenger, peddler, beggar, pimp? Even a backward country like Cuba could feed and educate its people if the monsters in government did not devour its wealth. Is Hitler really worse?"

161

I was carried away by Pierre. I remembered how when I was eight or nine, we had read *Treasure Island* together. Pierre stood for books and ideas; he knew it all. And now, watching him tell Suze off, I began to feel strong like him. Yes, one could do things, couldn't one? One did not always have to seek protection. In the end, it is what one tries that matters, not whether it is successful or not. I looked down at Alejandro, who seemed to be stirring. The first thing he'll do when he sits up will be to crack a joke. Alejandro is like that.

Suze turned to Pierre. "What a child you are," she said impatiently. "Hitler has nothing to do with this. It is I who count here. I, who struggled and risked all to get you out of Europe. You cannot do this to me! I don't want the police to walk in here and drag anybody out of my house. Not anybody, not one soul!" she shrieked, the telltale vein throbbing on the side of her neck. Then, looking at me, she cried: "Move! Get going!"

Wichito and Sergio exchanged embarrassed glances. Although they did not understand German, they must have had a pretty good idea of what had been said. I was sure that Suze's ranting had awakened Alejandro and, when I looked, I thought I saw him try to open his eyes. There was a glistening line running from the corner of his mouth to his weak chin. Could he have been drooling? I began to smell the mixture of blood and sweat that emanated from his body and wondered whether he had stained the sofa. It would be impossible to wash out. I then tried to imagine the police at the door. Would they wear the dark suits of the secret police or uniforms? Would they touch me? Could I still pass for a child? I suddenly had an enormous desire to be with my thin-lipped, austere Dieter at the Havana Yacht.

"You win," I said to Suze. "I'm leaving."

Pierre looked up and seemed on the verge of saying something. I turned my head away from him. Before I

162

left, I heard him speak softly to Suze. He had his arm around her and I think he was asking her to forgive him. "I'm an idiot," he was saying. "You have every right to be frightened. We'll move Alejandro right after the doctor has seen him."

XX

On this carnival Saturday before Lent, Margarita's uncle, a senator, had arranged to place us on the very steps of the Capitolio. We were eight—boys from La Salle and Belén, girls from St. George's—here in the center of a flamboyant Havana we rarely managed to see. Our lives were very sheltered in those days and this night city of red-faced tourists, drunken sailors, wisecracking vendors hawking, we suspected, forbidden pleasures, had an extraordinary effect on us. Any minute now the *comparseros*—slum-dwelling black and mulatto performers transformed into kings, princes, and folklore heroes for a night—would be stepping down the Prado vying for the big money prize.

We giggled and screeched, suffused by the crowd's rum breath, sweat, perfume. A stray firecracker landed in Marieta's lap; she uttered a tremendous "Ay!" and billowed her skirt to get rid of the thing. A Belén boy picked it up and threw it back at her seconds before it went off.

"Monstruo!" she screamed, unhurt.

And we laughed. All except Dieter.

I put my hand on his thigh. *"Qué pasa?"*

"Nada."

Why so moody? Leave him alone, I told myself. But I didn't.

"*Díme*," I insisted.

He shook me off, squinting into the distance as if he had already sighted the first dancers. I'll get you later, I thought, when you want to be close. But that was just talk, and I knew it. I can't bear to feel separated.

I thought about Alejandro, who never frowned. Even while Dr. Schnitzler patched up his arm, he had entertained everyone with stories about the bungling Cuban police. "There were six of them," he had said, "six foxes to catch one little chicken! I ran out of my house, jumped across a ditch, dove behind a car, and voom, got away." Yes, Alejandro's spirit was intact.

As star Cuban history student, I knew he was following a tradition begun in 1868 with Cuba's war of independence from Spain. In the twentieth century, Cuban rebelliousness had turned against the United States and, as recently as 1933, against the dictator Machado. Young men like Alejandro find it difficult to sit back and let events take their course.

Later that night, Pierre had reopened his discussion with Suze. She was much calmer and he again tried to convince her that we, who had been so terribly persecuted, had a special obligation to help. But she dismissed him with an impatient gesture of the hand and said that it was all *Kwatsch*, which means hogwash in German. "The safety of the family always comes first. *That* is the law of the survivor."

At around 3:00 A.M., Alejandro got up to go. "I can't do it," Suze cried, barring his way. He ended up staying with us for three more days, the time it took to arrange to get him out of the country until things cooled down.

Dieter, I thought, had certainly not acquired this very Cuban ability to joke his way out of a problem, out of a black mood. But then, neither had I, and perhaps that was the reason I belonged with him and not with someone like Alejandro. I could sense the crowd straining; conga beats vibrated in our ears and throats. Amid the foliage of the Prado, torches—one, many—moved to the beat like insane stick figures.

"*Mira!*" Marieta poked me.

The men seemed naked until one noticed their leather pouches, slung low on the hips, supporting the flaming poles.

"*Cálmate,*" I said, for she was jumping up and down. Calm yourself.

A live boa appeared draped around the lead dancer's torso. *Viva la santería!* someone shouted.

"Wards off evil," Dieter whispered in my ear.

Oiled to shine as if with sweat, files of "slaves" shuffled behind the torchbearers to the sound of kettledrums, tambourines, rattles, graters, and cowbells. The women's bare undulating midriffs incited our boys to whistle and catcall, and Dieter finally joined them with a guttural cry. Its rawness startled me.

Eyes darting, foaming at the mouth, the legendary runaway slave called *cimarrón* was being "whipped" into submission by his taskmaster. Sweaty, his near-naked body aglow in the torchlight, he flashed through the crowd like a spark. Hey, Fraulein Claudia, *you* calm down now. But the drumbeats, the runaway locomotive rhythms, had overcome us all; we joined the crowd as it stomped and clapped and yelled *Ya, Ya!* Many had broken through the barricades and were dancing alongside the *comparsa*. Dieter was finding it hard to sit still. I could feel his quick shallow breath at my side. Unable to contain himself, he got up and said hoarsely: "Let's go down into the street and I'll show you a thing or two."

A thing or two? What a funny way to talk. But I was tempted to accept anyway. At sixteen, I was more than ready, yet afraid of the consequences. Society girls had almost no contact with "life" except perhaps through servants or on visits to the family *finca,* where the peasant's thatched *bohio* was never far from the main house. But Max and Suze, far from owning a *finca,* disdained the interior. Rural Cuba was, for them, a huge insect's nest. Cuba, they insisted, had been imposed on us by tragic circumstances. We must grin and bear it. Except for an occasional visit to the mountains of Soroa with Marieta, I had seen nothing.

"We'll come right back," Dieter urged. "Nobody will notice our absence."

I hesitated again. It was not a good idea to go off alone with a young man at night. Not proper. But the drumbeat, the memory of the *cimarrón,* were too much.

"Okay," I said. *"Vámonos."*

In those days, Havana was known as the city that never went to sleep. Her *centro* was so brightly lit that every night could have been carnival. The animation of her squares and cafés, the vitality of her street life made her the sort of city that reduces one's sense of isolation. Her climate encouraged street camaraderie and made the people voluble, gregarious, quick of wit.

Beyond the giant whiteness of the Capitolio there lay a maze of streets so narrow they might have passed for medieval. Feeble turn-of-the-century lampposts were the illumination here, in contrast to the brightly lit *centro,* and even these usually deserted streets were crowded tonight. Dieter's hand, firm as always, led me past gates and barred windows beyond which, I knew, stood lush patios.

Here and there, clusters of *comparseros* were standing in the wings, so to speak, clapping and tapping, awaiting their turn to parade. Suddenly, I felt myself pushed from behind and thrown against Dieter. I watched costumed men and women trading insults and realized that Dieter and I were caught in a real melée. The boa *comparsa,* it seemed, had usurped the spot of the "Princely

166

Harem" *comparsa,* whose veiled women and pantalooned men were nervously awaiting their turn to go on.

A man pounced out of the boa cluster and I recognized the wild "runaway" *cimarrón.* Two "slaves" grabbed him, tried to restrain him.

"Look," Dieter said. "He's drugged. Shot himself full of God knows what and now they can't control him."

How does he know?

The *cimarrón,* so muscular and glittering from a distance, now appeared seething and sweaty. His primitive contortions had a violent quality that I found almost, but not quite, repellent. He continued to thrash about, still foaming, an incoherent animal vigor blinding him to the fact that the "Harem" platoon would be reluctant to fight because they feared for their costumes.

"Come on," Dieter said. "Let's move. There will be trouble here."

He eyed the machetes being flaunted by the "slaves" and I shivered. I did not want to leave. These half-naked bodies would soon be locked in combat and I knew that I wanted to watch the fray.

"Come on," he repeated impatiently. We continued to walk and I sensed a purposefulness to Dieter's pace. The crowd began to thin and I tried to slow my step, but Dieter would not. I wanted to disengage my hand, but he would not let me go. I recalled how, the night we had met, he had held me so hard that I had been unable to move back and look at his face.

"Stop," I said. "There's nothing here. I want to go back."

Just then, a beggar came flying toward us in a little wagon made from old crates. Legless, he rattled a tin cup.

"Mister, mister," he called to Dieter, "fi' cen'."

"Go and peddle your stumps to the *gringos,*" Dieter shouted in Spanish and laughed.

"Dieter, hush!" I said, putting my hand over his

167

mouth. "I'm not superstitious, but laughing at a cripple could make it happen to you."

"You *are* superstitious, you just proved it."

"Nonsense, I just don't like to hear you talk like that. I'm scared."

"Bah," Dieter said, "probably had his legs amputated so he could beg more effectively."

"Basta. Let's go back." But he seemed not to hear me.

"No," he finally said, looking at me. "I must explain something to you. Promise you will listen."

Dieter took my arm and led me to a nearby bench. The lamp on the corner cast a hazy beam that nearly reached us.

"I am going to take you somewhere," he said, his face close to mine. "Somewhere special. We are going to visit a *bruja.* Don't pull back like that. I know what I am doing and it will make sense to you after I explain it. She is a sort of priestess who can look into your soul. Afterward, you will feel different."

"What are you talking about? I feel fine."

"Claudia, Claudia the Lame," Dieter cried. "Why didn't they call you Esther so we might know what's what? Jews are no strangers to such rituals."

Jews! Is that what he said? What did he mean, "Jews"? Something terrible was about to happen. Of that I was sure. If he's found me out, I will insist. Look at me, I will say, can't you see that I am as unflawed as you are?

"Your mother, the so-called 'French lady,'" Dieter continued, "is president of a Zionist organization and your father is, of all things, a Polish Jew!"

I wanted to shout that it wasn't true. In a thin voice I whispered, "What do you mean?"

"Your brother Franz gave you away. He thinks it's a big joke. We lunched together during last week's tennis tournament. I beat him, by the way, 6-2, 6-2, 7-5." He

168

lowered his voice. "The *bruja* will purify you and you will become one of us. She can do it."

"One of us?"

He touched my cheek. "Yes, racially pure."

"What are you saying?"

"I can't explain everything," he said with impatience, "you'll have to trust me. She negotiates with the devil, you'll see."

He was so intent that I was beginning to believe he meant it.

"She won't hurt you," he said softly. "I have seen *santería* in the Sierra and it really works. Makes you see things and feel things you wouldn't believe. She will pray and dance all around you. I believe that if you want something badly enough, you should make it happen. Maybe that's what witchcraft is all about, too. Try it for me."

I reached for his hand. If I could touch him, all would be forgotten. But he pushed me away, gently.

I no longer cared about the late hour, the people who might be looking for us, the possible scandal. Without him, who would I be? Twin, I wanted to cry, you are my twin. The curve of your shoulders, the nervousness of your hands define what I am.

"Dieter," I pleaded. "I'm still me. Can't you see that?"

"I want to be able to love you," he said. "Don't be stubborn."

"But not this primitive thing—where did you get such an idea?"

He stared. "It's not primitive. You must will it, too."

Racially pure. Of course I knew what he was talking about. Hadn't I willed it often enough. Wouldn't my upturned nose do? And my green eyes?

Someday, he had once said, we will get married and live in a house so tiny that we will bump into each other all the time.

We got up and began to walk, Dieter's hand on my shoulder as if he were directing a compliant child.

"Let's go back," I said one last time. "Everyone is waiting for us."

We passed a low, peeling stucco wall that had once been blue.

"Here," he said, and pushed open a wooden door. He pulled me into a patio that smelled of unseen flowers. Dimly lit in the trunk of a ceiba tree stood a crude statue of Christ and at its feet lay a pile of feathers.

I reached for his hand. I would do anything for him after all. I no longer cared to defend myself. A small mulatto man stepped out of the doorway. Dieter motioned to him and together they escorted me into the house.

XXI

Smoking a cigar, the *bruja* was squatting on a red satin mat in front of a flickering shrine crowded with plaster saints, candles, and carnations in tin-can containers. A loose white cloth hung to the ground, giving the shrine the appearance of an altar. Veiled in incense and smoke, the dimly lit foul-smelling room felt like a cave.

Dieter ducked his head to get through the door.

"Aquí está," he announced as if she had been expecting me.

How long had he been planning this?

"Tiene el ñeque," Dieter said. The devil has got her.

The mulatto began a slow, soft drumbeat in the corner.

Was this some sort of prank?

"*Qué preciosa*," the *bruja* said admiringly, and came over to stroke my arm. I pulled away. Her stringy gray hair brushed against my hand. She wore a torn nightgown, or was it a cloak? Could the stains be blood?

"Get her away!" I shouted.

Dieter's blue eyes met mine. They seemed soft, gentle, and I prayed that it wasn't just the effect of the candlelight. He feels sorry for me. He will take my hand and lead me out of here.

The *bruja* gave a knowing laugh. "The *ñeque* is fighting back," she said. "I can feel it."

Dieter's eyes lost all trace of gentleness.

"*Vén.*"

The *bruja* reached out to take my hand. I saw that Dieter kept wiping the palms of his against his trousers.

"Let me out of here!"

I tried to run for the door, but the mulatto stepped forward and grabbed me by the shoulders.

"No," I screamed. "No!"

The mulatto forced me to turn around and face the *bruja*. She pushed me onto the satin mat and ordered me to kneel. The drumming resumed.

"Dieter, is this what you want? Answer me!"

"Let the *bruja* help you."

"Help me how?"

"You'll see."

"What?"

"You are impure, Claudia. This is what you deserve."

"No, I don't!"

Impure. Contaminated. Imperfect. Of course. This *is* what I deserve. I felt almost relieved. *Die Juden sind unser Unglück.* Shut off that radio. I don't want. I don't understand. I am a little Belgian girl, that's all. Let me. A little Cuban girl. A little German— *Please!*

"All right," I whispered. "I'll let her touch me."

The *bruja* indicated that I should rise. Then, she began unbuttoning my dress.

"What is she doing?"

"Hay que purificarla primero," she said to Dieter.

"It's like handwashing, a purification rite," he said.

"What is like handwashing, what?" I didn't recognize my own voice. Breathing had become so difficult that whenever I needed air, my throat made an ugly, rasping sound. The dress was now open to the waist and I could feel the cracked fingernails pulling at my shoulders.

"She is going to wash you. Wash you and cleanse you."

"Don't let her hurt me!"

Naked and quivering, I was made to stand before the altar. My hunched shoulders wrapped themselves around my breasts. I let my head fall forward and closed my eyes. Like a blind man, Dieter had known me only by touch. Touched at the movies, at the dances, touched on the couch and in dark corners. Now . . .

"Don't watch," I whispered, but I knew that even if he heard me, it wouldn't make any difference. Whether he realized it or not, he was here to see my buttocks bulging with excrement, buttocks I was pressing together to contain my shame. Could he also sense the stabbing pain between my shoulderblades?

The *bruja* approached with a bowl of soapy water and began washing me with quick, nervous strokes. The warm liquid felt almost soothing.

"Tienes enemigos hija?" she asked.

"No. No enemies. *Nada.* Nothing."

She crossed herself and kissed her thumb. She kept mopping the sweat from her face, then began tossing bits of coconut shell on the red mat before the altar. She studied the configurations and shook her head.

"Reveal yourself, *Changó!*" she cried, and turning to Dieter added: *"Tiene sangre mala."*

My blood is tainted.

She began rocking back and forth, puffing on her cigar, scooping and casting the shells, shaking her head as if the patterns were not telling her what she needed to hear.

She mumbled pitiful entreaties and rolled her eyes as if she were trying to fling them into the room. Suddenly, she fell back, rigid. The drumming stopped.

"Give me something to wear!" I howled.

The mulatto handed me a soiled robe. *"Changó! Changó!* God of thunder and lightning!" he invoked. "Save this creature!" He resumed his drumming.

The *bruja* sat up and echoed his cry. *"Changó, Changó,"* she implored. "Save this creature! Free her as only you can!"

Nothing happened, and the *bruja* fell into a downcast silence.

"Hay que buscar un gallo," she finally said to Dieter. We must get a cock.

I felt dizzy, lightheaded, without will. Maybe the magic was working. One image kept recurring—that of a bleeding stigmata. Maybe it will happen to me and then they won't have to send for the cock.

The *bruja* continued to chant and rock and fan her warm, filthy breath my way.

"Dáme tres pesos," she said to Dieter, and passed the money to the mulatto, who went out.

She lit two more candles. Like in church. The posting of miracles. Cancerous breasts restored, making the lame walk. Wonders of Christianity. We have nothing like that. But *santería?* Cockfights maybe. No, that's a sport. What then? Wish I could stop trembling.

I could hear the mulatto outside. Also a subdued chortle. Was it the cock? Were there two? I turned and saw that Dieter's *guayabera* was off and that he was wet. The room was like a furnace.

The door opened and the mulatto came in with a reddish cock under his arm.

Grabbing the animal by legs and wings, the *bruja* flourished him before a plaster Santa Barbara, all blue and red and gold with rouged cheeks, a bejeweled crown, and a castle in her hand. The woman turned toward me and tried to apply the animal to my body, too. I cried out and turned to Dieter one more time. "Save me!"

"Let her," he shouted. His face was contorted with excitement. "Let her. This is what you deserve!"

The *bruja* rubbed the bird against my head, my paralyzed arms and legs, its terrified pounding body fluttering against mine, echoing my terror.

"Santa Barbara, Santa Barbara," the *bruja* implored. "Deliver her, free her soul!" Then she dropped her voice and croaked: *"Changó, ayúdame!"* Help me, Changó.

Sweat poured from her temples, the gray mop covered most of her face, her hands were moving in a thousand directions. She snatched the bird's breast feathers in big handfuls and piled them over an amber bead necklace on the floor.

The cock let out an excruciating squawk. Then all was quiet. The *bruja* had twisted its neck off with one skillful snap and was pouring the thick, warm blood over the beads and shells. She came at me with her bloodstained hands.

I looked down and saw that my palms were sticky and covered with dark blood.

"It's happened," I screamed. "It's happened. Dieter, my darling, look! The stigmata!"

"Come in, Jesus," the *bruja* was calling. "Come into her and deliver her!"

XXII

"Sorry?" I heard Dieter ask. We were alone in a square, white room. The window, which was barred and high, gave it a cell-like appearance. Dieter was lying on a coarse mattress next to me. Flies were crawling on the ceiling.

You know the answer, I wanted to say. Why do you ask?

I had never seen him naked before, his beautiful, smooth, hairless body still taut with desire. He had penetrated me slowly, gently, asking every second whether I felt pain, pleasure, until the blood began oozing onto the sheet. He had made love to me then so very tenderly that I was able to think, at first, so this is what it feels like to be with a man. But then, when I had no longer been able to tell his body from mine, I had wanted to cry and hold him and have the pain last eternally.

He ran his fingers over my hips and along the curve to my waist. I moved closer. This nakedness of ours, mine translucent, his more opaque, was an offering of love. I could interpret it no other way. But the other had been the nakedness of defilement.

"I needed to keep you," he whispered. "Going to the *bruja* was the only way."

I knew that he was waiting for my absolution, but I could not.

"The only way? Couldn't you have spoken to me first? I would have tried to explain, I would have tried. For a whole week, you did not give yourself away, you plotted this night of horror instead. I'll never forget that creature last night and how you stood by while she went about her business."

"Claudia," Dieter said, "and you are Claudia now, even Lotte or Gretchen if you wish, please understand.

Amor mío, you had held out a promise of fulfilling my every dream. Only you on this throbbing island would see the world through my eyes. Only to you could I speak of Goethe and Schiller and . . . *Schwarzwalder Torte.*" He smiled. "And that first night in your long white dress . . . don't stop loving me now. When Franz revealed your secret, my grief was so intense that I stopped eating, honest, like a real Werther. It was as if you had died. Look, you had promised me everything and then, the dreadful blow. A Jewess. I was beside myself."

I was too young, too vulnerable to laugh at the desperate romanticism of this outburst. On the contrary, I almost responded to it. If only he had not used the term "dreadful blow." It brought everything back.

"That foul, smelly creature, that dreadful animal!" I cried.

How had I let him do it? Out of love? That must be one of the great ironies. Did I still love this man, this boy who had staged a pagan ritual? Talk of civilization, of biologically pure races. Dieter himself—so clear-eyed always—giving his soul to something like that? I didn't know him at all. Except his will. I had always sensed that.

What was this Jewishness that he had had to deliver me of? What did it mean to me? I couldn't touch it, I couldn't feel it. Whenever I tried to think about it, a vast empty desert presented itself. Was it the diamond handlers costumed in long black coats that even Max despised? Or the Kosher laws? Or Abraham and Isaac? Or lighting candles on Friday night? I couldn't see it. Was it Cecile Edelstein and Marianne Shapiro with their loud raucous voices?

He touched me again and I looked up. Last night's hard eyes were gone; these were young and gentle.

"When you made love to me, you erased everything, just like that," I whispered. "How is that possible? Can you explain it? Dieter, I won't know who I am if I don't stay with you."

"Stay with me," he murmured.

"I hate you," I said. "It is you who are possessed by the devil."

"Hush," he whispered.

I glanced toward the window and saw that it was light. By now, Max and Suze would have called the police, I was sure of it. How could I have let this happen? Stayed out all night. All night with a man, that's what people will say. Like a *guerida*, a "beloved," the Cuban euphemism for "mistress." I cannot show my face.

"My parents have called the police," I said.

"We'll fix it somehow, I'll think of something. I had to do it this way. Don't you see that?"

"No, I don't." I looked at my palms but they were clean. "Dieter, you don't believe . . . ?"

"Yes, I believe. Didn't you feel the presence in the room?"

"I don't know," I whispered.

"Look," he said, "it worked so well because Jews also believe in mysticism and witchcraft. Everyone knows that. They sacrifice animals and char their bones."

"Not true," I said. "You've got it all wrong."

"When I was small," Dieter said, stretching out on the mattress, "our maid took me to séances that make last night look like child's play. When I got older, I rode into the Sierra and observed the rites of the *guajiros*. You have no idea what goes on in those tiny villages tucked far away in the mountains—"

"But you are a German, Dieter. How do you get mixed up in things like that? You must have been over-joyed to discover that I was Jewish so you could have an excuse to experiment on me. Don't you know that things like the Kabbalah and Jewish mysticism are as foreign to me as they are to you? And *santería*, something so primitive, I can't get over it."

"But you went along last night. Don't deny it. You were possessed."

"By you. Oh my God!" I felt a burning sensation between my legs and wondered whether I would be able to walk. My face will give it all away. You can tell whether a woman is a virgin just by looking at her. That's what people say.

"Are we still here?"

"Yes, the *bruja* rents rooms as well."

I looked around for my dress. I had worn a white pique to the carnival, in another life. It now lay freshly washed and ironed on a crudely made wooden chair by the mattress. The *bruja* washes and irons too, I thought bitterly. I should be wearing red, or black. My head seemed to be flying in all directions.

"Where's the telephone?" I asked. "I must call home."

I got up carefully but there was no pain. I put on the dress. Did I feel different? I couldn't be sure.

"I'm done for," I cried. "Everyone in town will know."

Dieter stood up and put his arms around me. I let my head rest on his shoulders.

"Hold me," I said.

"You are my wife, my Gretchen," he murmured. "Listen, this is what I think. You are probably only partially Jewish but don't know it. One of your grandmothers was undoubtedly raped by a Cossack or some such thing. Just look at you, it's so obvious. You are now in a state of grace, believe me."

"Stop it. I don't want to hear any more."

I pushed past him and walked out of the room. I didn't see a phone anywhere. No matter.

Dieter overtook me in the hallway, barefoot and shirtless.

"I must go home to my mother and father," I said.

"Let me come too."

"No."

Even after all these years, the incandescence of the young Cuban sun continued to surprise me. It played on the narrow street strewn with carnival litter and brought to life the bits of costuming, dead flowers, and burst balloons lying on the cracked sidewalk. To my surprise, a tired-looking taxi turned the corner and its unmuffled engine tore into the ravaged street toward me. I held out my arm and it stopped. Dieter tried to get in with me, but I pushed him aside, very gently.

"I'll call you," he insisted. "Don't abandon me, Claudia. We are the perfect pair."

I sat back. Can I still believe that? Germans and Jews, two chosen people. Chosen for what? To suffer, to do great deeds? Such a union could only have been made in Hell.

XXIII

I could sense that outside, beyond the closed shutters, the purple bougainvillea had produced its daily quota of blossoms. And the thought crossed my mind that the cactus standing on the window sill, trapped in the twilight of my room, would somehow be damaged by lack of light.

But no. I've been reassured that the dimness will be soothing and restorative. Sleep, don't think. Tomorrow is another day.

And then? Slip into school just before the Lord's Prayer. But they'll only catch me at recess, or in between classes. One look and they'll know. That's all they think about, anyway. I'm *not* getting out of bed.

*   *   *

"A German, it figures," Suze said from my bedside the next morning. Although the clock read eleven she was still in her robe, which was not unusual.

"*Armes Kind,*" she said. "Of course, with a Jewish girl he would do anything he pleased." She patted me on the arm. "Don't worry," she whispered. "Everything is taken care of."

Armes Kind—poor child. She sees me as a victim. Wants to include me in that persecuted world. What does she know about me? In spite of everything, I belong with him, with Dieter.

She should be outraged. Nice girls don't. Her tone had implied: we women must stick together. I should respond. But the solidarity made me uneasy. I didn't like it. Patting me on the arm like that. Perfumed even in the morning. She's had her share of lovers. She knows about sex the way Concha knows about virgins.

"Señora!" Concha had said, pointing an accusing finger at Suze. "A daughter is a twenty-four-hour responsibility!" She had shaken her head and made a "tsk" sound with her tongue and palate. "*Dios mío,*" she had continued, "now that she's tasted it, she'll want it again and again."

Virgins and ex-virgins are Concha's specialty. She had asked me first thing and I had blurted it out like a fool. In front of everybody. Including the butcher's delivery boy and the weekly washerwoman. Might as well have shouted it from the rooftops. She had called me a fledgling and she had been right. Hardly three years since I had begun marking the twenty-eighth day on the calendar. My swollen breasts still seemed to belong to someone else.

"It will all blow over," I heard Suze assure me.

I opened my eyes.

"Doña Mercedes has been a true friend," Suze continued. "On the phone with me all night. We feared an accident. No question of anything else. Your reputation is intact."

Intact? She must be kidding. I touched my thighs under the covers. His rough, callused hands. Oarsman's hands.

"Spoke to the boy's father, too." Suze repeated Herr Müller's words to me. "If she's with Dieter, she's all right. You can trust my son one hundred percent."

"Why should fathers worry about their sons?" she sneered. "If your brothers stay out all night, does it bother me? But a girl! We checked the hospitals, even the police. *Ach*, the longest night of my life! But here you are, safe and sound." She knocked on the table. "Touch wood."

She had thrown her head back when she said, "*Ach*, the longest night of my life!" She had gesticulated to accentuate every one of her points. Calm down, I wanted to say.

"Where's Papi?" I asked.

"Hasn't been feeling well, and then this business with you. Complained of a heaviness on his chest. When he saw that you were all right, he lay down and went to sleep."

"How did he know I was all right?"

"He assumed. Saw you in one piece, I guess."

"I'm not in one piece."

"Nonsense. Of course you are. I've cooked up the most perfect story for you." She moved her chair away from the bed, to set the stage, so to speak. Her hands, her long red nails, pushed against the night table. She lit a cigarette and began unraveling an ingenious tale about a heel caught in a pothole, an injured ankle, pain and swelling, mazelike streets, unavailable taxis, more swelling, circulation problems, even gangrene.

"All Dieter can think of is to get you to a doctor," she announced proudly. "That makes sense, doesn't it? We'll make him a refugee doctor. I'll speak to Hermann Schnitzler—he'll back us up. It could easily be three, four o'clock in the morning by the time you get to him. And the examination—those things take time. So, your night is accounted for and we're all set. Doña Mercedes believes the story and you know this means it will get around."

I noticed that she was rocking slightly. She seemed to be waiting for something. Wants me to thank her, that must be it. Congratulate her on her quickness and nimbleness. She thinks that she's taken care of every little thing and that I should now get out of bed and pirouette with joy.

I cried, quietly, only with my eyes.

"Nothing to cry about," Suze said. "Everything is all right."

Ask me whether something hurts, sing to me, hold me . . .

"I'm not showing my face at school," I said.

"We'll talk about that later," she whispered. "After a good nap, the world will look different."

Desire's warm shafts rouse me whenever I try to sleep. Concha was right. Now that I've tasted it, I want it again and again. That *is* how it feels when all is said and done.

I scream in the silence of my dreams. I stuff a pillow between my legs to smother the longing but it runs higher and higher until, free at last, it shoots through me like hot wine. Dieter.

I could tell that it was afternoon because the canary had stopped singing. Suze was standing in the doorway with a tray. "Feeling better? Hungry?" I shook my head. "From Concha," she said, pointing to a cup of broth. "Beef extract. Builds up lost strength."

She placed the tray on the night table and sat down.

"Will you tell us exactly what happened?" She spoke very softly, but eagerly. "Tante Eva is here and she wants to listen in. Is that all right?"

I saw Eva by the door.

"What did it feel like?" Eva asked as she moved forward. She sat on the edge of my bed, depressing it with her weight.

"What did what feel like?"

"The deflowering, ha, you know."

So, Suze had announced it. Too good to hold back. Eva is my best friend, she will say when I cry betrayal.

"I mean," Eva pressed on, "did you enjoy it or was it painful? My own, I am afraid, is not much to brag about. I had to wait until I got married and then, after all the build-up, it was rather disappointing. But to have it happen spontaneously, when you are young and hot, that must be . . ." She swallowed saliva and smiled encouragingly, exposing her gap teeth.

"Stop pestering her," Suze said.

"Do you love him? Last question, word of honor. He took you to that house to take advantage of you, right?"

"No, Tante Eva, no! It wasn't like that at all. Dieter happens to be interested in witchcraft and at the house . . ."

"*Lieber Gott*, Suze, did you hear that? Now that's a different story. Let's have it."

You can't "have it," I wanted to shout. It's mine. I didn't need her wisecracks. Why had I begun at all? To defend Dieter? Would they find witchcraft more palatable than the loss of my precious virginity?

"He wanted to show me an authentic folk rite. He's interested in things like that, that's all. But the carnival had gotten us very excited and then the other happened too. It was an accident. Really."

"Witchcraft!" Suze exclaimed. "What does that mean? A savage, that's what he is. Trying to frighten my little girl. I don't ever want to see him around here again. Such a well-mannered boy, Eva. You wouldn't believe it. After all that Cuban informality, it was a delight just to greet him. He would stand very straight, look you in the eye, and shake hands. Just like back home."

"The important thing," Eva said, "is to make sure

she's not pregnant. Keep track of your periods, Claudia."

"Stop it, Eva, she's not pregnant."

Tante Eva winked. "If she is, leave it to me. I know where to go."

I loathed her wink. How many abortions had she had?

"And a medium, was there a medium?"

"Tante Eva," I screamed, "leave me alone. It's none of your business."

"*Perdón, perdón*, if I have offended you." Eva spoke with mock humility. I could have struck her. "Especially here in Cuba," she continued, "where every beauty mark is guarded as if it were gold bullion, one does not do what he did."

I sat up.

"He's not like that," I shouted. "He's German, Tante Eva, German like you. Doesn't that mean anything?"

"*Ja.* Germans I have up to here," she said, lifting her finger to her nose.

"I don't believe you. You love the Germans. I have heard you dream of Berlin. No city like it, you always say."

"Berlin was my city, but the beasts who live there now are not my Germans."

One minute she claims that Germany is perfection itself, the next it is peopled by beasts.

"What about Schiller and Beethoven?" I asked. "What kind of Germans are they? Beasts? And Wagner. Even Papi loves Wagner. Dieter believes in the greatness of Germany because of the geniuses she has produced. Is that so hard to understand?"

"Your Dieter is a fine example of Germany's greatness. I could be charitable and call him a confused young man, but no. Let me call him a true German. *Pfui.*" And she spat.

She reached for Suze's cigarette pack, tapped the bottom, and caught one with her mouth. She turned to me, unlit cigarette between her lips, and spoke slowly:

"What happened in Germany is unspeakable. It erases everything else. Why should you defend it?"

Eva was trying to trap me, but I wouldn't let her. I stared at her dangling cigarette, waiting for it to drop, but it had somehow attached itself to her lower lip and only wobbled. She looked like a gangster.

"I'm not defending anything," I replied. "It's just that the whole world does not revolve around the fate of the Jews—it seems to me."

"You are telling me," Eva said, "you are telling me *that!*" She lit the cigarette and let the smoke come out through her nose.

"Don't you dare!" she shouted, and walked out of the room.

"You do love the Germans," I called after her. "You do. I know it!"

"Hush," Suze said. "What's come over you? Why do you want to hurt her feelings?"

Why indeed?

When Max came, he sat at my side like a mourner, eyes downcast, as if afraid to meet mine.

"You should have looked out for yourself, Claudia."

How typical. Better if the whole thing had not happened so he wouldn't have to deal with it.

"What good does it do to make a comment like that?" I said.

He smiled his embarrassed, lopsided smile. "I'm sorry," he murmured.

Unlike Dieter, he would never, never have disregarded the code, and yet Jews are accused of being too aggressive.

"Look at me," Max said. "Are you going to be all right? Would it make you happy if you got your room back? For good this time. I haven't the strength to snore anymore." He smiled again.

He had spoken with the solicitude accorded a

gravely ill person. So meek and soft. Are all Jews expected to behave like that? And I am a Jewess. Look at me, Papi. You are my Jewishness. Put him on a separate train or he'll get us all arrested.

I looked at him. Those gray eyes. Not of steel.

"Tell me about your mother," I said.

"There is not much to tell," he replied. "She had many children, of course. Couldn't worry about clothes and the WIZO the way your mother does. Once, she took me for a walk in the forest behind our little town. We went along a path covered with moss. I see it now. We stopped at a birch grove and picked mushrooms. She identified the edible ones for me. I remember that as a very happy day."

"You've never told me things like that before."

He cleared his nose and gave a little cough. "There was nothing to tell."

He moved forward and sat on the edge of the chair. He looked uncomfortable, as if it were no longer designed to fit the contour of his body.

"Would a new dress help?" he asked solicitously, reaching for his wallet.

Over the years, the wallet had sunk deeper and deeper into his back pocket. He used to whip it out with a flourish. Waiter, give *me* the check. *Ici*. But the *fábrica* had folded. Swallowed his money and spirit. There, now you are ruined, I had overheard Monsieur Mendelsohn say. Satisfied?

Who would have thought, Max had replied, that the United States would produce civilian goods before the war is even over. Cuban zippers—suddenly they're a joke.

He went around complaining that his nerves were shot. And his digestive tract, too. It's those mangoes, he would cry, and the crickets, the humidity, the tropical storms and, worst of all, no winter. No winter! I feel like an old man already.

I shook my head about the dress and he understood.

186

"Promise me," he said softly, "promise me that you will go back to school. You are my A-1 girl. Don't forget that. I count on you."

Obsession with education is supposed to be another Jewish trait. Would I rather be a Cuban Philistine?

He got up, glad to be rid of the confining chair.

"And we'll keep that Dieter fellow away," he said. "It was that fine-looking German boy, wasn't it?"

Yes. I have followed in Grandmother's footsteps.

"Things could be worse," Franz said from the doorway. "At least it happened with a good tennis player."

So, my affair was even Franz's business now. All your fault, I wanted to cry. Blabbermouth! But I knew that wasn't true.

"You remember Graciela, my girl," Franz continued, taking a step into the room. "She's called *la gran Graciela* at her ballet studio. Yet at school, at your fancy school, she gets no invitations, goes to no parties. The mamas call her an entertainer. Graciela couldn't care less. Yes, male dancers hold her on stage, in front of everybody and not in dark movie theaters, I might add. And she gets applause. Nothing like applause, she insists. Graciela likes you very much, Claudia, and she'll stand by you in school."

I had never heard Franz say so much all at once. I was touched by his effort to console me.

"If I ever go back, I will try to befriend her," I said. "But you know, Graciela is used to being an outcast. It's different for me. Dieter and I—you know how it was, Franz. You saw. We stood out, were admired, thought superior somehow. That's how Dieter made me feel. It isn't only tennis he's good at. Dieter does everything well. And he is smart, and tender."

Franz's face reddened.

"All right, *vieja*, cut it out," he said. "I get the picture."

I kept quiet. I could see that having said his piece, Franz was anxious to leave. The condolence call was over.

Finally Pierre came, a thin volume under his arm.

"For God's sake, let's have some light," he said, reaching for my bedside lamp.

He might as well. Examine the curiosity. Lost it. Lost it. Does one always lose it? Given it away then. That doesn't sound right. Come, Pierre, look around like everybody else. Under the bed, too. But you won't find it. It's gone for good. Surely the redrawn lines of my face make that clear.

He tapped the book. "Here," he said. "You two have a lot in common. *Rien ne nous rend si grand qu'une grande douleur.* That's Musset."

Poetry. "Oh, Pierre, part of you still believes poetry can cure all ills."

"Well, not quite. But he treated you badly, or madly, your Dieter, and that qualifies you for poetry. You have paid your drop of blood. What did you have, you two, a secret society? Don't give me that look. I got the picture a long time ago. Physical perfection! What have you been reading, Nietzsche? Well, now you know not to trust philosophers. All hell can break loose when you least expect it. I tried to warn you."

I described our visit to the *bruja* with apprehension. Would he be outraged? Mock me for having allowed it? Why did I allow it? Why? For I had no doubt, at this moment, that I had been an accomplice. But why should I want to be humiliated and frightened like that? I pulled at my sheet to cover my naked arms. The tepid bedclothes reminded me of the warm feathers of that terrified cock. Oh, why didn't I fight back? Or say, Yes, I'm a Jew. Affirm it like Suze. But even now, at this very moment, the thought is repugnant.

"If not with Dieter, where do I belong?"

"Who would have thought that it would come to this?" Pierre mused.

"I don't know," I said. "I don't know what it means."

"It's harder for people like us to place ourselves. We've had no childhood indoctrination. There were no expressions of affection and loyalty for either Germany or Belgium. No parental musings about life in a Polish shtetl. On that subject, Papi was certainly mum and Mutti too proud of her so-called westernization to bring it up. Look at them now, no interest whatsoever in Cuba as a country, perfectly content to remain on the outside."

"Am I so rootless that I must borrow alien myths? And why did I choose that one, the German one?" Lowering my voice, I added: "I didn't really resist enough."

"Why? That's for you to find out. It took me years to realize that I was hiding behind all that philosophizing and poetry. I was paralyzed. I've finally lost the need to belong anywhere at all, and does it feel good! I am whole at last and able to commit myself. My political activism is not so much in the interest of Cuba as it is in the cause of mankind. For those who have wandered the way we have, there is only the big world. We cannot fit into cozy nooks."

"Pierre," I asked, "could there have been a real miracle, a *real* one?"

"Listen," he replied, "your experience is as valid as the next person's. You tell me that you saw the stigmata and that it later disappeared. Not impossible. What do you think happened to Bernadette of Lourdes? No witnesses. Only fourteen years old and the Virgin 'appeared' to her eighteen times. Eighteen!"

"But," I said, "the blood could have come from the *bruja*'s hands."

"Yes, it could have. You will never know for sure and it doesn't matter. It's what you believe that counts."

His features were becoming sharper, more pointed. His face had that quizzical look. He was enjoying the metaphysical aspects of the conversation. He was the old Pierre, temporarily free of his political pragmatism.

"I don't understand you," I insisted. "Was it real or not?"

"Don't look at it that way, don't be so categorical. Miracles fall into a different class. Highly personal, hallucinatory, if you will. Who, besides Jeanne d'Arc, heard her voices?"

"You're making fun of me, as usual."

"Word of honor. Just don't try healing lepers."

"I want to believe it," I whispered. "Is that crazy?"

For the first time, his eyes focused only on me. He stopped smiling.

"Since that night," I said, "I've been going mad trying to figure out what it is in me that Dieter loves. Whom, I should say. Whom does he love? He calls me his Gretchen, and so you see . . ."

"Not that again. You're both trapped in an unwholesome fantasy. Whom does he love, you ask, Claudia or Gretchen? He loves *you*, I guess, you who are part illusion and part reality. It's just like the miracle, but you won't believe me. You want clear answers."

"I do," I said, "with all my heart."

"Poor little mouse," Pierre replied. "What a hard time you are having. Tomorrow," he murmured, stroking my hair, "go out and get yourself the sweetest cake the Chinaman sells. I'm sure he wonders where you've disappeared to. After that, the ligaments in your 'injured' ankle should feel a little stronger and you can begin to think about returning to school. People are fickle, they tire quickly of even the juiciest scandal."

"It is a 'juicy' scandal, isn't it?"

"No, Mutti has woven a good tale. Take advantage of it. You are strong, courageous."

"That's easy for you to say . . ."

"No, it's not. I'm here to help."

"I'm sorry, *mon* Pierre. I didn't mean it. You are the only one . . ."

He was. The linen of his *guayabera* soaked up my tears.

"Poor little mouse," he murmured again before leaving. "You have so much to learn."

I turned the light off. Like all gifts, I thought, these visits, these offerings of wisdom and solace had fallen short of the mark. *Une grande douleur.* How grand that sounds. How far from the truth. Instead of pain, I felt only the numbness of fear and loss of face. Surely not the stuff to inspire a poet. And I was tired. Hardly willing, hardly able to feel. Tomorrow, when I woke up, everything would not be all right. But now, as I sensed sleep overtake me, I gratefully surrendered not only my lost face, but my limbs, my breasts, to the promise of no tomorrow.

XXIV

══════════════════ Make a wish now and when the war ends, it will come true. I will buy it, whatever it is. When you first said that, back in 1941, I didn't know what to ask for. But I knew it would have to be something big, something like a trip around the world. As the years went by and you kept repeating the offer, my appetite grew more ordinary: bicycles, cameras, radios, aquamarine rings. But you died too soon, Papi. Now that the war is finally over, what I want is to have you back. Buy me that.

They buried you so quickly. Not because it's the

tropics. They know how to keep a body cool here. It's the law. Jewish law. The next day—pouf, you were gone. That's the way to do it, people said. Keel over and die. No sickness, no suffering. I couldn't believe they envied you.

We were seated in a proper semicircle; Franz and Pierre were in jackets and ties.

Monsieur Mendelsohn was the first to walk in. Perhaps, I later thought, he had actually planned to leave early but had been seduced by the prospect of mingling with people again.

He laughed self-consciously as he picked up a glass of rum. He quickly poured himself a second, spilling a little onto the table. "Is rum then the schnapps of the Caribbean?" he quipped.

Suze had had conflict about sitting *shiva* from the start. She had said that a week at home awaiting condolence calls would drive her mad. She had compromised on two days, because, she claimed, to ignore the custom entirely would offend her father's memory.

"I will even rip my dress as a sign of sorrow," she had said, "but you," meaning me, "don't have to. Children are excused."

I was never really his child, I think.

I search and search for the feel of his coat, his skin, his hand. Only the pinched cheek comes back. Affection? Anger? Did he resent me then?

He was so proud of my looks, my performance, but he did not feel comfortable with me. I embodied only his illusions. He endowed me with a wisdom I didn't really have. Why didn't I tell him I'm only a child?

Over in a corner, Eva, Heinrich and Freddy Bauer stood whispering . . .

"His wife had the decency not to show her face."

"Why is he here, anyway?"

"Friendly with Max, didn't you know?"

"Pas possible . . ."

Dare I stand up for Max and Monsieur Mendelsohn? I began to walk toward the large, clumsy man, aware that Eva was following me with her eyes and frowning.

Monsieur Mendelsohn leaned over and whispered in my ear. "I'm going to give you a set of records," he said. "All nine Beethoven symphonies."

"Beethoven, all nine!" I exclaimed so everyone could hear. "I'll need a truck."

When I embraced him, he seemed flustered but pleased. Then he said that he would go get his hat.

"No," I called. "Don't go just yet." I grabbed the *Nusstorte* on the tea wagon and offered him a portion. He ate quickly.

"I must now," he said, looking wistfully about the room. No one had spoken to him.

I watched him smoothe his wrinkled linen jacket, then he straightened his tie, shifted his weight from foot to foot.

"A word about Max before I say goodbye," he announced, his bald head glistening. Suze turned on the electric fan.

"For a man of humble origins," Monsieur Mendelsohn pronounced, "our Max had big dreams. Overdeveloped dreams for a country such as this. He paid the price."

"Yes, poor Max," Suze joined in. "Couldn't adapt. Insisted on wearing suits to work every day. Said *guayaberas* looked sloppy, ungentlemanly, and would not command respect."

I remembered that I had once heard her confide to Eva that Max was not a survivor. Never could switch gears fast enough, she had said. Clung to the status quo as if it were sacrosanct and in time of war, well, that's suicide.

193

One thing is obvious, he died and she didn't.

Heinrich shook his head. He faced Suze as a clear indication that he was responding only to her comment. "Max threw all caution to the winds with that *fábrica* of his. Lost a fortune. This was not the place for big manufacturing ventures."

"A brave man," Mendelsohn insisted. "He took risks."

Brave? His smile was too broad, too unguarded. Not of pleasure, or even of sadness. Ingratiating. Inappropriate. He spoke with his hands as if he were afraid of losing the listener's attention. Leaned forward, touched people like a conspirator fearful of being overheard.

Always afraid.

I was ashamed of him.

Sometimes I wanted to shake him, hit him, mutilate him.

Why, then, this immense sadness?

Mendelsohn reached for another glass of rum.

"Pierre!" Suze hissed. "Watch him—and the rum."

Mendelsohn hesitated. He was poised at that exquisite instant when a person is on the verge of committing a foolishness but has one last second of ambivalence. He looked as if he might let the glass fall from his hands before it reached his mouth. But no, with an energetic tilt of the wrist, he downed the shot.

"A man is defined by the risks he takes," Mendelsohn repeated in a loud, firm voice.

"That must include you, Monsieur," Heinrich said.

"I'm proud of what I did. Does that surprise you? People bought their way out of Europe with the money I helped them procure. You might say that I saved lives. Who can match that?"

"You handled Nazi money," Freddy Bauer said. "You are living off it now."

"You, Herr Freddy, will be the first to run and do

business with the Germans once the war is over, mark my words."

Freddy was heaving. He crossed and uncrossed his tennis shoes. Finally, he stood up.

"Monsieur," he said, "I must ask you to leave."

Suze looked alarmed. "You can't quarrel here," she said. "We are sitting *shiva*."

"What an amusing Yiddish word," Eva said, casting about for a laugh. "*Shiva*."

Suze flushed.

"*Shiva* is Hebrew, not Yiddish," Pierre said. "I'm surprised you didn't know that."

"Why not simply say 'mourning' or something ordinary like that?"

"For God's sake, Frau Eva," Mendelsohn burst out, "this is Havana 1945. We are not sitting *Unter den Linden* using 'ordinary' words!" Then, Monsieur Mendelsohn looked at Suze, and in a calmer voice said that he was ready to go. Pierre stepped forward and led him to the door like a tame elephant.

Still heaving, Freddy Bauer stood up to take his leave as well.

"Frau Suze," he said, "allow me to apologize for this unpleasantness and to place myself at your service. I will be leaving for America very soon. My family awaits me there. If we can do anything for you, please write. Our real estate business is thriving again and I have a position already."

Real estate. You and I, Papi, how we loved the little house set in the wild banana field of Marianao. Tiled pink bathroom with movie star illumination. A back door that would lead to a garden.

But you bowed when Madame Olivier rattled her keys.

You froze when Suze said, Out of the question.

If only . . .

It would have made a difference, I'm sure.

I am his fears and his illusions, and sometimes I hate him for it.

For weeks after Max's death, Suze wore no makeup and her face acquired the drab yellowish cast of a suntan gone stale. The house in those days seemed exceptionally quiet, but Suze claimed that she liked it this way. Uncle Vitya, a frequent visitor, walked about in stockinged feet, out of deference no doubt. I wondered whether I was the only one who missed the sound of Max's radio and considered asking whether I could move it into my room.

And now, five years, eight months, seven days after it began, the war was finally over. We heard a radio commentator describe V-E Day in New York. Everyone dancing and kissing, he said. Flag waving, cigar smoking, confetti raining from the sky. On the front page of the *Havana Post,* a blow-up of New York gone wild.

It had always been held out as the best of days to come. But when Uncle Heinrich and Tante Eva brought champagne, Suze drank little, and when she said that the worst lay before us, I felt cheated.

She insisted on examining a picture in *Aufbau* that showed mounds of corpses by a concentration camp gate. Quoting a survivor, she read aloud: "'A mass grave was dug and we threw them in like they were nothing.' *Schrecklich,*" she said, and Heinrich and Eva nodded in agreement.

A familiar blueness pressed on my heart and I realized, perhaps for the first time, that it would never lift completely.

XXV

I finished the school year a woman among schoolgirls, a moist Magda Lupescu among laughing, white-misted Carmens and Margaritas. My prince had already come.

Like everyone else, Marieta pretended that nothing had happened. Pretended, I say, because of course she suspected a great deal. By holding back, I had closed off the artery that fed our friendship, and sometimes we even ran out of things to say. We would stand in the bare schoolyard, unable to walk away from each other. Marieta would fiddle with her headband and I would pick at the polish on my nails, a mannerism that had always irked her. One time she called out "Stop it!"—giving me a playful slap—and, for an instant, everything was as before.

Chica, I burned to say, let me confess to you, for you are my best friend.

Possessed by the devil because I am a Jewess? Marieta will find that very odd. I don't see the connection, she will say. *Hebreos* are just *hebreos,* who cares?

Don't trouble your little head, Marieta.

What happened, then? she will insist.

Released by a bongo-playing African god, I will say, and then possessed by my hairless boy-lover on a dirty mattress, of course.

I could never. No matter how I tell it, she won't understand and I would have to explain everything, beginning with the Garden of Eden. Even then, I don't think I could shatter her innocence. I have left her behind. I am wrinkled and used. New World Marieta, let me spare you our old complexities, our dirty, scheming past.

Only when Dieter takes me to a *posada,* closes the door of the rented room, and slowly unbuttons my schoolgirl blouse do I feel restored. I can't help it. And now that the Germans have lost and it's V-E day and Dieter says that it changes nothing, that Germany has a long history, even now I want to believe him, although I know he's wrong.

But we usually talk later. As soon as we have stepped away from the door, his hands are on my blouse; it and the jumper fall to the floor and I stand before him in a short white slip. He begins, as always, by kissing me on the ear, then the neck, the shoulders—quick, alluring, provocative, enticing, flirtatious kisses that make me wild for his mouth. I reach for his face and his breath, fresh as new apples, flutters over my features. He carries me to the bed and lowers me slowly. The sheets are starched and crackle slightly as they succumb to my weight. I watch him kick off his shoes, trousers, blue La Salle shirt and tie. I do not think of him as a schoolboy. Naked, blond, lean, white, we could be each other's reflection. In the instant before he possesses me, his blue eyes never look away, never close. Neither do mine.

We are just two. We have stopped going to parties and we are no longer part of the crowd. I am afraid to talk about the past, about what happened, and I think he is too. But now that Max is dead, I feel there are things I must explore.

Lovemaking never drains me, on the contrary I feel fuller, brighter, braver. "I read in the paper," I said, "that General Jodl surrendered at a little red schoolhouse in Reims. He said that he was delivering the German people, for better or worse, into the victor's hands."

"Who said?"

"General Jodl."

"Poor fellow, that must have hurt."

Stretched out at my side, my athlete was at rest. Hands behind his head, Dieter's biceps formed an almost feminine curve; the blond hair under his arm caught the afternoon light.

"Sympathy for Jodl?" I asked.

"He was a career military man. The war was lost fairly."

"Was Hitler fair, too?"

"My father always despised Hitler, you know that. Yet he was sometimes tempted to believe that Hitler would restore the glory of Germany. You should have seen Father do his imitations of Hitler. We would laugh till our sides split. But Germany, that's something else."

Dieter yawned. Today, for some reason, I wanted to push him against the wall. I watched him turn over and heard him ask me to scratch his back, right below the left shoulder.

My hand reached out automatically and I saw my nails trace whitish tracks below the blade, then along the spine.

"Germany and Hitler are one and the same," I said quietly.

"Come on, Hitler was just an episode—ten, twelve years, what's that? A dot in the book of history. Don't think that intellectuals like my father didn't suffer. Hitler," he shuddered, "was so coarse . . ."

"Let's leave your father out of this. How many people did Hitler kill?"

"Wars are wars, not picnics."

"I don't mean in battle. Don't you read the papers? A Russian communiqué this morning—about the camps . . ."

"The Russians are first-class liars. Everybody knows that. Anyway, with your luminous blondness, *Liebchen*, you would have been whisked away to *Lebensborn* to breed racially superior children."

"What? With only one Cossack grandfather? That's only twenty-five percent . . ."

"What's come over you?"

"Nothing—I feel as if I were standing on the edge of the world looking down, that's all." My fingernails dug deeper into the fair flesh. I wanted to draw blood.

"Don't be melodramatic."

"In May 1941, the Germans rounded up thousands of Jews in Paris, foreign Jews, many Poles. I was living there at the time."

Now that sounded really important. Made Dieter look like a bystander. All of a sudden, I felt quick and alert. I remembered how gray Paris had been that spring, how the gendarmes had not shed their winter capes.

"Dieter, it rained, it was cold, I could have been . . ."

"But you weren't in the roundup, so cut it out."

I was glad that he had not let me finish. I would never be ready to hear myself say it.

We were sitting up now, on the edge of the bed. I was fanning us both. My hair, usually held back with a velvet band, fell around my face. I lifted it up and tied it in a knot.

"I was over there while you were sitting in the tropical sun eating bananas." What I was doing was cheap, and I knew it, but I couldn't stop.

Dieter straightened his shoulders. Dieter the swimmer. I had gone too far. Maybe, if I rubbed his back again . . .

"Why turn on me?" he said, pulling away. "After all I've done for you."

"Done for me? I don't understand."

"Yes you do. I am your secret wishes. I've included you, I've given you the myths of my childhood. It's a misfortune to be born a Jew, and I gave you the illusion that you had escaped it."

There was something so wounding in what he had said that I could barely grasp it.

"Illusion? Favors?" I cried. "My fine German *novio* has been doing me favors?"

Damn the tears. Why do women always . . . ? Somehow, he will convince me that I am wrong no matter how

200

much I rage, and I will continue to let him trick me.

"I thought you believed it," I screamed, "really believed it!" I lost all restraint. I was wild with sorrow and anger, and the only release was to pound and pound his chest and scratch at him with my nails.

"*Basta!*" Dieter cried. He grabbed both my wrists and forced me off the bed. I felt him guide my head until it was between his legs. I almost gagged. Never, not even in books. It was over in a few seconds.

Dieter fell back. "There," he said quietly, "there, now we both feel better."

XXVI

My hardest moments come in the morning when I wake up too early for school and the whole day looms empty and without desire. Everything is an effort: watching the little travel alarm that used to belong to Max, thinking about the energy it would take to get dressed.

Dressed in what costume? The mirror refuses to tell me who I am. I'm fully rounded, almost seventeen, and the chaste uniform with white ankle socks and convent shoes seems more perverse than ever. The hair, perpetually light in this sunful country, gives the impression of health. The freckles the mask of childhood. It is curious, the way I examine myself in the mirror, unable to find what I am looking for.

Dieter's girl. I am still me, I had said. I knew what that meant then. Or at least I thought I did. But afterward when he had denounced the deception, *my* deception, I had wanted to shout that our pact did not suit me anymore.

Look, look again. Is this my reflection? I turn and, yes, I see it, the start of a growth, a small mound that turns into a shoulderblade only if I keep rotating. A fraction of an inch of counterrotation and it reappears as a hump. It wouldn't be all that surprising. One has so little control over one's body. Some are born deformed, others straight. Nothing is fair. Take Mushka, the manicurist. Not only a hump, but her hands too—as if in a perpetual spasm. And she chose to become a manicurist. I have heard it said that people deliberately choose professions that compensate for handicaps. Is that courage, or just the opposite? I am so confused, I don't seem to get anything straight.

Humpbacked Claudia. Claudia the Humpback and other grotesque German fairy tales. Story of a princess turned freak. Tell me another, Mother dear . . .

Suze loves an audience and, facing her across the little work table, Mushka was only too eager to oblige.

"Those Americans," Suze raged, inhaling her cigarette so deeply I thought the smoke would burn down to her soul. "There's no getting around them. In their so-called innocence, in their excessive bounty mixed with self-interest, they know exactly what they are doing. Their politicians fear losing gentile votes so they have told Roosevelt to keep the Jews out and their immigration quotas way down. And he did what he was told. What an orgy of obedience we are having all of a sudden!"

It used to be, "When the war is over." Now, all I ever hear is quota, quota, quota . . .

"Things could be worse," Mushka said. Her voice seemed to rise from the floor. My God, she is so short that she need hardly bend over to lift the napkin that covers her workbasket.

"Worse? Five years of waiting!" Suze was irritated by Mushka's resignation. "The waiting list, my dear Mushka, is long enough to hang yourself with ten times. My husband's legacy, that Polish quota. And the irony is that they stripped him of citizenship to protect themselves against the return of unwanted Jews. Is there such a thing as a wanted Jew, I ask you?"

"No," Mushka declared, busy with soapy water, bottles, and jars. "Frau Suze," she added, "if anyone can get a family into America, it is you." She looked up and gave Suze an admiring glance.

"That's where you're wrong, exactly wrong. I can do nothing. They refuse to notice me at the consulate." She freed her hand from Mushka's hold and picked up her cigarette for a quick puff. How she hates feeling helpless, I thought.

"Worldliness, chic, *chien*," she ranted on, "nothing counts there. If you're over twenty-five, you're invisible. Finished. I should send Claudia in my place."

She! Ready to pass the mantle? Hell, no. I've watched her flash the old dazzling smile too often.

"Here in Cuba, the *señoras* give in too graciously," Suze continued. "They let themselves grow old and fat without a fight. But in America, where the women insist on putting on a ghoulish show, it's just as bad. Have you seen the tourists?" She began to sing.

I got the sun in the mornin'
And the moon at night . . .

"Singing like innocents, vapid faces unlined as if life had not touched them. And those sunback dresses, I ask you! Exposing flesh that has lost all resilience! *Ach*, give me a woman who knows her age but wears it well. A civilized woman!"

Mushka nodded. She was so flattered by Suze's banter that she forgot to ask her to select a color.

203

"No! no!" Suze shrieked, pulling her hand away. "This one, the deep red!"

I observed the quick, experienced movements of Mushka's hands, the way she whipped out the acetone and deftly took off the rejected polish. How, earlier, when she had soaked the hands, she had dried them without rubbing. A professional patting motion only. How skillful she is. And now, the deft brushstrokes of color and those beautiful half-moons.

I noticed that her own fingers were painted, too. Do people like Mushka experience vanity? Does she really believe there is anything she can do to enhance her appearance? What could it feel like to be born a Mushka with a Polish childhood like Max's? Born before the turn of the century, both of them. Were their villages part of Poland then, or was it Russia, or Austria . . .?

"I hear that Herr Heinrich and Frau Eva have left with little Friedl. Those Germans, they get all the breaks . . ." Mushka stopped in mid-sentence to repair a stroke that had run beyond the nail.

"Yes," Suze said. "You can say that again. But Frau Eva writes that New York's streets are not paved with gold after all."

"Too bad." Mushka laughed. She looked up from her work table. Her pale eyes had narrowed and seemed to be set in an aureola of fine wrinkles.

"Monsieur Mendelsohn, I hear, is having a mountain of difficulties." She grinned. "Americans don't like collaborators."

Am I a collaborator, too? If the Americans knew, wouldn't they keep me out as well? I looked away although I knew that my face no longer betrayed my emotions the way it used to. I've managed to control that. Now it's my hands. At this moment, for instance, they are like ice.

I forced myself to look in Mushka's direction. Her bowl of warm soapy water seemed inviting. Her little fingers would fly over mine, wash them, cure them—oh yes.

"I'd like Mushka to give me a manicure today," I said.

Suze looked up surprised. "Really? Why the change of heart?"

But Mushka was enthusiastic. "Congratulations," she said. "Welcome to the club."

She spread a fresh white towel for me.

"Claudiachen, try this delicate rose color, it suits you."

I was allowing her to touch me for the first time. I noticed that she was proceeding more slowly than usual, as if she were savoring every moment. Suit me? Surely you, Mushka, are the delicate rose. Help me. Make my hands warm up, come to life.

Mushka hummed as she pushed back my tender cuticles with her rounded wooden instrument. "What lovely soft hands," she murmured. "So white, yet why so cold?"

For her touching me must be like brushing against youth and beauty. People see what they want to see. I feel old. The manicure is not working.

Mushka was bending over so low that I could feel her breath on the back of my hand. I had not anticipated that; I wanted to pull out . . .

"What will I do," Mushka said, "when you leave and I lose all my best customers?"

"Nonsense," Suze said, waving her hands in the air to make the polish dry faster, "you will come to America like the rest of us. At the consulate, they did tell me, just the other day, Lady, they said, you've waited all these years, be patient a little longer. Your turn will come. That applies to you just as much, Mushka."

"I wouldn't go," she whispered. "The thought of picking up one more time . . . no, thanks. I'll manage here, get my business from the *hebreos,* and sit tight until my dear brother returns."

Suze didn't reply. There was nothing even she could say. There had been no news of Mushka's brother in years. The last boat out of Lisbon left in 1942. Neither the International Red Cross nor the Joint Committee had been able to come up with a clue.

Let me change places with him.

Let me raise him from the dead, become his ashes.

Look up, Mushka, your dear brother is here.

He will take care of you . . .

But who was I to offer comfort? That sort of comfort. I clasped my cold, dead hands together, then rubbed them in an attempt to restore circulation.

"Don't!" Mushka cried. "You're not dry!"

XXVII

From a distance, Suze looked naked in her flesh-toned underwear. Naked and full. Especially her waist, I thought. It *is* getting thicker. I leaned beyond the dining room table to get a better look and caught the quick heart-shaped movement that is her mouth. The mourning period must be over.

"Can't find my glasses," she called without turning. "Would you check the paper for Mushka's ad?"

"What ad?" I spit out the *mamoncillo* pit I have been sucking for the past ten minutes. Even after the pulpy white flesh has been chewed off, the pit holds the fruit's sweet-sour flavor.

"Sweeter than the roses in May . . ." She was singing. An American song. I couldn't believe it. Getting ready for New York, I suppose.

"What ad?" I repeated.

"The one about her brother."

"Oh."

The latest edition of *Aufbau* was lying next to the fruit bowl. The German-American *Zeitung* had almost doubled in size over the last months, thanks to the classified ads searching for survivors.

I began thumbing through the paper.

"Here, I found it."

Suze walked in, dressed.

"Desperate for news of beloved brother Leo Berkowitz, it says. Last domicile, Paris. Last heard from, August 1941. Contact Mushka Berkowitz, Havana, Cuba."

I reread it. Was there hope then?

"Mutti, will she find him?"

"Who knows," Suze said. "A chance in a million."

"In a million!"

I looked down and directly below Mushka's ad I saw many more:

> —Who can give me information about Emma
> Katz?
> —News of our mother, deported June 1942.
> —Of Helga Aronstein and son Konrad, fourteen.
> —Of Herman Blau, born Budapest, December 25, 1895.

My eyes moved to the opposite page. "*G.I. Journal from Dachau*, it says. An American writes: 'People that are nothing but skeletons . . . I shall never forget a seventeen-year-old Austrian boy, his face full of abscesses, his parents burnt . . .'"

"Forget?" Suze said, reading over my shoulder, "Who can forget?" She flipped through the paper until she found what she wanted. "'From a survivor,'" she read. "'I only wanted to live in order to tell this, and now that I am, it is not affording me the release I had hoped.'" I heard her give a small, almost inaudible gasp. When I looked up, I saw that the choking sound had been an effort to stifle a sob. I felt her hand on my shoulder and realized that we had lost the habit of physical contact. Could she be turning to me for consolation? No! I wanted to cry. Leave me out of it.

"Claudia, what shall we do?"

I leaned forward as far as I could, pretending to be engrossed in the paper.

—Camp survivor seeks wife, formerly Leipzig, now Bolivia.

—Camp survivor seeks father, formerly Berlin, now Brazil.

Formerly Warsaw, now Brooklyn, formerly Prague, now Tel Aviv, or Shanghai, or Swaziland, or Johannesburg . . .

Formerly Antwerp, I thought. *Now Havana.*

Anton Hanner seeks brother in Lansing, Michigan.

Anton! I felt a flush of shame.

"Mutti, look!"

"Not our Anton, dear. His last name wasn't Hanner."

We continued down the page together, in silence. Suddenly, she took me by the shoulders and pointed to a headline that read: "Fate of Jews in Czechoslovakia."

> —In Prague, one hundred left out of a population of sixty thousand . . .
> —Typhus epidemic holds Theresienstadt inmates captive a while longer . . .
> —Rationing cards stamped "Jew" to be exchanged for normal cards by Prague Nutrition Committee.

Yes, of course, she was Czech.

After all these years in Cuba, I had almost forgotten. One might say, quite accurately. that she was a Czech refugee. But what kind of refugee was I? Better yet, was I a refugee at all? If so, from where? Previous domicile: Antwerp. Next domicile: New York. And so on. If a refugee is simply someone who seeks refuge, then I am, after all, a bona fide refugee. The rootless variety perhaps; not torn from anything deep. To be a Czech. There is something simple and definitive about that. I wonder how it feels? Why am I always asking questions? Don't I know anything at all? One time, long before this war, and before the other one, too, Suze had a normal childhood somewhere. A small-town childhood protected, she often said, by the image of her beloved Kaiser Franz Josef. He was, she said, everyone's father. In our prayers we asked God to watch over him.

So many stories. Her childhood. In the attic, she would say, my three sisters and I. We would dress up in our grandparents' clothes, take them out of wooden chests and carefully put them back. A most ordinary thing. Children at play. Where are they now, those chests? And the sisters? The only one we know is safe is Tante Caro in Brazil. The other two I have met only once, before the war, when I was four or five. Their names are Luisa and Anna, who is the youngest, but that, too, always slips my mind. When the Kaiser died in 1916, Suze had already completed her first decade. History books refer to it as a prosperous and secure one. What will they say about mine? It isn't fair!

If she is Czech, then what am I? A forged document? Exposed, will I burn, or starve like those *Aufbau* skeletons Suze exhumes so eagerly? All through the war she had feared Maidanek or Terezin for her sisters. I can't remember which. Now, she haunts the ads and talks of placing one of her own. Those *Aufbau* people, those *Aufbau* survivors, haven't I known about them all along? Didn't Max and Suze often speculate that such camps existed? I should be grateful to Dieter for having given me a taste. Now there's less to be afraid of.

"What shall we do?" Suze cried. "How do we live with this?"

We? She's right. I should be crying like her.

I pulled the paper toward me again and examined a framed epitaph at the bottom of the page. It read:

> We have only just heard that our dear father, brother, grandfather, Herman Kipnitz, was killed at Belsen, January 1943. No time to say goodbye.

No time to say goodbye. Jesus!

"Mutti," I cried, "that name again? The youngest sister . . ."

"Anna, I've told you a thousand times."

"I'm sorry," I said, and embraced her.

Anna. As in *Anna Karenina.*

There are three novels on my night table. *Anna Karenina, Jane Eyre,* and *Gone With the Wind.* I have become a reader at last, for I prefer to toss in bed, on my back, on my side, book held this way and that until my arms fall asleep. I banish reality late into the night, transformed into the heroines of my dreams. Scarlett and Jane give me the illusion, briefly, that I can be strong like them. But Anna is the one I feel for. I don't want to end up like Anna, and so bury myself under the covers to dissipate the chill of death.

In the morning, when I finally walk into the dining room to drink my orange juice, I watch Franz, who now works as a diamond cutter and earns lots of money, devour a colossal breakfast that includes mango and papaya, just like Max. Fleshy, healthy Franz. Is he the sanest of us all? He has announced that he will not be going to America. Even when the papers come, he says: "I'm going to marry Graciela when she graduates. *Esta islita me conviene* —This little island suits me fine."

Not so with Pierre. He has been conferring with Suze and together they have decided that he should complete his studies in Mexico. Why Mexico? I howl. Because, I am told patiently, calmly, Pierre's life is in danger here. Do we have to explain? And besides, the university is so strike ridden that even if he doesn't get gunned down or arrested, it will take him forever to finish. Why does he have to become a lawyer? That, Suze, says, is the silliest question of all. The world needs lawyers. And his beloved causes? Is he just going to walk out? He's going to survive, Suze says. That comes first. After things calm down, I'll come back, Pierre promises.

Pierre, don't go! Pierre has always given me an hour or two of tenderness when I needed it most. People like Pierre have the capacity to imagine everything. There is rarely a need to explain. He phrases things better than you can yourself. But his needs come first; I should have realized that long ago. He asks my forgiveness and listens one more time as I tell him I don't understand ambition and appetites. How does one find the right role? I cry. I have no sense of the future. I'll have no one to talk to.

He's going to go, no matter what. Nothing I can say will make any difference. He is Pierre and I am I. I'd like to wish him well, but I can't. I will say goodbye to him the way I said goodbye to Dieter. With bitterness for the things that keep being taken away from me without being replaced.

I had been so sure: Only Dieter would do. Did he give me exactly what I asked for and is that why I found it so hard to let go? Do I want it still? Will I always?

She should have saved me. Isn't that what mothers are for? Even now, she's better off than I am. She can cry and feel her loss. She knows what side she is on.

At first, Dieter had not believed me when I told him we were through. We were riding one of the ramshackle buses to Miramar, to the club. It was literally coming apart and I could see the road through cracks in the floor. The driver had rigged up a mini altar with dusty artificial flowers over the dashboard. Even bus drivers have their patron saints.

"Why?" he had asked.

"I know more than I used to but not enough."

"What are you talking about?"

"I knew, all my life, I knew. Now I read it in the papers and I can't even cry."

He turned in his seat. "It's the camps, isn't it?"

"Yes."

"But I'm the fellow who sat out the war in the tropics eating bananas."

"But you are German. Sometimes I believe that you always knew that I was Jewish, and that was part of the attraction."

"Like Romeo and Juliet, perhaps?"

"I'm not trying to be funny!"

Out of the blue, the bus driver began speeding, ignoring six or seven stops in a row.

"He won't halt until he sees something worthwhile," one of the passengers quipped, drawing a curvaceous female figure in the air. Others stuck hands, heads out the window to catch the breeze. Dieter's blond hair bobbed on his forehead. Everyone was laughing.

"Anyway, *Romeo and Juliet* doesn't apply. Sometimes I believe that we loved because of our differences, not despite them."

"Maybe Shakespeare intended that as well."

"Forget Shakespeare."

We got off the bus and crossed the street to the club's entrance. I looked at the manicured flower beds, at the porter's desk, at the airy dining room beyond. The porter waved us in. Today I was Dieter's guest. I will give that up, too.

"Come," he said. "Get into your bathing suit and we'll go for a swim."

I reappeared wrapped in my terry robe *à la cubana*.

"Not in the pool," he said. "In the sea."

I followed him. We swam to the end of the jetty and beyond. "Let's go to the raft," he said, and I moved quickly and effortlessly. I was glad that I was a good swimmer. I placed my elbow on the raft but Dieter toured it twice before stopping. My legs were moving rhythmically, treading aqua water. I could see the sun sparkle on my wet arms. I was glad we had come. My face felt hot, my body cool and alive. I won't want to leave Cuba when the time comes. Maybe I belong here amid the sudden downpours and the brightness that always follows.

"Don't." His leg was between mine. He began kissing me on the neck. We rolled in the water and I swallowed a mouthful. I placed both hands on his shoulders. Weightless, we touched each other with hands and feet. Dear God, let it always be like this. He put his hand where his leg had been. I let him. And I loved him back.

I turned over and began to float. I was tempted to let the current take me, not out to sea, of course, but on a smooth passive journey parallel to the shore. Neither in nor out. The route of least resistance? No, even that would require an effort since the current was pulling me out, and Dieter was calling and gesturing toward the raft. I will have to go through with it after all. What was he thinking now, at this very moment, as he motioned impatiently for me to come? Will he take me seriously? And if he does, then what?

Did I fear him? I looked at him as I swam back with a slow, deliberate breaststroke, thinking that if it weren't for his swollen biceps and pectorals, he would look like a boy still. I hoisted myself onto the raft and looked around. It was early and we were the only swimmers. Most people

213

preferred the pool anyway. I shuddered pleasurably as the sun touched me. I would be dry in minutes. I closed my eyes.

"Look at me," he said.

"No puedo."

"I must have drunk some sort of anti-Semitism with mother's milk," he said, "for I never heard my parents speak out against the Jews. Never."

"What about me, where did I drink it?"

"You?"

"I let you, don't forget. I know I did. The question is, why? Sometimes I'm on the verge of understanding and then it disappears. Something inside me *knows*. Let me look at you." He turned. His body, copper-hued, had a tinge of gold. No matter how much time he spent in the sun, his tan never dulled. "Let me try to know what I feel when I look at you. Maybe I admire Germans, just like my father. For he did, although he feared them. Or maybe it was my mother—she could hate them, but then she managed to use them and enjoy that, too. I never told you how we got out of Europe, how she manipulated, how fiercely she fought for us. Maybe I sensed the danger of what she was doing . . . and envied her. All my life I heard: 'They want to get rid of the Jews.' Get rid of the Jews! If she could save us from that, she must have a secret I don't possess."

"I don't remember ever seeing a Jew until I met you. Not knowingly, at least. Still, all my life, I too had heard . . ."

"The perfect pair, all right. Is it possible that we crave our punishment so as to get it over with?"

How odd to be telling him this in full view of the *pepillos* flirting by the pool. If one of the chaperones, rocking in the shade, overheard us, she wouldn't even know what we were talking about. I will envy the Cubans their innocence for the rest of my life. At least with Dieter there was a shared sensibility.

"I did it out of love. I didn't mean it as a punishment. I swear."

"*Dios mío,* Dieter, how can I manage this? I don't feel anything anymore. My mother and I . . . read a German-American weekly called *Aufbau,* Jewish German-American, I should say, full, full of things about the camps, and I'm like a zombie, while my mother cries and wails. My mother can do it all. She always has the right response. What am I supposed to do? I cannot grieve."

"You're not a zombie with me. Doesn't that tell you something?"

"When I think of our night at the *bruja*'s, I know that I cannot imagine my life without that experience. I remember opening my eyes afterward and seeing you naked beside me and realizing that at last you were really mine just like . . ." The pain shot into my brain. My jaw locked and I bit my tongue. I had seen her then, for a second, no more, before she slammed the door. Lieutenant Ducek, clean, smooth, naked beside her, a rumpled sheet at his feet.

"Like what?"

"Leave me alone." Let me drown.

"You're upset. Forgive me."

"Nothing to forgive. Haven't I explained that it's all my fault? I allowed you into my twisted illusion. I can't go on with it—"

"Without illusions, what's the good of anything?" He touched my hair. Dieter the gentle, so hard to resist. And I wanted to argue with him. I tried to picture life without him and I feared that I would just find a substitute. The same thing, over and over again. Is that all I'm capable of? Maybe if I could explain, he would understand, even help me. But I would have to talk about Suze and Ducek, and I can't. The only thing clear to me is that I don't want to be Fraulein Claudia anymore.

In the fall, Dieter will leave Havana to attend a college in the United States. Why not wait until then? Wouldn't it be much easier to let time take care of things? The world is full of cowards anyway.

I began to swim and Dieter followed. Alongside me at first, then reaching out, his arm around my waist.

"I own you," he said.

"I love you, too," I replied.

"I own you," he repeated. I understood this time. I pulled away. I have no choice. He is helping me to make the gesture. It has to be now.

Only Suze remains. My mother. I realize now how fine is the line between knowing and not knowing, how one can cross it suddenly, without preparation. Dieter knew about me all along, he just couldn't face it. And I knew about Suze and Lieutenant Ducek.

I owe my life to her once and surely twice. How dare I hold anything against her? If I confront her, she will say *Ach,* Ducek, he wasn't really a German, you know. A Czech in German uniform, a lamb in wolf's clothing. Won't bother her one bit. And Papi? I will ask. Max? Dumped the whole mess in my lap. What did he expect? She'll shrug her shoulders and go on to the next thing while I ponder my role in all this. Stop playing the innocent. You know. You wanted it all, from the very beginning. Hand-kissing Don Estéban, Schiaparelli finery, broad-shouldered Ducek, roses, wine, soft laughter . . .

"I don't worry about things I can do nothing about," Pierre once said. Maybe he gets that from her. She does not seem remorseful. On the contrary, flaunts it, tells her tale over and over again and, every time, I want to scream, Shut up! Grow up, Claudiachen. You are a partner in her virtuous crimes.

America, she says—in America, we will start all over again. By we, she means the two of us. Mother and daughter. She has already begun to make plans. I'll show them, she says. I'll make money in their land of opportunity. I'll open a boutique for fine accessories, the little things that make a woman chic—gloves soft as butter, chiffon scarves, hand-stitched bags, hats, costume jewelry. Maybe even perfume. The sort of things cosmopolitan women can never get enough of.

Youth, beauty, brains, four languages—you have everything going for you. How do you talk to someone who says things like that? Use face cream at night, this sun dries your skin. I know about evil, I want to cry, but goodness is more elusive. Always dress as if a movie director were awaiting you at the next street corner. But I want options and moderation. Don't bother your little head, an attractive girl like you will find someone just like that. Snaps her fingers. She believes in romance. So do I. But it isn't enough. She has something else, something I am lacking. The WIZO ladies, the bridge partners, the shopgirls, even the merchants at the *mercado* sense it. What is it? How can I find it?

We stand side by side, I a woman too, though taller, thinner, blonder, frailer, and without the opaqueness of her eyes. Mine are liquid, blue-green—a reflection of my mutability. Hers brown and solid like the earth of Ostrava. Yes, strength and fear sit in the eyes; the mouth is malleable and can be twisted to deceive. My mother's eyes, I want them.

If we must move again, let it be for the last time. Cuba was just a stopover, after all. We can't stay. We are driven to America, to New York, our final destination. Over there, I will make good use of my sharpened perceptions. Claudia learns quickly. Before you know it, she will have figured out the right way to walk, to talk, to dress. No one will suspect. She may be young, but don't underestimate her talents. She even speaks without an accent.

I graduated before leaving. At the head of the class. For Max. I cradled a bouquet of roses and made a speech before the assembled parents, schoolchildren, and as much of the diplomatic corps as Miss Vance and Mrs. Maple could snare. I spoke about the rebuilding of the world, about the United Nations—and the triumph of democracy. I said all the right things. Quite a speech, except for the stutter at the end.

Once again we share a cabin. It is a ferry, small and festive; there's gambling and dancing aboard. Ninety miles of this, across the Straits from Havana to Miami. Back and forth. Americans and Cubans taking their pleasure. Everybody needs a change.

She is humming and smoking as she moves between dressing table and bathroom. I told her to go first and she said, Don't rush me, I'll be out in a minute. Twenty have gone by. I am lying on the bed, waiting; a moment ago I had to fold my leg to avoid being grazed.

"Meet me in the bar."

"*Sí, señora.*" I give her a mock salute.

It's like a nightclub. I had no idea. Evening gowns and mink stoles. This time, she said, we're doing it first class. Bartenders flourish cocktail shakers like court jugglers: daiquiris and pink ladies. Men with rings on their fingers down shots of rum and raise their voices. The air is humid—I'm perspiring. Beads above my lips, like Max. When the band strikes up, I realize there's a dance floor just beyond the bar. She must be in there, kicking up her heels, doing her number. Not again. I turn around and head for the deck and some air.

Cuba is no longer visible. I'm at sea. I suddenly miss the babble in the cocktail lounge. It's so dark, so quiet here. Once upon a time people shunned night air like the plague. I wrap my angora cardigan across my chest.

"Aren't you . . . ?"

"Yes, of course . . ."

A whole family has materialized and I recognize a classmate from St. George's.

"*Chica,* what are you doing here standing in the dark like that?"

"Waiting for the end of the world."

They don't know whether to laugh or not.

"*Oye,* wasn't that your mother in there doing a mean tango?"

"My mother? Impossible. I'm traveling alone."

Epilogue

Years later, I received an invitation to Marieta's daughter's wedding. I had not seen Marieta since 1954, when she and Doña Mercedes had come to New York to buy her trousseau. Every Christmas, however, there had been cards with bits of handwritten news tacked on. She had fled Castro's Cuba within a year of the revolution and settled in Miami with her husband Pablo and two babies. After Pablo's fatal auto crash, she had managed on public assistance until the children were old enough for school. Then she had begun teaching piano and eventually developed a local reputation as an accompanist. During a college tour, she was offered a position in Augusta, Georgia. She accepted and installed her parents in a ranch house next door to hers.

I picked out Marieta's calm brow by the gate. Hair still pulled back from the forehead but now held in place by spray instead of a velvet band. At her side, an old woman in black—Doña Mercedes. She looked withered, and the gray chignon at the nape of her neck offered little protection to the fragile skull, the empty sagging ears. Don Andrés, in an open shirt, also displayed gray, but his body had kept the limberness I remembered. He seemed to be dancing on the balls of his feet as he awaited my arrival at the end of the ramp. Would I, who had been "up north" these thirty years, know how to respond to a Cuban *abrazo?*

Elena, the bride-to-be, and her brother Carlos had also come. As they waved and blew kisses in the glaring Georgia noon, I wanted to drop my bags and gambol over the gate into their arms.

Marieta held me, kissed me, scolded me for being too thin, insisted that I marry and grow ripe on babies and black beans the way she had.

"Too late for all that," I said, hugging her back and enjoying the weight of her sturdy body against mine.

"Nonsense, in America you're never old," she said, and from my throat came girlish giggles that echoed our adolescence.

At the airport coffeeshop, Don Andrés tested my Spanish while Doña Mercedes asked, as tactfully as she could, what I did all day long. If I'm not married, she must wonder whether I'm being kept.

"I work as an interpreter," I said. "The U.N. sends me around the world and back . . . I have words coming out of my ears. I once believed they could do some good, especially after the war; now I think they can do no harm."

"I'd give anything to travel and know languages the way you do," Carlos, Marieta's oldest, said. He had a summer job teaching horseback riding at the local country club and his face was very burnt.

"The words I use are never my own."

"Who cares, if you can say it four ways?"

I laughed. "Languages are the refugee's campaign ribbons. Consider yourself rooted, Carlos, if you have only two."

Don Andrés wanted to know whether my mother was still as attractive and charming.

"Her new rich husband thinks so," I said. I told them how she ran a big house in the suburbs, gave lots of parties, and went on at least one cruise a year. "Her only regret," I added, "is that I wouldn't let her get me a husband as well. But you, how have you weathered the transplant?" Never, not in a million years, would I have dreamed that the Cuba I knew could disappear.

Don Andrés shrugged his shoulders. "This heat could fell a cockroach," he said lightly. "I'll take Havana's breezes any time. If you must know, I miss my porch and my rocking chair. Air conditioning is only good for sleeping."

"Don't mind him," Elena said. She shook her heavy Spanish hair. "He spends every morning on the golf course, has a marvelous time—beats me why he's always yearning for the good old days."

"Cuba is home," Carlos said.

"Bah," Elena answered between cigarette puffs. "Georgia is my home and this is where I belong."

I touched Elena's hand and stroked it. "Elenita, don't frown. Tomorrow is your wedding day."

Doña Mercedes was shaking her head. She who had wielded an iron hand over maids, chauffeur, and gardener now sat with her spotted hands folded to keep them from trembling. With a nod in Elena's direction, she let out a wail. "Ay, Elenita, thank God you're getting married at last! *Americana* or not, it is immoral to carry on the way you did, out every night, no chaperone. The flesh, you know, is weak—and people talk, you have to be careful."

I bit my tongue. How I had pleaded with Suze to chaperone me. I'm not ready to sit and watch, she had replied. In Europe we don't have such barbaric customs.

Marieta sighed. "You have no idea what it's been like, trapped between these two. Though she's only eighteen, getting married is the best solution for Elena. Jimmy, her fiancé, is a Georgia boy but steady-headed."

Elena's wedding gifts were laid out on a long white table like a body at a wake. A conical statue of our Lady of Cobre, patroness of Cuba, stood surrounded by candles and gladioli in a corner of Marieta's formica-and-chintz living room. At the Virgin's feet, three about-to-be-shipwrecked fishermen knelt in prayer in the midst of a storm. The air was cool yet stale. Still, it was preferable to the 103 degrees that cooked the suburban avenues. People hurry from house to car to work as in other climes they might seek refuge from the cold.

Fresh from Miami, Marieta's brothers Pepe and Manolo looked splendidly tanned and too energetic in their impeccable linen suits. Their buxom, perfumed wives, in low-cut summer dresses displaying perfect skin, mirrored the matrons of *Vanidades,* Miami edition. How do they manage to turn magazine pages with those *ancien régime* fingernails? We were introduced and I pecked the women's cheeks. Then, turning to the men, I looked for traces of the little brats who used to shatter my idyllic afternoons with Marieta in the scented decaying garden in Miramar.

"Why, you're all grown up!" I said. "But this is more like it." Manolo's nine-year-old lacked only the blue school shirt and navy tie of La Salle. "The resemblance is uncanny."

"And look at her," Manolo nudged his brother. "She certainly hasn't lost her looks or shape. We had our fantasies, you know . . ."

"But she's a little less naive," I replied, though I relished their compliment. Even now, in this world of my past, I need the reassurance that I look attractive and frail and distant. I tell myself that with luck, I'll age gracefully.

At the other end of the room, Carlos was arguing with his grandfather. Their voices silenced everybody else.

"Listen for once," Carlos pleaded. "Castro has wiped out illiteracy, built schools and hospitals. The *bohios* are gone, no more dirt floors—everyone has running water! Doesn't that count?"

"*Bohios* are eternal," Don Andrés mumbled.

"*Basta,* Carlos," Doña Mercedes cried. "How many

224

times must I tell you not to mention that man's name in this house. He is the devil."

Alejandro, I wondered, could that be you hiding a weak chin under Castro's devilish beard?

"On top of it all, *es un mujeriego,*" she ranted. "He snatches any woman that strikes his fancy."

For a while, he had eyes only for me.

"Who cares? It's what he accomplishes that matters."

"Sh," Marieta said. She looked my way and for the first time I noticed a bluish line across her forehead where a vein was gently throbbing. "Mami is hysterical when it comes to Castro and the revolution. She's been through so much."

"And the piano," Doña Mercedes wailed again. "Do you remember Marieta's Steinway? I wanted to give it to a friend. God knows, we left everything else behind. But no, that swine refused." She quickly crossed herself, then added: "The piano, he said, belongs to the state."

"Of course I remember. A baby grand near the French doors leading to the garden."

She gave me a grateful squeeze.

Manolo shook his head. "Castro would be out by now if the country had only listened to Nixon."

"*Sí,*" Don Andrés agreed, "the *americanos* are unbelievably naive." He looked in my direction and I wondered whether I was a *gringa* to him now, dressed in my Saks wraparound and tailored blouse.

"Nixon was a crook," Carlos said. "*Abuelito,* admit it. He was a gangster just like Batista. Batista, with his gold faucets and bedrooms full of carved angels and roses, ugh!"

"Who's defending Batista?" Don Andrés said, rubbing a finger over his wrist as a reminder that Batista had mixed blood.

I felt a chill. Max had often pointed out that Batista was a friend of the Jews. If to be a Jew means you must color everything with a unique perspective, will I ever want to qualify?

Juggling Cokes and potato chips, Marieta marched up to Carlos. "That's enough," she said. "Have a Coke and hold your politics until after the wedding!"

All eyes turned to Elena, who was fingering her gifts. Silver for twelve—soup spoons, serving spoons, dessert spoons. She lifted the lid of a copper chafing dish and examined the interior.

"Elenita, don't fall in," Carlos called, but she ignored him. She touched the blender, the mixer, caressed the table linens. Fine china and everyday china. Blue blankets and flowered sheets. Tiffany wineglasses from me.

"Look at this," she cried, holding up an oversized towel. "Just like velvet."

I watched her drape the towel around her shoulders and rub her cheek against the nap. Poor naked bride. I felt a rush of tenderness for Elena and her enormous needs. Once again, I found myself reaching to touch her. There was an awkward silence until Manolo began to sing "Here Comes the Bride" and his children started to walk in a mock procession. The youngest, a little girl of six, pretended to be strewing petals. The butterfly ribbon in her black hair matched her starched cotton dress. A film of talcum powder clung to her neck and arms.

The altar's candles were low. The Virgin's rouged face, softened by shadows, beamed approval on the family gathering. Over in a corner, on the brightly patterned sofa, Don Andrés pulled Doña Mercedes close by putting his arm around her.

"*Qué pasa, vieja?*" he said softly, stroking her arm.

She gave him a contented smile, evoked perhaps by the sight of her two sons holding hands with their wives like perpetual adolescents. Yes, this family has survived the transplant, I thought, and my throat felt dry. I reached for a sip of Coke. Kind lady, I murmured, help me weather the storm. I felt an overwhelming desire to get up and sit by Don Andrés near the little altar. I would lift his free arm and place it on my shoulders. I would sink into the tender gaudy pillows, close my eyes, safe at last.

When I looked up, my eyes met Marieta's. She was sitting alone on the corkscrew piano stool and I moved to be near her. Tomorrow, she would host a reception for a hundred Georgians, people surely as alien to her as the Cubans had been to Suze so long ago. Could Suze have carried herself with such loving calm? Could I? Certainly not Max, who had had no such thing as golf in his ghetto spectrum to ease the pain of exile and business failure. He's a good kid, Marieta had said of the bridegroom, and it had seemed to satisfy her. That *is* what counts. To know a good kid when you see one.

"Ever hear from Dieter?" Marieta asked.

"Yes, one letter soon after my arrival here. I returned it unopened."

"How could you?"

"How could I not? Think of the temptation. I was busy becoming an American. Now, Dieter is only a cherished ghost."

"A cherished ghost?"

"Oh yes. Our past ends up becoming very dear to us. It *is* us.'

"Sometimes Havana seems as remote as Mars to me," Marieta said. "When I think what my life would have been like had there been no revolution, I shudder. I look at my mother, so bitter, so dependent still, and I want to shout *Gracias, Fidel!* There but for the grace of Castro go I."

"Curious how events can announce themselves as calamities and then get completely turned around."

"Yes, just think, at this moment I'm preparing a recital with a wonderful soprano. There's even talk of our
touring in New York."

"I'll take you to lunch at La Grenouille."

"*Magnífico,* wherever that is." Marieta was looking
me full in the face without blinking. Cuban women have a
directness that is lost in all that New York cleverness. I
miss it.

"You seem so sane," I said. "How do you do it?
Don't you harbor any secrets?"

"What do you mean?"

"You move, you flow, from one role to another—
daughter, sister, mother, artist. You are a link between
generations."

"And you? Don't you have anybody?"

"Yes, a friend in New York. He proposes every New
Year's Eve, but we just go on, he in his apartment, I in
mine."

"Why?"

I shrugged my shoulders. "Don't know. I like my
life the way it is. Without mess. I've been at the U.N. for
twenty years; it feels like home."

Elena had folded the towel but was clasping it to her
breasts like a child.

"Elenita," Pepe called to her, "I've polished my Mercedes especially for you!"

"You and your fancy Mercedes," Carlos said. "Tara-
tara—introducing Mr. Cuban Success Story. The Miami
Cubans," he added, turning to me, "are known as the Jews
of the Caribbean."

"Jews of the Caribbean? My dear Pepe, don't worry,
you're no Jew of the Caribbean.

Carlos blushed, deepening his sunburn. "I was only
kidding," he said.

"Carlos meant Jew in the larger sense of business
sagacity, cunning . . ."

"I realize," I said, uneasy at the turn the conversation was taking yet unable to let it go. "What's so funny, then?"

"Of course we are not Jews," Don Andrés pronounced. "We are Spanish Catholics one hundred percent. Well, not quite," he added with a laugh. "Mami here has some French blood in her. Anyway, we are Cubans, at least five generations."

"I never think of you as Jewish," Doña Mercedes said. "More *alemana,* I would say. You speak German, don't you? And your blond hair, you know. It really stood out. I always told Marieta the boys would be crazy about you. I'm surprised you didn't stay and marry that handsome German boy. He . . ." She stopped and her hand flew to her mouth.

"You were so glamorous, Claudia, we envied you," Marieta said.

"Envied me? But I was a refugee. We had come to Havana to escape Hitler's camps. For seven years, we waited to get into the United States. My father was a Polish Jew, and our quota was hopeless."

"*Un polaco?* Really?" Doña Mercedes wrinkled her nose. "I had no idea," she said.

"You had no idea because I turned myself inside out to act the Cuban *señorita* like everybody else."

"Oh, we knew you weren't Cuban." Doña Mercedes laughed. "But come to think of it, we were never sure what you were."

"A Jew in the Caribbean."

"Cut it out, Claudia," Marieta said. "No need to put it that way."

"To be a Jew in the Caribbean is a sorry business," I said, picking up the wedding gifts one by one. "You have to lose your mixers and your toasters and your fine linens a hundred times; it has to happen to your father and to your father's father. You have to lose," I added in an unfamiliar register, "you have to lose relatives whose names you refuse to remember."

I had been holding a Tiffany glass and felt it slip out of my moist hand. I watched it shatter on the floor. So did the children, sitting cross-legged on the rug. The *Vanidades* matrons clasped their pearls. The room seemed extraordinarily quiet. Had I been shrieking? I felt hot. Was the air conditioner off? I've blown it, I thought. I won't be able to stay for the wedding.

"Some days, even now, when I brush my teeth in the morning, I'm amazed to find myself performing such an ordinary task." My lips began to tremble. "When I bite into an English muffin thick with butter and jam, I feel that I'm pressing my luck." My nose was running, my cheeks were drenched, my palms, my armpits soaked. Marieta came to hold me up.

"*Muchacha,*" Don Andrés said, walking toward me, "what are we arguing about? We're all survivors, aren't we?"

I looked away. "If only I could be sure I deserve it," I said. "If only somebody would teach me how to live!"

I walked over to Elena and embraced her. "Elenita, forgive me. When I get back to New York, I'll send you the glass I broke."